"I'm here to see Ellie ~~...~~" P9-BYM-259
"I'm Santa Claus."

Marisa just stared at him. He was in his seventies and fit the Santa persona to a T, including the rounded stomach and red cheeks, although he wasn't wearing a costume. But that was minor. The store had done a great job in hiring someone so authentic.

He sat down on one of the office chairs and Ellie climbed onto his knee. "What did you want to see me about, little angel?"

"I wrote you a lot of letters asking for a mommy, and you never sent me one."

"Don't fret, Ellie," he said. "You'll have your mommy before Christmas."

Ellie threw her arms around his neck. "Thank you." She leaned back and tugged on his beard. "My friend Lori says you're not real and that your beard's fake, but it *is* real, just like I told her."

He stood, setting the child on her feet. "Yes, I'm real. Never be afraid to believe, Ellie. It's a very powerful emotion."

The man walked to the door and then stopped. He touched the back of his hand to Marisa's face. "You're never too old to believe, Marisa."

She was so surprised by his touch and the sincerity in his eyes that words eluded her. *What did he mean? And how did he know her name?*

Dear Reader,

Fifteen years ago I had an idea for a book. At the time I was recovering from several surgeries and my mind was clouded by medication. That's my only excuse. But I'd read Harlequin romances for years, so I was sure I had an understanding of what was required in a story. Even today as I think about my stupidity, it's hard to keep from laughing.

I started writing longhand in a spiral notebook. I wrote every day and soon I had a stack of notebooks. My husband bought me an electric typewriter, and it took me several months to type and edit my story into manuscript form.

When I finished, I mailed my treasured work to Harlequin. I promptly got a rejection. Then another. And another. One editor sent me a nice two-page rejection letter. Ten years later I made my first sale (a Harlequin Superromance novel called *The Truth about Jane Doe*) to that editor. In one of our talks a while back, she asked me about my first manuscript. I was stunned. She suggested I write another proposal based on that idea. I did. She bought it. *The Silent Cradle* from long ago is now *The Christmas Cradle* for American Romance.

This book is very dear to my heart and I hope you will feel some of the real emotion that went into its creation.

Warmly—and with best wishes for a wonderful Christmas,

Linda Warren

P.S. I love hearing from readers. You can reach me at lw1508@aol.com or visit my Web site, www.lindawarren.net or write me at P.O. Box 5182, Bryan, TX 77805. I will always answer your letters.

THE CHRISTMAS CRADLE
Linda Warren

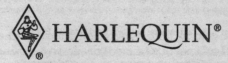

HARLEQUIN®

TORONTO • NEW YORK • LONDON
AMSTERDAM • PARIS • SYDNEY • HAMBURG
STOCKHOLM • ATHENS • TOKYO • MILAN • MADRID
PRAGUE • WARSAW • BUDAPEST • AUCKLAND

ISBN 0-373-75046-3

THE CHRISTMAS CRADLE

Copyright © 2004 by Linda Warren.

www.eHarlequin.com

Printed in U.S.A.

To Paula Eykelhof, who gave this book a second chance

and

to Beth Sobczak. Without your loving generosity,
this book would never have been published. Thanks.

Acknowledgment:

Thanks to Carolyn Lightsey and Brenda Mott
for sharing your knowledge of horses and the rodeo.
And to Amy Landry, pediatric nurse,
for the crash course on childbirth.

Any errors are strictly mine.

Chapter One

Dear Santa,
I've been real good this year, but could you please send
Daddy and me a mommy for Christmas? Someone
who's nice and pretty and likes dogs and horses. That's
all I want for Christmas.
Love,
Ellie Kincaid

Ellie was stuffing the letter into an envelope and licking the
flap as Colter Kincaid walked into the room.

"What are you doing, angelface?"

"I wrote a letter to Santa. Could you mail it for me,
please?" Her bright green eyes waited for an answer.

A knot formed in Colter's stomach. He knew what she'd
written because this was the same letter his daughter wrote
every year—asking Santa for a mother. He'd helped her when
she was three and four, but after that she'd printed them herself.

She was seven now, a mother was all she ever thought
about. Instead of enjoying her childhood, Ellie spent her time
thinking of ways to get a mother; she'd landed him in a few
embarrassing situations by asking women out to the ranch.

He didn't have the heart to tell her he'd never fall in love
again and that she'd never have the mother she wanted. Life

was cruel and love was painful, but he wouldn't tell his daughter that. She'd learn soon enough.

"First thing in the morning," he replied, taking the letter from her. "Now it's time for bed."

Ellie made a face. "Why do I have to go to bed at nine? I don't have school tomorrow 'cause it's Saturday. We're going shopping with Aunt Becky in Dallas."

"Because we have rules around here."

"Tulley doesn't obey the rules. He goes to bed when he wants to."

Colter pulled back the covers. "When you're Tulley's age, you can go to bed when you please."

"Oh boy." Ellie crawled into bed. Her dog, Sooner, jumped up beside her. "How old is Tulley? How long do I have to wait?"

"Tulley's seventy. You do the math."

Her face fell again. "I'll never be that old."

Colter gathered her in his arms. "Yes, you will, but you'll always be my little girl."

"I love you, Daddy." She gave him several loud kisses.

He kissed her soft cheek. "I love you, too, angelface."

No matter what happened in his life, this child would always be the center of it, and he would do everything in his power to ensure her happiness.

And that meant he couldn't tell her the truth about her mother.

MARISA PRESTON SAT at her desk and wondered what she was doing in her Dallas office on a Saturday afternoon. She didn't usually come in on weekends, but today she had to stay busy, to keep from thinking. She got up and headed down to the busy hub of Dalton's Department Store. The firm she'd hired to do the Christmas decorations had done an outstanding job, or so her secretary and father had informed her. Maybe looking at the decorations would inspire a little Christmas spirit. This time of year always left her with a lonely, empty feeling that was hard to shake.

She found herself in the gift section full of special items they'd gotten in for the holidays. Her eyes went to it immediately—the Christmas Cradle. They had one every year. A man who lived in Austin designed and crafted them, and each one was made from a single block of wood. He didn't use a single screw or hinge. His wife sewed the delicate bedding of white silk and lace. It was an antique design, and the wood was stained, not painted. All the intricate designs carved on the cradle denoted "The Twelve Days of Christmas," making it one of a kind.

Unable to stop herself, she walked over and touched the beautiful cradle. As it rocked gently, she suddenly felt suffocated. Closing her eyes, she drew several deep breaths, but she couldn't block out the sound—the sound of her baby crying.

She was powerless to halt the memories. This was the day she'd met *him.* She remembered it vividly; her friends, Stacy and Rhonda, had wanted her to go on an adventure to Las Vegas early in December. Back then, she'd lived in a New York penthouse with her mother and adhered to a strict regimen of training to be a concert pianist. While her mother was away in Europe, she had the opportunity to escape. She'd yearned for fun and freedom.

The National Rodeo Finals were taking place, and Stacy and Rhonda wanted to attend some of the events, to get a glimpse of a real cowboy. Once they were sitting in the audience, all of Marisa's attention was on one cowboy. He wasn't bigger or taller than any of the others, but he rode with such self-assurance and confidence, and he seemed to have a genuine respect for the animal he was riding.

He was the best and they all knew it. Not only had the announcer said he was the top rider in the country, he had numerous awards to prove it.

He'd been very impressive to a young girl from New York. She hadn't been able to take her eyes off him. Once, when he'd finished a ride, the pickup riders let him down right in front of where she was sitting. He'd bent to retrieve his hat and as he straightened and slapped his hat against the side of his leg, he'd looked directly at her.

He had the most unusual green eyes. They were light green, the color of grapes in summer. She remembered that first stirring of desire she'd experienced gazing into those eyes, and she'd known he would be far more stimulating than any nectar grapes could produce.

And he was. He was a true-blue Texas cowboy, with a brooding look that could make a young girl's heart flutter. He was handsome, exciting and very much a man. She'd fallen in love with him instantly.

If her mother… She exhaled a painful breath as other emotions crowded in—the shock, the heartache that followed. But those were only minor compared to the pain of her son's birth and his death. She still wasn't over it, and she believed a woman never got over losing a child. She hadn't. The memory of her son was always with her.

That was why at Christmastime she always managed to find her way to the cradle. It would soon be sold to a lucky expectant mother, but for a moment she could imagine… *No, no, don't.*

Shoving the memories away, she glanced around the large store, its merchandise and salespeople upscale and the very best. Dalton's was important to her and her family. Her grandfather, her mother's father, had started the business in the 1930s, and today it was one of the most successful family-owned chains in Texas. This was her heritage and she was proud of it.

She just wished she felt more enjoyment, more pleasure in her work. What she actually felt was trapped. As senior vice-president, she should have more responsibility for making decisions, but her father, Richard Preston, was the driving force behind Dalton's and nothing was ever done without his approval.

The decorations were perfect, she thought, studying the

beautiful gold and silver bells and garlands and the red accents that seemed to reflect the cheer and enthusiasm of the busy shoppers.

Several of the employees watched her, but none spoke. She hated her father's rules: no fraternizing with the staff and vice versa. She'd been reprimanded more than once for speaking to employees while on the floor. If she had something to say, her father had told her, she was to summon that person to her office. Since her best friend worked on the floor, it was hard to follow the rules, but then, her father didn't need to know every little detail of her life. Although she resented his rigidity and control, she'd always be grateful to him because he'd been there when she'd really needed someone. Her mother she refused to think about—especially today.

She stopped abruptly as she caught sight of a man standing by the gift-wrap counter. *No.* Her breath congealed in her throat. *It can't be. It can't be* him! *Not today.*

Was she hallucinating? Thinking about him too much? The tall lean figure had to be a trick of her imagination. But as she took in the long legs in tight-fitting Wranglers, the silver buckle, the cowboy boots, the brown leather jacket, she knew this was real. *He* was real—as real as he'd been eight years ago.

Colter Kincaid, the man she'd loved so passionately and promised to marry when she was seventeen, the father of her son, was standing a few feet away.

She hadn't seen him even once since that morning in the motel, but she would've known him anywhere: the proud way he held his head, the sharp lines of his face, those broad shoulders. All these things were the same and yet he seemed so different. It was as if time and maturity had added another dimension that she knew nothing about. What was he doing here? Marisa fought an unwelcome surge of excitement as she trembled with an awareness she thought she'd long forgotten.

She felt that awareness like a raw wound, deep in her heart. Her first encounter with love had almost destroyed her. That all-consuming passion had controlled her mind, body and soul, and she never wanted to experience it again.

Yet she couldn't look away, couldn't move, was unable to do anything but stare at him. The years had enhanced his appeal, not dimmed it, but there was a hardness around his eyes that she didn't remember. She had waited so long for this meeting, for a chance to explain about the past. But the words wouldn't come and she felt as tongue-tied as the first time she'd met him.

COLTER GLANCED IMPATIENTLY at his watch. How long could it possibly take to wrap three packages? God, he hated shopping. That was part of being a parent, though. He did a lot of things he didn't really enjoy. Like having a multitude of little girls over for a slumber party and listening to them giggle all night, not to mention listening to music that could easily break the sound barrier. But when his daughter put her arms around his neck and said, "You're the best daddy in the whole world," it was all worth it. He sighed, checking his watch again.

His impatience vanished as an eerie feeling came over him. He could actually feel the hair on the back of his neck standing up, as if his body sensed danger. Raising his head, he received a jolt that he would remember for a long time. He felt winded and gasped, struggling for breath. It couldn't be. It couldn't be *her*. But he knew it was as he looked into the brown eyes of a woman he'd hoped never to see again.

They stood there silently, staring at each other, and against every conscious objection on his part, the years rolled back. He remembered that time in Las Vegas, the love they'd shared, the days and nights of sensual magic only their bodies could create. The happiness and pleasure of those weeks flashed through him, only to be overshadowed by the pain left in its aftermath.

Colter's first instinct was to turn his back on her and walk away. He didn't want to acknowledge her presence, but a force deep inside moved him forward until he was standing in front of her.

From a distance he could tell she'd changed, but he wasn't prepared for the impact of seeing her face-to-face. The young girl he remembered had matured into a beautiful woman. His eyes made a quick, thorough assessment of her, taking in the ash-blond hair around her oval face, the dark eyes that shimmered like brown satin, the delicately carved facial bones and the soft curve of her mouth. His appraisal missed nothing, not the beige linen dress and matching jacket, nor the way she nervously pushed her hair behind her ear. A provocative gesture he remembered well.

She was beautiful; he'd thought that years ago, too. Bitterness quickly filled his mind, reminding him what a fool he'd been—a stupid, infatuated fool. Her beauty was only a facade. She was not beautiful on the inside.

"Marisa Preston?" Her name erupted from his lips and came out as a question, and he couldn't imagine why, because he definitely knew who she was.

"YES," SHE ANSWERED with a quaver in her voice, feeling as if her knees were going to buckle. "It's been a long time. Do you live in Dallas now?"

His eyes narrowed. "Why do you ask?"

She shrugged, not knowing how to answer. She'd only been trying to make the best of an awkward situation.

"What are you doing here?" he asked.

The bluntness of the question took her by surprise, but she answered without a pause. "I work here."

He frowned. "Work? Here?" He made no attempt to hide the incredulity in his voice as his eyes slid over her again.

"In the executive office," she amended.

"The executive office?" The frown deepened. "I assumed you'd be playing in concert halls all over the world by now. Isn't that what your mother planned for you?"

"You know I never wanted to do that," she answered almost inaudibly, wondering if that was what he'd believed—that she'd left him to pursue her career as a concert pianist.

"I never knew what you wanted," he said in a harsh tone. "I never knew you at all."

Her stomach tightened. She hadn't expected him to be so cold, so angry. After all these years, she'd expected idle curiosity about why she'd left him, but he didn't seem too concerned with her reasons for leaving. Her head began to throb and she lightly touched her temple to ease the ache.

His eyes caught the small gesture. "What's the matter? Do thoughts of the past upset you?"

If he only knew. Feelings of guilt mounted inside her. "Some thoughts," she acknowledged, forcing herself to meet his eyes. "But that was a long time ago, and I was very young." The statement sounded inane even to her own ears, so she tried again. "I made a lot of bad choices that I'm not proud of, but I've managed to put them behind me."

"How convenient for you," he muttered, urging himself to walk away. He couldn't do it, though. What was wrong with him? *Why* couldn't he just leave? It had to be the shock of seeing her, of knowing what she'd done to his life. She'd ruined him for other women. After her, he couldn't trust a woman again. He'd tried, but he couldn't, and he couldn't fully love again, either—the way a man should love a woman. Not even for his daughter had he been able to do that. All because of *this* woman.

She called it a bad choice, said she'd been young. Was he supposed to accept that and now have a pleasant conversation with her? Her gall was unbelievable! He mentally shook himself, fighting to keep his emotions under control.

Marisa had imagined this meeting a thousand times, but she was unprepared for this hostile stranger, especially since he'd married Shannon four months after Marisa had left him. Her mother was glad to tell her the details. So why would he still be so angry with a young girl who'd broken her promise of marriage?

She blinked nervously under his hard stare, unable to stop herself from asking, "Don't you think you're overreacting? After all, it was a long time ago."

"Overreacting!" he repeated, his voice sharp as a whiplash. He jammed his hands into the pockets of his jacket. "Doesn't it ever bother *you?*"

How dare he ask her that? He was a married man. He had no right to judge her without knowing the truth. *The truth.* She suddenly knew she had to tell him that truth, the truth that had tortured her for years.

"Yes, it bothered me for a while," she began, lifting her chin, meeting his icy gaze as she struggled for the right words. "But as I said, I was young and—"

"Oh, please," he cut in. "Spare me your pretty speech. Why don't you just admit that you were a spoiled rich girl who couldn't handle responsibility or commitment, so you ran home to mother?"

"It wasn't like that," she denied, hating the picture he held of her in his mind.

"It was just like that. Tulley warned me. Shannon warned me, but—"

"Please," she begged, her head beginning to ache in earnest. "You don't understand."

"No. I'll never understand."

"If you'd just listen, I can explain."

"It may surprise you, but I'm not interested in anything you have to say—now or ever. I've moved on."

"I didn't mean to hurt you," she said, hoping for a weakening in his implacable attitude. He quickly disillusioned her.

"No, of course not," he replied in a scornful voice. "You never thought about me or my feelings. You just left."

"Please, listen—"

"I told you I'm not interested in anything you have to say.

I had a feeling you were trouble the first moment I met you, but you seemed so different from the other girls who hung around the rodeos—or so I thought. You had me wrapped so tight around your little finger, I couldn't see the real woman behind the beautiful face." His eyes slid over her, sending a tiny shiver through her body. "It's hard to imagine I ever considered myself in love…with you."

"Mr. Kincaid, your packages are ready," a woman called from the gift-wrap counter.

Colter whirled toward her.

"Daddy," a little girl shouted, running up to him with a pair of low-rise jeans in her hands. Rhinestones glittered on the pockets and around the hem. "Can I have these? I really like them."

Colter grabbed his packages and turned to face the child. "You're too young for jeans like that."

"But all the girls in my class are wearing them."

"Ellie—"

He and Shannon had a daughter—a beautiful little girl with blond hair and green eyes. The Kincaid green eyes. She appeared to be around six or seven, and Marisa couldn't look away. Through the panic rising in her, she realized Colter and Shannon had started a family very soon after she'd left.

Before she could assimilate this piece of information, another child with blond hair came running up.

"Daddy said I can't have them," the girl called Ellie told the other one.

Marisa's stomach tensed in pain. *Colter has two daughters.*

"Go put the jeans back," Colter said.

"Aw, Daddy."

"Ellie."

"Okay, c'mon, Lori, we'll find something else."

They ran off and Colter followed. He didn't give Marisa a second glance.

Colter stopped and put his arm around a woman who had her back to Marisa. Marisa couldn't see the woman clearly, but it had to be Shannon Wells—Colter's wife.

Almost in slow motion, Marisa walked to the executive elevators. Once the doors closed, she jabbed the stop button and the elevator stalled. She sank to the floor, wrapped her arms around her trembling body and began to cry. Tears rolled down her cheeks and she didn't bother to wipe them away as pain encompassed every part of her. *Why today?* Why did she have to see him and his perfect family today?

And why, after so many years, did it still hurt so much?

"Ms. PRESTON? Ms. PRESTON? Are you stuck in the elevator?"

Marisa heard the man's voice over the intercom and rose slowly to her feet. She hit Talk and released the stop button. "I'm fine, thank you. The elevator's moving now."

When it reached the executive floor, the maintenance man was waiting. "Ms. Preston—"

"I'm fine," she murmured again, brushing past him and hurrying to her office, not wanting him to see she'd been crying. The news would quickly get back to her father, and she couldn't deal with that right now.

She went over to the window that overlooked downtown Dallas, she didn't see anything except Colter's angry face. So many years she'd waited to tell him about their son, yet she couldn't even bring herself to utter the words in his presence. *We had a son. He died.* How could she say that to him? Oh God, she had to talk to someone.

She picked up her phone. "Send Cari Michaels to my office, please."

"Yes, ma'am," her secretary responded.

Marisa wrapped her arms around her waist again to still her agitated nerves, and waited, staring out the window. Within minutes, Cari came through the door. Petite with dark eyes and hair, Cari had started working at Dalton's as a sales-clerk. Today she was head of staff and, even though she had an office, she spent a lot of time on the floor making sure the store ran smoothly. Marisa had met her the first year she'd returned to Texas and they'd become fast friends, best friends. Cari knew all of Marisa's secrets.

"You're going to get me in trouble," Cari teased. "You keep forgetting I'm not allowed on the executive floor."

The executive floor was for the Preston family. Her father had a large suite of offices, as did she and her brother, Reed.

Marisa turned from the window.

"What's wrong?" Cari asked immediately.

"I saw him."

Cari frowned. "Him? Who?"

"Him," Marisa emphasized.

"Oh, no." Cari understood now, and Marisa blurted out what happened.

"He was awful and I...I don't understand." Marisa was trembling visibly, and Cari quickly got her a glass of water.

"Here—" Cari handed her the glass. "Sit down before you collapse."

Marisa sank into her chair and took a sip.

"Are you okay?"

Marisa nodded. "Seeing him was such a shock and he was so hateful, not at all like the man I once knew. It brought back so many memories. I wanted to tell him about our son, but he wouldn't listen. I wanted to tell him how sorry I was. I wanted him to know—" Her voice wavered as emotion closed her throat.

Cari knelt beside her. "Marisa, don't do this to yourself. You were so young, and you did the best you could under the circumstances."

"Did I?" Marisa jerked to her feet and began to pace. "I don't think so. I was weak and I let my mother control my life."

Cari stood, too. "Marisa, what good will it do to—"

"My mother has these priceless crystal eggs that have figurines in them. I feel like one of those figurines, encased in glass, sheltered from the world, not allowed to live or make my own choices. That's how both my parents treat me—like a piece of crystal."

Cari didn't say anything.

"Everyone knows my father created this job for me. I'm nothing but a figurehead. I'm allowed to decorate the store. That's rich. That's a joke."

"Marisa, please—"

"But not anymore, Cari," she said with renewed vigor. "No one's going to treat me like that—including Colter Kincaid."

"What are you going to do?"

"I have to see him again and tell him what really happened. That's the only way I'll have any peace." She drew a deep breath. "But I don't know where he lives. I never knew, even when we were together."

"Do you really not know?"

Marisa swung to face her friend. "What?"

"I guess it was inevitable that you'd run into him one day."

"What do you mean?"

A look of momentary discomfort crossed Cari's face. "He has a large horse ranch somewhere outside Mesquite."

"How do you know?" Marisa asked, pushing hair from her face.

"A couple of years ago, he was featured in *Texas* magazine. The story talked about his success as a horse rancher—and in the western wear business. His name's on everything from boots to belt buckles."

"What?" she whispered. "He was just a cowboy when I met him. And now he…"

"Marisa." Cari's eyes filled with compassion. "I never said anything because I didn't want to upset you—and what good could it possibly have done? You've come too far to let this get the better of you."

Marisa licked her dry lips. "Where's his ranch?"

Cari shook her head. "I've just read about it, that's all."

"Please, Cari, I need his address." Marisa stared into her friend's eyes with a silent plea.

Cari sighed. "Marisa, I have this feeling you're going to get hurt."

"More than I'm hurting right now? I don't think that's possible."

Cari flung up her hands. "Okay, let's try the Dallas and Mesquite phone books."

Marisa opened a drawer and pulled out the directories. Colter wasn't listed, but his company had a Dallas address.

"That doesn't help," Marisa said. "And I'm sure his company won't divulge his home address."

"Your father has a lot of contacts," Cari suggested. "I'm sure he could find the address in no time."

"I don't want my father involved in this," Marisa replied, her tone abrupt.

Cari shrugged. "Just an idea. Now, let's think. There must be a lot of people who know him." Cari grew thoughtful. "Wait a minute. Why didn't I think of this before? My sister's husband works for one of those large feed-supply places. Colter has horses, so maybe he buys feed from them."

"Call him, Cari, please."

As Cari punched out a number, Marisa's nerves were taut. She knew she should just forget about Colter and get on with her life. He had, so why couldn't she? She didn't have an answer. All she knew was that she had to find him.

Cari haggled with her brother-in-law, it was clear he didn't want to give out the information. Finally Cari scribbled something on a pad and Marisa's heartbeat accelerated.

Cari hung up, then handed her the paper. "I had to use a little family blackmail, but there it is."

Marisa hugged her. "Thanks, Cari. Thank you so much."

"Just don't tell anyone where you got the address, or Charlie could lose his job."

"I won't breathe a word. I promise." She grabbed her purse and coat.

"You're going now?" Cari asked, sounding dismayed.

"Yes. I need to do this and I need to do it now."

"But sleet's in the forecast. Why don't you wait until tomorrow?"

"No, I can't," Marisa said. "I'll be back before the weather turns bad. Mesquite is only about fifteen minutes from Dallas, and the ranch can't be much farther."

"Marisa—"

A tap on the door interrupted Cari. Reed Preston, Marisa's brother, walked in and shook his head at Cari. "You know you're not supposed to be on this floor," he said.

Cari didn't bat an eye at Reed's censure. "Don't worry, junior, I was just leaving."

"Don't call me that."

Cari lifted an eyebrow, then glanced at Marisa. "Call me later." She sauntered out the door.

"I don't appreciate it when you talk to my friends like that," Marisa said once the other woman had left.

"Cari? She's tough as nails, and if I didn't reprimand her, she'd think I was ill."

"Still, she's my friend and I invited her here."

"Point taken." Reed grinned at her.

He was five years older than Marisa and a younger version of their father, very tall and handsome with a disarming smile. She was four years old when she and her mother moved to New York, and nine-year-old Reed had stayed with their father in Dallas. It was well known that Harold Dalton had arranged the marriage of his only daughter, Vanessa, to Richard Preston. His daughter didn't have much interest in the stores, and her grandfather wanted a man who could control her and control the empire he'd built.

The marriage had been a disaster from the start, but they'd stuck it out until Harold Dalton passed away. Then they'd received a shock. Harold had left half his estate to Vanessa and the other half to Richard. If they divorced, they'd lose everything. Her grandfather had sentenced them to a life together. But her parents figured out a way around it—living separate lives without a divorce, and in the process making their children's lives a nightmare.

"I stopped by to see if you wanted to go with me to the airport to pick up Mother."

"Oh, no, sorry. I have other plans." She couldn't believe her mother's visit had completely slipped her mind. She'd been dreading it for days. Now other, more important, matters took precedence.

Reed watched her for a moment. "Are you okay?"

"Sure, why?"

"You seem a little nervous."

"It's nothing."

"I know you and Mother have had problems, but that's all in the past, isn't it?"

"Yes."

In her youth, her mother's complete domination of her life had turned her into a shy, insecure teenager. Vanessa had dreams and plans for Marisa—dreams Marisa didn't share. She'd rebelled only once, when she'd run away to Vegas, and that had been the happiest and yet most debilitating part of her life. She had thought she'd never recover, but after the death of her son, her father had brought her back to Texas. With his love and support, she'd stood up to her mother and refused to return to New York. For the first time in her life, she made her own plans. She went to university and earned a degree in business and then began working for Dalton Department Stores, much to her father's delight.

She'd grown confident and stronger and was now able to cope with her mother on an adult level. She still had difficulty sorting out her feelings about Vanessa, but she did love her, although at times she found it impossible to like her.

"I really have to go," she said, brushing past Reed.

"Where are you going?"

"I'll be home in time for dinner." She threw the words over her shoulder.

As she drove out of Dallas, her nerve began to falter, especially when she thought about Colter's wife. Shannon had been crazy about him back then and she hadn't liked it when Colter took an interest in Marisa. Colter had said they were just friends, but Marisa knew it was far more for Shannon. In the end, Shannon had won. Colter had married her. That hurt, even now, but she didn't want to cause any problems in Colter's marriage. However, she had to tell him the truth, for her own peace of mind, her sanity. She couldn't live with the guilt any longer, and there was only one solution. To see Colter—and to tell him about their son.

Chapter Two

Colter sat at his kitchen table clutching a cup of coffee, unable to get *her* out of his mind. What was she doing in Dallas? Working, she'd said, but somehow that didn't fit the Marisa he'd known. She'd lived in New York with her mother who was wealthy, and Marisa was a daughter of that environment. She was so far out of his realm that he didn't understand why he'd gotten involved with her in the first place.

He shifted uneasily. What did she expect from him? She was the one who'd left. What did she hope to gain by trying to make amends?

He squeezed his eyes shut. He'd somehow known that someday they'd meet again. But she would not make a fool of him again—not now that he had his daughter. Ellie was his top priority, and ever since her mother had decided she didn't want to be a mother, he had devoted his life to her, making sure she had roots, stability and a home. He didn't bring other women into their lives and he realized that had probably been a bad decision. He'd thought his sisters would fill that void in Ellie's life, but they hadn't.

Ellie's quest reminded him of the mistakes he'd made after Marisa had disappeared from his life. Marrying Shannon had been one of them. He hadn't loved her the way he had Marisa, but he'd honestly believed they could make it work and raise a family.

Early on, it became clear he couldn't get Marisa out of his head, and Shannon had reacted in anger. After a heated argument, she left and went home to Wyoming. She never called or asked about Ellie, which bothered him. He'd received divorce papers in the mail. Shannon didn't want a thing and didn't even ask for visitation rights. She'd severed all ties.

He should have taken Ellie and gone to Wyoming to talk things out. Once she saw Ellie, she might have changed her mind. He couldn't do it, though. Shannon was as miserable as he was in the marriage, and staying together for Ellie's sake wasn't the solution. But he'd thought Shannon would make some effort to see Ellie. When she didn't, he'd decided to raise his daughter alone.

Ellie was the best part of his life, and he didn't want Marisa anywhere near her. That might be a little extreme, but it was the way he felt.

A familiar anger welled up in him. Seeing her, listening to her rekindled that pain of rejection, and he knew that he hadn't learned to control his feelings for her.

And he didn't know if he ever would.

AS MARISA DROVE, memories of Colter wrapped around her. In the early days, thoughts of him had been painful, but time had eased the pain and she could now think calmly about the past. Or some aspects of the past, she reminded herself. Not her baby...

She'd first seen him at the rodeo, then later at one of the parties given for the cowboys. She'd never met anyone like Colter, and without knowing how, she'd realized he was going to change her life.

He had made her feel so special, so alive, so much a woman, and when he'd asked her to marry him, she had happily agreed. They loved each other and nothing else seemed important. The stupidity of youth still astonished her. Why had she ever thought—?

She inhaled deeply, but it didn't stop the memories. When her mother had returned home and found her gone, she'd called Stacy, who was then back in New York, and got the whole story—that Marisa had decided to stay in Nevada and was getting married. Announcing the news was like putting a match to gasoline, and the scenes that had followed were not pleasant. It had been the beginning of Marisa's nightmare.

A sob left her throat and she forced herself to look at the directions in her hand. She turned off the highway onto a blacktop country road. As she did, she noticed the dark thunderclouds. A storm was brewing, as Cari had said, but she'd be back in Dallas before it broke. Dinner with her mother would be an ironic ending to the task ahead of her.

TULLEY CAME THROUGH the back door, removed his hat and folded himself into a chair opposite Colter. Jackson Tulley was like a father to him. Everything Colter knew about riding, Tulley had taught him. He'd been there for every win and every loss. He also understood every hurt and pain Colter suffered, because he suffered them, too.

Tulley and Colter's father, James Kincaid, had been best friends, riding the rodeo circuit in their off time. James died when Colter was ten, and Tulley nurtured the boy's rodeo interest with his mother's approval. Looking back, Colter didn't know what he would've done without Tulley in his life.

"You still brooding about seeing her today?" Tulley asked, watching Colter's dark expression.

Colter tightened the hold on the cup. "I can't get it out of my mind. I turned around and there she was. I couldn't make myself walk away from her. I wanted to say so many things, but I'm not sure what I actually said. I just don't know what she was doing there."

Tulley ran one hand through his thinning gray hair. "Think about it, boy."

Colter raised his head. "What?"

"Marisa Preston."

"Yeah. What are you getting at?"

"Either you're getting dense or you have a mental block."

"What the hell are you talking about, Tulley?"

"Richard Preston, owner of Dalton's Department Stores. Marisa Preston. There has to be a connection."

"God, I never put it together." Colter ran both hands over his face. "She said her father lived in Texas, but she never mentioned what he did."

"Back then you two didn't do much talking."

Colter thought they had, but in reality Tulley was right. They had hardly known each other. He couldn't understand why his memories of her were still so strong.

"So what are you going to do?"

"Nothing," Colter replied. "She's obviously working for her father now. What happened to the pianist career I don't know, nor do I care. She's not going to get her hooks into me again."

Tulley's eyebrows shot up. "Did she show any interest?"

"No, not really. She wanted to tell me something about the past and I didn't want to hear it." He ran his hands over his face again. "God, Tulley, why can't I forget her? It's been years and yet—"

"You know the answer to that."

"Yeah." Colter gazed out the window, his eyes matching the dark clouds gathering outside. "When I won at the finals in Vegas and she was there, I felt like king of the world. I spent a lot of my winnings on a ring, and when I got back to the motel room, she was gone. I hit the ground so hard, I've never recovered. No other woman ever made me feel like that. Not even Ellie's birth dimmed it."

Tulley just nodded. He'd heard the story before, and he cursed the young girl who had the power to hurt this man so much. Changing the subject seemed like the best thing to do.

"Becky got everything set for the stores in Austin?"

Colter took a long breath. "Yeah. She's worked nonstop to get Kincaid Boots into more western stores."

"That girl has a good head on her shoulders. Both girls do. You've done great with your sisters."

Colter's mother had died when he was eighteen and he'd become solely responsible for his two younger sisters, Jennifer and Rebecca. Tulley and his wife, Cora, had moved in with them and Cora had stayed with the girls while the men were on the circuit. But his sisters had always been level-headed and responsible and never given him any problems.

Becky and Jen had business degrees, and together they ran the Kincaid Boot Company. Colter put his expertise into the design of the boot, and Bart, Jen's husband, who had a marketing degree, had turned Kincaid Boots into a thriving enterprise. Thanks to Becky's drive, Jen's management skills and Bart's commercial savvy, a lot of western stores were carrying the Kincaid Boot. Accessories had recently been added.

Years ago they'd all lived in a small three-bedroom house, and when Colter had built this house he'd wanted it big, with enough room for everyone. But by then everyone was older and going off in different directions.

The girls were in college when Cora passed away. It had been a difficult time for all of them, but they'd had each other, and had adjusted. Jen was already dating Bart and soon married him. Becky lived in the house for a while, but then she became so involved in making Kincaid Boots a success that she was gone a lot. He'd encouraged her to rent an apartment in town because he didn't want her to feel honor-bound to stay because of Ellie.

Ellie was *his* responsibility, and Becky deserved her own life. After many discussions, she finally rented a place not far from the Kincaid offices, but he still kept a room for her and Jen to use whenever they wanted to come home. It was just the three of them there now—Ellie, Tulley and him.

Colter took a sip of coffee. "I'm very proud of them.

They've done wonders with Kincaid Boots. Of course, Bart helped a lot, too."

"I think your name had a little something to do with it."

"Yeah, but they did all the work." He stared at his cup. "I was busy raising Ellie."

There was silence for a second.

Tulley cleared his throat. "Jen will probably spend less and less time on the business now that she and Bart are expecting."

"Jennifer's always been a homebody, and if she wants to stay home with her baby, then I'm all for that. A baby needs a mother."

Silence again.

"Dammit, Colt, boy," Tulley said, reading his mind. "Shorty's fine without a mother." That was what he called Ellie—and had since the first day he held her.

"I don't know. She has a dog that she insists talks to her and she writes all these letters to Santa. I've mailed four already this year. I'm at a loss as to how to deal with some of these problems."

"She's a little girl and she'll outgrow them. All I see is a happy, imaginative child—and so should you."

"Speaking of my child, where is she?"

"She's at the corral looking at that new horse you bought."

Colter jumped to his feet. "I don't want her anywhere near that horse. He's not broke."

Tulley shook his head. "Lordy, boy, you're jumpy. Give Ellie some credit. She knows not to get in a pen with an unbroke horse. We taught her better than that."

Colter sank back into his chair with a groan. "I'm not thinking straight and I'm all keyed up."

Before Tulley could answer, Ellie and Sooner came charging through the back door. Ellie rarely walked; she was always in a run, her ponytail bouncing. She slid onto Colter's lap, and Colter held her tight, maybe a little too tight.

"That horse is real mean, Daddy," she told him. "He's pawing the ground, and Sooner growled at him. Sooner said he's not scared of him, but I think he's lying."

Sooner barked.

"Yes, you are, Sooner," Ellie said, and Colter closed his eyes briefly. He didn't want to have another conversation about whether or not she could hear Sooner talk, not today. He had to get rid of this restless energy.

"Let's go see just how mean that horse is."

Ellie's eyes grew big.

Tulley swallowed a curse word.

Colter got to his feet. "A good ride will calm him right down."

"Have you noticed the weather?" Tulley asked. "There's a storm coming and the temperature's dropping fast. This is no time to be breaking a horse."

"Getting soft?" Colter teased, but he knew he was about to do a stupid thing. It wouldn't be the first time, he told himself, but if he could obliterate Marisa's memory for those few minutes, it would be worth it.

COLTER HAD A RURAL ADDRESS, but it was easy to find. A couple of miles down the country road she came to a large brick entrance with a huge overhead sign in wrought-iron letters that read Circle K Ranch. She drove over the cattle guard onto a gravel road that led to a house.

Her eyes opened wide in appreciation of the scene that met her. The land was flat and a two-story brick colonial house nestled among huge oaks. Now bare, the trees stood proudly against the chilling wind, enhancing the beauty of the house with its white pillars and mullioned windows. Beyond the detached four-car garage were various barns, outbuildings and corrals, all neatly maintained. She couldn't help thinking that even her mother would be impressed.

Parking on the circular drive, she took a steadying breath,

then ran up the paved walk to the front door. The wind bit through her clothes; it had definitely grown colder. She pulled her cashmere coat tighter around her and rang the doorbell.

There was no answer, so she rang it again. Still no answer. She felt a deep sense of disappointment. It'd been difficult to make the trip at all, and now that she was here, she hated to leave without seeing him. But it seemed she had no choice. It was after four, anyway, and she needed to return to Dallas for the dinner party her father had planned.

As she left the circular drive, a movement from one of the corrals caught her eye. A small child sat perched atop a fence, and Marisa drove in that direction. She stopped some distance away, got out and ran over, hoping she might find Colter.

The child, huddled in a winter coat with the hood pulled over her head, was too engrossed in what was going on inside the corral to notice Marisa. Following the child's gaze, she caught her breath at the sight of Colter astride a big red stallion.

The horse jumped and twisted, determined to dislodge his rider. Bending his head close to the ground, the horse struck out with his back legs, to no avail.

Marisa walked closer so she could see better. Too late, she realized her mistake. The child turned to look at her at the same time Colter did. As his concentration was diverted, the horse gave a wild kick that sent him flying against the fence.

Stunned, Marisa watched the horse run wild, his hooves threatening to trample Colter's inert body lying in the dirt. Without thinking, she hitched her skirt high and climbed over the fence. Someone yelled, "Stay back! Stay back!" but she didn't stop until she heard the sound of hooves close by.

She saw a man waving a rope above his head, trying to guide the horse into another pen. She felt a wave of panic as she realized she was in the corral with a wild horse. All those years ago, she'd been afraid of horses, that hadn't changed. She held her breath as the horse thundered past her through a gate.

Her high heels hindered her progress over the loose dirt but nothing deterred her as she hurried to Colter's side. When she reached him, the child called Ellie was already there, holding Colter's head, crying, "Daddy, wake up! Please wake up."

Marisa squatted beside them, her hand gently brushing the brown hair from his face. He was completely motionless, and her whole body felt a chill that had nothing to do with the weather.

Ellie glanced up at Marisa, tears streaming down her face. "Is my daddy dead?"

"No, no," Marisa insisted, staring into green eyes so much like Colter's. She quickly looked back at Colter, feeling the cold hand of fear grip her heart as she stared at his eyelashes, so dark against the pallor of his skin. His broad chest moved slightly, and she sucked in a breath of frosty air.

Her eyes traveled down to his legs. "Oh, my God," she said. Something on the fence had ripped his jeans and blood was soaking through the denim.

The man came running over. "Is Colter okay?"

"He's cut his leg. Would you get me a clean cloth to stop the bleeding?" she asked him.

The man hesitated for a second, then walked off to the double doors that opened into the barn and came back with a small towel. She pulled the jeans away and saw a gash about three inches long. It wasn't deep. That was good, anyway. She pressed the towel against the wound and gave a sigh of relief as the bleeding slowed.

Colter's eyelids fluttered open.

"Daddy, Daddy," Ellie cried, kissing his face.

"Oooh," he groaned, his eyes blinking. "What happened?"

"That mean old horse threw you," Ellie told him.

"Damn." He sat up, and as his hand went to his head, his eyes caught hers. "What are—?"

"You cut your leg on the fence," she broke in.

Colter's dazed eyes focused on her.

"Please leave," he muttered in a thick voice.

"Colter, you're hurt and…" Her voice trailed away as he struggled to his feet.

Marisa and Tulley immediately tried to help him.

Colter shook off Marisa's arm.

"Who are you?" Ellie asked, staring at her.

"Uh—I'm Marisa Preston, a friend of your dad's. I knew him a long time ago." Silence followed.

"Lots of people know my daddy," Ellie declared a moment later. "He's a famous rodeo rider."

The two men walked slowly to the house, Ellie and a grayish brown dog running ahead. There was no invitation for Marisa to come in, but she hesitated only a fraction of a second before trailing after them. She had to talk to Colter.

As they walked to a covered walkway, a light sleet began to fall and the cold wind tugged at their clothes. Shivering, she followed the others through the door and down a hallway—there was a laundry room to the right and a closet on the left. They entered a spacious breakfast nook and a kitchen decorated in a lovely country style. Touches of cobalt-blue and white milk glass were here and there, and the white-and-blue tiled floor only added to the feeling of warmth.

Marisa looked around for Shannon but didn't see her. It suddenly dawned on her that this was inappropriate. She shouldn't be here interrupting his family life. She should have called and arranged a meeting—that would've been the proper thing to do. Since confronting him in the store, though, she hadn't been thinking too clearly.

"Ellie, turn up the heat. It's getting cold," Colter said, and slumped into a chair.

Ellie disappeared, and the man knelt in front of Colter with a first-aid kit and began to clean the jagged cut.

"Can I help?" she asked.

"I've been fixing his cuts, bruises and broken bones for more years than I care to remember," the man replied. "So, no, I don't need any help."

That voice finally jogged her memory. "I'm sorry, Tulley, I didn't recognize you."

Tulley slit Colter's jeans slightly to bandage the cut, then rose and faced her. "It's been a long time, Marisa, and under the circumstances I think it'd be best if you left."

Marisa bit her lip for fear it would start to quiver. This man had been kind to her once, but now kindness was not extended. She should leave; she'd already acknowledged that, but for some reason she couldn't make herself go. The urge to talk to Colter was still strong, overriding good manners and common sense, and it kept her rooted to the spot.

"Daddy, what's all that noise?" Ellie asked, running into the kitchen.

The adults had been so involved with one another that they hadn't noticed it was sleeting in earnest now and that the wind howled.

"It's just sleet, angelface."

"Oh boy! Is it gonna snow, Daddy?"

"I don't think so."

"C'mon, Sooner, let's go see," Ellie shouted, and rushed out the door with the dog behind her.

"Ellie…"

"I'll get her," Tulley offered, glancing from Colter to Marisa. Colter nodded and Tulley left.

"I apologize for the intrusion," she said as his eyes bore into her. "I shouldn't have interrupted your life with Shannon and your daughters, and I…"

Colter looked confused. "What are you talking about?"

"I just saw Shannon from a distance in the store and I assumed the other little girl was yours, too."

"If you saw Shannon, you have very good eyesight. She lives in Wyoming. The other little girl is Lori, my daughter's best friend. The woman was my sister, Becky. It's just Ellie and me now."

"Oh." Marisa didn't know quite what to say. She'd pictured

a perfect, happy marriage for him, and she wasn't sure how to deal with the situation now that she knew differently. Leaving would be the best course of action. But she couldn't go without telling him about their son. It was now or never.

"After seeing you today, I felt I needed to explain about the past," she plunged in.

He shook his head. "Marisa, I thought I made this clear, but evidently you didn't understand. I'm not interested in anything you have to say. We had a brief time together. It was over years ago. Nothing you say can change a thing, and I don't care about your excuses anymore. It just doesn't matter."

It just doesn't matter. Their son didn't matter. She swallowed hard, trying to accept that, but nobody, not even Colter, could ever make her believe the short time their son was alive inside her didn't matter. Their son had changed her life, and her perception of life in general. Losing him had given her the strength to stand up to her mother. She was still struggling to find herself, to find her niche in the world, but that had been a start.

It just doesn't matter, he'd said. Maybe to him it didn't. He had a new life, a new child, and Marisa was the only one not able to accept the past and move on. Suddenly she could see that Colter was right; telling him wouldn't change a thing except maybe to cause him more hurt. And what would that accomplish? Nothing.

Losing their son was her own private pain and she had to deal with it on her own. Mistakenly she'd believed that sharing the truth about their baby with Colter would ease her heartache. But she was the only one who could overcome that grief.

"Please leave and don't come back." Colter's voice penetrated her thoughts. "There's nothing left to say."

They stared at each other like strangers, total strangers, and Marisa felt the numbness of that reality. She had to leave.

But before she could move her feet, Ellie burst through the back door, followed by the big dog.

"Daddy, you should see," Ellie shouted, pushing back the hood of her coat. "Ice is everywhere. It's like a big skating ring, and Sooner says it's gonna snow, too."

Momentarily diverted, Marisa patted the dog's head. "Sooner?" she repeated.

"Yeah, he's part German shepherd and we don't know what else, and Daddy named him Sooner 'cause he'd sooner eat and sleep than do anything else." Ellie gave the dog a big hug. "Daddy, Sooner says he's not going back outside 'cause it's too cold."

"Ellie, that dog does not talk."

"Does, too." Ellie pouted. "You just can't hear him."

"Ellie." There was a note of warning in Colter's voice. "We've been through this before. Sooner does not talk."

Marisa didn't understand how Colter could be so harsh. Lots of kids had imaginary friends, especially the lonely ones like her. She'd talked to a doll when she was about Ellie's age, and she'd outgrown it, as would Ellie. She could offer Colter some reassurance, but she knew it wouldn't be welcomed.

Ellie wriggled onto Colter's lap and put her arms around his neck. "Does your leg hurt, Daddy?"

"Naw," Colter answered, kissing her cheek.

Clearly Colter had a good relationship with his daughter. She couldn't help thinking that while she'd been lying in a New York clinic in labor with their child, he'd already married someone else, started a new life, a family. A pang of jealousy pierced her as she realized he'd gotten over her with remarkable ease.

She wondered about his marriage. Were he and Shannon separated? Divorced? She couldn't imagine Shannon ever leaving Colter or their child. What had happened?

Ellie didn't look much like Colter, she thought, but the green eyes were definitely his. They'd said her son's eyes were blue. Most babies were born with blue eyes, though. Later, would he have had the Kincaid green eyes or— *Stop it.* Her son was dead.

It was time to let go of the memories. It was time....

Chapter Three

Marisa turned to leave and just then, the electricity went out, shrouding the house in darkness. Outside the light was fading and nightfall wasn't far away. She should've left already.

"Oooh, Daddy, what's happening?" Ellie curled closer against Colter.

"The storm's probably taken down some power lines. The electricity's been out before, remember?"

Ellie raised her head to look at him. "Yeah, and we lit candles. I'll go get the candles." She jumped off his lap and ran to the cabinet, opened drawers.

"Top drawer on the left, angelface," Colter said, and Marisa noticed how gentle and reassuring he was.

He was a great father. She felt an ache deep inside her, in a private place kept only for her son, a son Colter would never know.

Tulley came into the room with a battery-operated radio, and Marisa switched her focus to him, unable to deal with all the emotions railing within her.

"The Dallas-Fort Worth area and Mesquite are under a weather advisory," Tulley said. "Some places, like here, don't have power, and people are being advised to stay off the roads because of the ice."

Ellie plopped several candles on the table, then handed

Colter a box of matches. He absently lit a couple, and Marisa could see he was absorbing Tulley's news.

"I need to get back to Dallas," she said.

Tulley shook his head. "Not tonight."

Colter's eyes darkened in the glow of the candlelight. "Are you sure?"

Tulley set the radio on the table and turned it on. Through the static they heard, *"...Do not drive unless it's an emergency. Road conditions are hazardous..."* The warning faded away into silence.

"DADDY, aren't you gonna light another candle?" Ellie piped up.

Colter stared into Marisa's eyes, trying to accept that she was here for the duration, trying to accept that he had to deal with her presence and, above all, trying not to lose his temper.

Ellie tugged at his arm. "Daddy?"

"Uh." His gaze swung to his daughter. "Okay." He lit several more candles.

"I'll take one to the den," Ellie offered.

Colter grabbed her before she got too far. "Walk, don't run, and be careful."

"Okay." Ellie slowly walked to the den with the candle held tightly in both hands, Sooner at her heels.

Colter stood, his eyes holding Marisa's. "I don't want your death on my conscience, so it seems I have no choice but to let you stay here."

"I'm sorry," she said, feeling a need to apologize.

"I don't think you are. You barge into my life, my home, without any regard for my feelings. I fail to understand how something that happened more than eight years ago could be so damn important. Say what you have to say and then get the hell out of my life."

She gritted her teeth, the words stalled in her throat. She couldn't tell him like this—not when he was so angry.

"Nothing to say, huh?" he asked, his words loaded with sarcasm.

"No." She stiffened her backbone, tired of being the recipient of his insults. "And I will not apologize again. You don't deserve it."

His eyes narrowed to mere slits, but before he could vent his rage, Tulley stepped in. "Calm down. Ellie's in the next room."

Colter swerved around her and grabbed a big coat off the peg of a closet door. "Ellie, let's go," he called.

Ellie came running, with Sooner, as usual, right behind. "Where we going?"

"We'll check on the horses and make sure they have enough feed and water to outlast the storm, then we have to bring in more wood for the fireplace. It might be the only heat we have for a while."

Tulley spoke up. "I can do that. You should rest your leg. You were knocked out for a bit, too."

"It's just a scratch." Colter dismissed Tulley's warning. "And I've been knocked out so many times I've lost track."

"All the more reason—"

Colter cut him off. "Let's go."

Ellie secured the hood of her coat over her head, glancing at Marisa. "Aren't you coming?"

"No. Ms. Preston is not coming," Colter said before she could find her voice. He quickly ushered Ellie out the door.

Tulley stared at her with a sad expression.

"I'm sorry. I shouldn't have come." Colter might not deserve an apology, but she felt Tulley did.

"Not sure why you did."

"I'm wondering that myself."

Tulley removed his worn hat and scratched his head. "When you left, it was worse than when that horse trampled him in Cheyenne. He recovered from those bruises, but he's never fully recovered from what you did to his pride, his heart."

For the first time she realized how much she must have hurt

him. But he obviously didn't suffer long. She gestured at the darkened room. "He seems to have moved on rather easily."

Colter's dream had been to own a horse ranch. He'd already bought the land and was saving to build a house when he retired from the rodeo circuit. After meeting her, he'd decided it was time to quit and settle down, and she'd wanted so desperately to be part of his dream. But she never had the chance....

"Not so easily," Tulley said dryly. "I thought he'd kill himself with the drinking and the partying, then something happened that turned him around."

She raised her eyes to his. "Ellie?"

"Yeah. When he found out about her, it changed his whole life. Her...her mother decided she couldn't be a mother, and Colter took full responsibility."

To say Marisa was shocked was putting it mildly. She couldn't imagine Shannon not wanting their child. Shannon had been crazy about Colter and they had shared the same interests—horses and the rodeo. What had gone wrong?

She swallowed. "Colter's a good father."

"Does that bother you?"

"A little," she admitted reluctantly. *A lot* would have been closer to the truth. Colter should know he'd had a son, too.

Tulley crammed his hat back on his head. "That little girl is the center of Colter's world. Everything he does, he does for her. Please don't come between them."

"Oh, Tulley, I would never do that."

He nodded. "I'm glad. And for good measure I'm asking you not to hurt him again. He didn't deserve it eight years ago, and he certainly doesn't deserve it now."

"Tul—" But Tulley was gone and all she heard was the slamming of the door.

She watched the candles on the table, her emotions flickering and wavering like the glow of the flames. One minute she wanted to tell Colter the truth, the next she didn't. She took a deep breath, recognizing that her actions were thoughtless and inconsiderate. She'd only been thinking about herself. Maybe Colter was right that she hadn't changed. Maybe her mother— Oh God, her mother! Her parents were probably waiting for her this very minute to sit down to dinner. She had to call.

Through the dimness she saw a phone on the kitchen wall. She reached for it, but the line was dead. Now what? Her cell phone might work. Looking around for her purse, she realized it was still in her car at the corral. She'd have to go herself, because she certainly wasn't asking Colter for any favors.

She opened the back door, then immediately closed it. The temperature was freezing, and she needed a heavier coat. Her eyes settled on the closet full of coats—surely Colter wouldn't mind? She rummaged until she found a heavy navy windbreaker with a hood. Holding the jacket to her face, she breathed in the leather and musk scent—Colter. She remembered that tantalizing fragrance, and for a moment she was lost in its magic.

She slipped on the jacket, which was rather large but would do. She zipped it up and tucked her hair beneath the hood.

Outside she stopped as the frigid air took her breath away. It was bitterly cold—the temperature had dropped at least twenty degrees. Light sleet fell to the ground. Icicles hung from the roof and the trees, and the wind added to the chill factor. She had to get her phone in a hurry.

There was no ice under the covered walkway, but as soon as her heels touched the grass, it crunched beneath her feet. Suede heels were not the ideal footwear for this weather. They'd be ruined, but she didn't particularly care. Her goal was to reach her car without breaking her neck.

She judged each step carefully, but a few yards from her car her feet slid out from under her and she landed on her butt with a thud that jarred her whole body. Sleet peppered her head, and her face, hands and feet were numb. Tears weren't far away. Everything seemed to close in on her at once.

What am I doing here? What am I doing here?

Sitting there, miserable, she felt her life become as clear as the chill in her bones. She'd believed she'd grown stronger and more confident, but in reality she hadn't. That was why she was so dissatisfied with her work. She'd traded living with her mother for living with her father, and he was just as domineering and controlling. Yet she clung to that security. Why? At almost twenty-six, she should be making a life for herself. She was a pampered little rich girl, just as Colter had said, unable to stand on her own two feet.

At the moment, that was the actual truth. Her body shook with cold, and she made a promise, a vow to herself. She was going to change her life completely—get away from her parents. Now if she could just get to her feet…

Colter dumped fifty pounds of feed into a trough under the eaves of the barn. He turned—and saw Marisa as she fell. He dropped the bag and ran for the gate. She wasn't getting up. Was she hurt? His feet slowed as he realized what he was doing—going to her aid. The past came full circle, and so many feelings were choking him, he fought to breathe. *I don't care about her. I don't.* He'd help anyone who needed help. *I don't care about her. I don't.* Over and over, he repeated the words, but he never stopped in his movement toward her.

"Are you hurt?"

Marisa glanced at him, squinting against the sleet. "No. Just my pride."

"Well, get up. It's freezing out here."

"I've tried, but my feet keep slipping out from under me."

Without a word, he held out his leather-gloved hands.

She placed her cold hands in his and he pulled her to her feet. When she slid into him, he caught her, holding her steady. He hadn't touched her in eight years and the sensation radiated a warmth that dispelled the cold. It brought back so many wonderful memories of touching her, loving her, until the warmth became a blazing flame. He hated the fact that he could remember those emotions so clearly.

"Were you trying to leave?" he asked, suddenly releasing her.

She brushed sleet from her nose. "I was trying to reach my car to get my cell phone. I need to call my parents, and the phone at the house is dead."

At the mention of her parents, he stepped away from her. "Mommy still keeping tabs on you?" he asked, unable to disguise his sarcasm.

She stuck out her chin in defiance. "I live with my father in Dallas."

"I don't—" He stopped and sucked air into his lungs. "Get in your car and drive into the garage and call whoever the hell you have to." Saying that, he strolled back to the barn.

Marisa shoved away the pain of his words and quickly drove her car into the garage. Not because he'd told her to, but because it was the sensible thing to do. She let the motor run, hoping the interior would soon warm up. She found her cell phone, but when she tried to call, there was nothing but static.

The clock on the dash told her it was seven o'clock. Dinner was at six, so by now they would be wondering where she was. Lamar Norris and his son, Adam, were dinner guests, and her father was not going to be happy she wasn't there. He'd been trying for the past few months to arrange a date between her and Adam. She had stoically refused. She was not attracted to Adam. He didn't wear cowboy boots or a Stetson hat or have green eyes. Every man she met she compared to Colter, and they all came up short. She'd never admitted that to herself before. She hadn't moved on at all. She continued to wallow in the emotions of the past.

The man in question didn't want her anywhere near him or his daughter. He'd made that very plain. Yet here she was, stuck for the night.

She wondered if her mother had arrived safely. If she had any idea where Marisa was, she'd have a fit. Cari was the only one who knew. She hoped her parents assumed she'd sought shelter from the storm. They'd be worried, but there was nothing she could do about that.

Hearing voices, she turned the motor off and climbed out. She grabbed her purse, then followed Colter, Ellie and Sooner into the house. Colter carried an armload of wood and Ellie held the door for him. Tulley was outside piling more wood on the patio.

Colter had a roaring fire going in a matter of minutes, and Marisa realized she had a problem: her clothes were dirty and wet. But she wasn't going to mention it. She'd caused enough trouble. She huddled closer to the fire.

Tulley came through the patio doors with a couple of flashlights. "Ah, it feels better in here already."

"Ellie, take the flashlight and see if you can find Ms. Preston some dry clothes in Becky's room." Colter spoke from the doorway, and she could feel his eyes on her.

"Are you wet?" Ellie asked, still wrapped in her big coat.

"Yes. I went out to my car."

"You have to walk fast. That way you don't get wet."

"I'll remember that," she replied with a grin.

"Ellie, the clothes," Colter said in an impatient voice.

"Okay. Okay." Ellie took the flashlight from Tulley and headed for the stairs.

"I'll go with you," Marisa offered.

"There's no need," Colter snapped.

"She has to put them on, Daddy," Ellie said, as if she were talking to a child.

There was a long pause. "Okay, but hurry. It's cold up there."

Marisa trailed Ellie and Sooner up the stairs onto a balcony overlooking the den. She could see the fire blazing and Colter and Tulley silhouetted against it. They were talking—probably about her—and she wished this night was over.

Ellie found her a pair of jeans, a T-shirt, a sweatshirt, wool socks and a corduroy jacket. The jeans were a tad big in the waist, but everything else fit fine. Her cashmere coat was ruined, as were her shoes.

Ellie shone the light on her high heels. "Wow. Can I try them on?"

"Sure, but let's take them downstairs. It's warmer there."

"Okay." Ellie took off running with the heels, and Marisa followed more slowly.

In the den, Colter and Tulley had made a pallet with blankets and quilts, and there were more quilts on the sofa.

"Oh boy," Ellie cried, falling down on the pallet, the heels forgotten. "We're having a slumber party."

"It's not a party," Colter said, his voice stern.

"Is, too," Ellie insisted.

Colter sighed. "Tulley's put out some cold cuts, fruit and soft drinks, so eat, and then we'll all get some sleep."

They sat on the floor around the coffee table. Colter ate sitting on the sofa, and she noticed a telltale grimace when he leaned over to reach for the mustard. His leg must be hurting, but he'd never admit it.

Marisa wasn't aware of what she was eating. The fire was warm and cozy and the candlelight flickered hypnotically. She felt as if she'd slipped into another time, another place, where she should've been eight years ago—here with Colter... She stopped those thoughts immediately.

Tulley gathered up the leftovers. "I'll throw this in the trash, then I'm off to my featherbed."

Ellie ran and gave him a kiss. "'Night, Tulley."

"'Night, shorty."

"Tulley's tough," Ellie told her. "He grew up in the— What did he grow up in, Daddy?"

"The Depression."

"Yeah, and sometimes all he had to eat was bread and water. He didn't have any shoes, either, and he had to walk ten miles to school."

"Tulley's pretty impressive." She smiled.

"He also tells impressive stories," Colter said under his breath.

"'Night, everyone," Tulley called, and Marisa could hear the laughter in his voice.

Colter stood. "You take the sofa." He didn't call her by name, but she knew he was talking to her.

"No. I'll sleep on the floor."

"You'll sleep on the sofa." His words were final.

"Let her sleep with me, Daddy, please," Ellie begged. "We're having a slumber party."

"Ellie." He groaned in frustration.

Ellie quickly removed her coat and crawled beneath the covers, Marisa did the same before Colter could object.

"'Night, Daddy," Ellie said.

Marisa heard a long, irritated sigh, then the squeak of the sofa. He was giving in, and she felt as if she'd achieved a small victory.

"Oh, oh." Ellie jumped up and ran to Colter. "I forgot to kiss you."

In a moment she was back. "I kiss Daddy every morning and every night. He can't live without my sugar—ain't that right, Daddy?"

"Isn't that right?" Colter corrected.

"Yeah. It is."

Marisa smiled as Ellie crawled beneath the covers again. Sooner nuzzled his way beside her. How could any woman give up this child? She was adorable.

"Do you have kids?" Ellie asked.

"No—" she answered with a catch in her voice.

"Are you married?"

"Ellie." Colter's voice rang out.

"Daddy's kind of grouchy," Ellie whispered to her.

"Go to sleep," Colter said.

"It's too early."

"I'm not in a mood to argue about that tonight. Just go to sleep."

"He's *real* grouchy," Ellie amended.

COLTER CLOSED his eyes, hardly able to believe that Marisa Preston was here in his house, talking to his child, and there was nothing he could do about it. This was going to be the longest night of his life.

He knew Ellie wouldn't stop asking her questions. She did that with every woman she thought might be a mother candidate. He wasn't sure how to tell her that Marisa wasn't the motherly type, that there was no way in hell he'd ever get involved with her again.

No way. Under no circumstances.

Chapter Four

"Where the hell is she?"

Richard Preston paced back and forth in the library of the Dalton mansion in Highland Park. Vanessa Preston and Reed watched him.

"The police haven't been able to find her car, so she's not stranded on any of the highways. Where could she be? It took me forever to get Lamar and Adam here, and she does a disappearing act. This isn't like her." Richard turned to Reed. "She didn't say where she was going?"

"I've already told you, Father. She said she had somewhere to go and that she'd be back for dinner."

"Why the hell did you allow her to go out in this weather?"

Reed's eyebrows darted up. "Allow?"

"She's not strong like you. She needs protection."

"I—"

"Lay off Reed, Richard." Medium height with blond good looks, Vanessa Preston crossed her legs and smoothed her silk skirt over her knees. "You're missing the obvious, as usual."

Richard glared at her. "What are you talking about?"

"Me, Richard. She's avoiding me."

"That's absurd. Marisa's gotten over the past."

"Mother might be right," Reed said. "Marisa was very nervous about something, and Cari…" He snapped his fingers.

"That's it. I interrupted Cari and Marisa talking, so she's either with Cari or Cari knows where she is."

"Call her," Richard ordered.

Reed dialed Cari's number and she answered on the second ring. "Cari, this is Reed Preston."

"Hi, junior, what can I do for you?"

Reed's mouth tightened. "I'm looking for Marisa."

"Isn't she at home?"

"No, and it's late and we're getting worried."

"Oh, no."

"What? Where's Marisa?"

"I'm not telling you anything, junior."

Reed took a deep breath. "In this weather she could be stranded somewhere, maybe needing medical attention. Please tell us where she went so we can check on her."

Reed listened for a few seconds, then said a curt goodbye and hung up. He stared at his parents.

"What?" Richard demanded. "Where is she?"

"She…she went to see Colter Kincaid."

Silence.

"Oh, my God," Vanessa muttered.

"No, no." Richard shook his head. "She wouldn't do that, not after what he did to her life."

Reed shrugged. "That's what Cari said."

"Richard, do something." Vanessa twisted the pearls around her neck.

"I will," Richard said. "I'll make sure that man never hurts my daughter again."

THE FIRE BURNED BRIGHTLY, enclosing the room in its inviting warmth. Marisa stared into the darkness, listening to the howl of the wind and the icy refrain of the storm, but she wasn't afraid. Oddly, she experienced a peacefulness that was comforting.

"Are you asleep?" Ellie whispered so Colter wouldn't hear.

"No," Marisa whispered back.

"Me, neither." Ellie scooted closer. "Are you married?"

Marisa smiled. Ellie remembered she hadn't responded to that question earlier, and it seemed Ellie needed an answer.

"No. I'm not married."

"Daddy's not, either." A slight pause. "He's handsome, don't you think?"

At seventeen, she'd thought Colter the handsomest man she'd ever met. Her opinion hadn't changed. "Yes. I suppose."

"Did Santa Claus send you?"

"Excuse me?"

"Well, you see, I wrote Santa for a mommy, and you appeared out of nowhere, so I figured he answered my letter."

Marisa hated to disappoint Ellie, but she couldn't lie. "No, sweetie. Santa didn't send me."

"Oh, gee, that's not fair. Why *can't* I have a mommy?"

"You have your father," Marisa reminded her, not sure how to handle this conversation.

"Yeah, and he's the best daddy in the whole world, but he doesn't know any girl things."

"Like what?"

"Well, my friend Lori has a sister. Her name's Ashley, and she started her period. Lori and me didn't know what that was, so her mom explained. When I got home I told Daddy, and his ears turned red. He said I was still too young, but it happened to all girls and when it did I was supposed to tell him and we'd buy what I need. That's gross, though. Aunt Becky said she'd come and help me, and Lori's mom offered to help, too. But I don't want Aunt Becky or Lori's mom. I want my own mommy. She'd know all about things like that."

"I'm sure she would." Poor Ellie. Clearly she wanted a mother any way she could get one. "But you have to leave that up to your father."

"Oh, no. My mother broke his heart and he's never falling in love again, but I'm not giving up."

Colter had been in love with Shannon. She couldn't believe how much that hurt—and it shouldn't. She'd left him, so he had had every right to get on with his life. How she wished she'd been able to do the same.

"Lori and me heard Santa's coming to Dalton's Department Store, and I'm going to see him. I want to ask him why he hasn't sent me a mommy. I've asked a bunch of times. Lori says Santa Claus isn't real, but I believe in him. Do you believe, Ms. Preston?"

Ellie's words danced in her head with childish candor. "Yes. I believe." She believed in anything that made another person happy, and believing in Santa made Ellie happy—that was obvious.

"Since I work at Dalton's, I'll make sure you get a private sitting with Santa. How's that?" Colter wouldn't like her interfering, but she couldn't help herself. She certainly wasn't telling Ellie there wasn't a Santa Claus.

"You do?" Ellie sat up, her voice excited. "That's awesome."

Colter lay listening to the conversation, biting his tongue and clamping his jaw so tightly his head hurt. If he stopped Ellie, she'd just start again with the questions. They'd been through this many times, and Ellie never gave up. He didn't understand her strong desire for a mother. He'd done everything he could to fill that gap, but he'd failed. And he had never felt that more than he did at this moment.

The menstrual cycle talk had caught him off guard. Considering the nature of the subject, he thought he'd done a good job. Clearly he hadn't. He wasn't even aware his ears had turned red.

Ellie needed a woman to discuss things with, that was very plain now. However, Marisa Preston was the last woman he wanted Ellie talking to.

"Are you *sure* Santa didn't send you?"

"Ellie Kincaid, go to sleep this instant." Colter's voice

shot through the darkness, and Ellie dived beneath the covers.

"I gotta go to sleep before Daddy has a coronary," she said. "That means a heart attack—Tulley told me." Then she whispered in Marisa's ear. "I'll be at Dalton's." Ellie snuggled against Sooner and silence prevailed.

Marisa stared into the glow of the fire with so many questions running through her mind. Why hadn't Colter remarried? Ellie had said he'd loved Shannon. Maybe he still did.

She'd thought the love she and Colter had shared was special—a once-in-a-lifetime love. She saw now that as a naive young girl, she'd been in love with love. She also saw that she'd needed to come here—to see Colter and his family. It was cathartic. This was what she needed to bury the past and get on with her life.

And she prayed she could.

COLTER TOSSED AND TURNED so much that his leg started to throb. Dammit. Would this night never end? At least Ellie had fallen asleep, and the quiet outside signaled that the storm had stopped.

He sat up, grabbed a flashlight and made his way to the bathroom near the laundry room. A couple of Tylenols would help. He got a bottle of water, swallowed two pills and headed back to the den. As he did, the lights came on. Thank God. Looking at his watch he saw it was 5:00 a.m.

The heat came on, but he stoked the fire and threw on a couple of logs. He glanced down at Marisa and Ellie sleeping on the floor. His eyes centered on Marisa, her blond hair disheveled, her features serene. She had that same appeal, that same look of innocence and beauty she'd had back then. He drew a deep breath. She wasn't innocent or beautiful. Try as he might, though, he found himself wishing she could've been Ellie's mother. The pain of that stabbed him.

Marisa stirred and sat up, pushing her hair behind her ears. His stomach tightened at the gesture, and he remembered mornings like this when she'd wake and smile at him and the world became a brighter place. It had all been a lie, though. At the first sign of trouble, she'd given in to her mother and left him behind without even saying goodbye.

"The lights are on," she said in a sleepy voice.

"Yeah. They just came on." He walked to the sofa and sat on the arm, gazing down at her. He had to do this, so he might as well get it over with. "You came here to tell me something. What?"

She blinked, unable to believe what she was hearing. He wanted to listen, and she welcomed this opportunity. She'd decided it would be better for him not to know, but suddenly she changed her mind—maybe because his voice wasn't so angry anymore.

Searching for the right words, she glanced at Ellie, unsure of whether to talk in front of her.

Colter followed her eyes. "She's sound asleep and she doesn't wake up until about seven."

Marisa swallowed. "I wanted to tell you why I left."

"Does it make a difference?"

She looked him in the eye. "Yes—to me."

He shrugged. "You let your mother force you into leaving, and that pretty much said how you felt about me and the future we'd planned. What can you add to that?"

"Have you ever wondered *how* she forced me?"

"From what you said about her, she wielded immense power over you and your life. When she showed up, you caved and went home like the dutiful daughter."

Marisa shook her head. "No, it didn't happen like that. I refused to go with her."

His eyes narrowed. "But you went."

"She didn't leave me much choice. When I refused, she said she'd have you charged with statutory rape."

"What!"

"There was a policeman waiting outside, and I knew she meant what she'd said."

"You were twenty-one."

She locked her fingers together. "I lied. I was only seventeen, a month from my eighteenth birthday."

He stood and jammed both hands through his hair. "*Seventeen?* I was ten years older than you. You were seventeen?"

"Yes. My friend Stacy had a friend who knew someone who made fake IDs. We just wanted to have some fun, and that was the only way we could get into the casinos."

"You never said anything."

"You never asked."

"I just assumed— God, you were seventeen."

"Yes." A flush of guilt stained her cheeks. "I couldn't let you go to jail, so I went with my mother. As soon as I reached New York, I called the motel, but you'd checked out. I was devastated. You didn't give me an address or a phone number, and I didn't know how to get in touch. I kept trying for weeks, then I hired a private investigator."

Colter's gaze sharpened. "Evidently he didn't find me."

"I made the mistake of writing him a check. My mother had access to my account, and she contacted him. She was furious at what I'd done and we had a big scene. In the end she gave me the information the investigator had found out— that you'd already married someone else."

"I wasn't married then," he said in a controlled voice.

The fire crackled behind her, and daylight peeped through the blinds, but she was only aware of his words. They didn't make sense. "What?"

"I married Shannon after Ellie was born."

"Oh."

His eyes flared. "Your mother lied to you."

It took a moment to assimilate this, to believe her mother would do that to her. But then, her mother would've done anything to keep her away from Colter. That little lie was supposed to make Marisa forget all about him. It had done just the opposite. Every day she'd carried their son she had thought about Colter constantly, and over the years he'd never been far from her mind.

"Let's stop playing games, Marisa. The decision you made years ago, under whatever circumstances, is final. The past is over and it's been over for so long that I don't even care anymore. Ellie's birth may not have been the way I wanted it, but that's something I'm honest about. I don't think you even know what the word means." He swallowed visibly. "As soon as the ice melts, I want you out of here."

She paled at the cruelty of his words. The anger was back, and his eyes blazed as hot as the fire. Before she could retaliate, someone rang the doorbell, then knocked loudly at the front door.

"What the hell?" Colter hurried to answer it.

Marisa got to her feet and realized she was shaking. She wrapped her arms around her waist to still that reaction. After a moment, she heard raised voices and moved toward the foyer, surprised the racket hadn't awakened Ellie.

"I'm sorry, Colter. I have orders," a man was saying. "I have a warrant to search your house. Richard Preston says you kidnapped his daughter, and he has the Dallas Police Department in an uproar. The sheriff wants me to check it out before they call in the FBI."

"Search away," Colter replied. "But you might want to ask the woman herself what she's doing here."

Marisa stood in the doorway, her eyes big and troubled.

"Ms. Marisa Preston?" the man asked.

"Yes," she answered in a weak voice.

The man stepped forward. "I'm Deputy Jimmy Walsh. Are you being held against your will?"

"Of course not! Why on earth would you think that?"

"Your family believes Mr. Kincaid kidnapped you and they're very worried."

Mother. She wasn't going to stop…until Marisa stopped her. The only person who'd ever kidnapped her was her mother. She'd taken away her childhood and now she was trying to destroy what little peace Marisa had managed to find. A white rage filled her.

"Mr. Kincaid doesn't even want me here. I came of my own free will, and you can tell my mother—"

The deputy held up his hand. "I've only spoken with your father, so if you'll get your things, I'll take you back to Dallas and your family."

Her mother could manipulate her father into doing anything. This time she wasn't giving in. She was fighting back.

"Are the roads passable?" she asked.

"The highway department's been working all night and I managed to get here without too much of a problem."

"Then I'll follow you in my car."

"It'd be better if you came with me."

"Am I under arrest?"

His face turned slightly red. "No, ma'am."

"Good. Then it's settled. I'll drive my own car." She whirled toward the den.

"Sorry for the intrusion, Colter," she heard the deputy say.

She sank onto the pallet, where she found the corduroy jacket and slipped it on. Ellie stirred and sat up, rubbing her eyes.

"The lights are on," she said.

"Yes," Marisa answered, looking around for her shoes.

"Are you leaving?" Ellie asked.

"Yes. I have to go."

"Then Santa didn't send you." The forlorn voice bothered Marisa.

"No. Santa didn't send me, but here's an early Christmas present." She handed her the high heels.

"Cool."

Marisa stood. "Goodbye, Ellie."

"'Bye. You sure you don't need your shoes? It's cold."

"I have wool socks on, so don't worry about it."

"Okay." She stroked Sooner. "Can I still come and see Santa?"

Marisa could feel Colter's eyes boring into her, but she wasn't going to disappoint Ellie. She didn't care how angry he got. "Sure. Anytime you want."

Ellie smiled. "Thanks."

Marisa picked up her purse and walked toward the back door. Tulley was in the kitchen drinking coffee. "'Bye, Tulley," she said, but didn't stop. She had to get away.

Colter caught her at the door. "Let's be clear about one thing."

She'd had all she could take from him. "No," she snapped. "I'm not listening to any more of your nastiness or your insults. I made some bad choices—very bad choices—but I had my reasons. Reasons I thought were valid at the time. If you could stop thinking about your pride for one tiny second, you might want to hear those reasons. Until then, I have nothing to say to you."

Chapter Five

Colter walked into the kitchen and flopped down into a chair. Tulley placed a cup of coffee in front of him, but he barely saw it. All he could see was Marisa's angry face.

Ellie tottered in on the high heels.

"Take those shoes off," he said, more sharply than he'd intended. "We're sending them back to Ms. Preston."

Ellie stuck out her lip. "She gave them to me."

"They're going back."

Ellie stepped out of the shoes, picked them up and ran to her room, slamming the door. Sooner barked. The door opened and then slammed again.

Tulley sat down. "You were a bit rough on her."

"I'll apologize in a minute—after I cool off." He looked at Tulley. "She lied to me."

"About what?"

"She said she was seventeen in Vegas, not twenty-one."

"Yep, that's a whopper, but I told you she looked too young and inexperienced for Vegas. Back then you weren't listening to much I had to say."

"I wore rose-colored glasses where she was concerned, but they were brutally ripped away and I can see her for the woman she really is."

"Are you sure?"

"What do you mean?"

"The young Marisa was weak, but this Marisa seems strong. Remember the time you scratched your arm riding Diablo at the rodeo in Vegas? She almost passed out when I changed the bandage. But yesterday she climbed over the fence, with the horse running wild, to get to you. She even stopped the bleeding. The young Marisa wouldn't have gone anywhere near that horse and she certainly couldn't have attended to your leg."

"So she's matured. That doesn't change anything."

"Guess not."

"What does she expect from me?"

"Forgiveness."

"No." He shook his head. "I can't ever forgive her—yet last night, when she fell on the ice, I ran to her without thinking. I could feel her pulling me in with those soft eyes and that sweet smile—just like in Vegas. She was sitting with all those people and the only one I could see was her. That connection was there, and it wouldn't have mattered if she was seventeen or twenty-one."

"Nope. Probably not."

Colter took a gulp of coffee, hearing the truth of his words but not wanting to face it. "I can't believe any of this. Her parents sending the cops out here was the last straw, and it seemed to be for her, too. She was furious when she left, but I hope they convince her to stay away."

"That would be best."

Colter got to his feet. "I'd better go soothe Ellie's ruffled feathers."

"What would it hurt if she kept the shoes?" Tulley asked. "She's a little girl, but she's starting to like big-girl things."

"Yeah." Colter glanced toward Ellie's room. "She's growing up too fast and I'm lost when it comes to this girl stuff."

"Yep. Ellie's reminded you of that on more than one occasion."

"I thought I could be everything to my daughter, and it hurts that I can't. She still keeps asking for a mother…."

"Then let her keep the shoes." Tulley stood and grabbed his hat. "She'll feel like a big girl. What harm can it do? That's my two cents. I'll check on the horses and be back to fix breakfast."

Colter watched him go with a bitter taste in his mouth. He didn't want any reminders of Marisa in his house—not even a pair of damaged shoes. But it was a little late for such thinking. Marisa had invaded his carefully built world in more ways than he cared to think about.

As MARISA FOLLOWED the deputy, her anger mounted. How dare her parents treat her like a child! That was what she'd always been to them—a child who needed protection, guidance and supervision. When her parents separated, the agreement had been that her father would raise Reed and her mother agreed to raise Marisa, and they would do so without interference from each other.

It had worked, more or less, until her father had come to New York for a visit and found her an emotional wreck. She'd just lost her son and she couldn't bring herself back from that dark place of grief and intolerable sadness. When her father learned what had happened, he and Vanessa had argued bitterly, but he had ignored Vanessa's threats and brought Marisa home to Texas to heal.

She'd had a strained relationship with her mother after that, but they'd reached a degree of understanding. Vanessa was not to meddle again. But Marisa had never been in control of her own life; one or both of her parents had. That was going to change. She'd been thinking about this earlier and now she had to put it into action.

The deputy didn't stop at the outskirts of Dallas. He obviously had orders to deliver her, like an expensive package, to her father. The drive had taken twice as long because of the icy roads, but soon he pulled up to the security gate of the Dalton mansion.

When he got out and came to her window, she pushed a button to lower it.

"I've been instructed to take you to your father. Could you open the gate, please?"

"Yes," she answered with deceptive calm, and punched the code into her remote control. The gates swung open and the deputy ran back to his car.

She parked behind him in front of the palatial home that had belonged to her grandfather. Normally, she'd drive to the garage, but today she wasn't planning on staying that long.

Before the deputy could ring the bell, the door opened and her father stood there. His eyes went immediately to Marisa. "Oh, sweetheart, you're okay." He tried to put his arms around her, but she sidestepped him and walked through the foyer into the living room.

Vanessa ran to her. "Darling, thank God you're home." She tried to hug Marisa, but again Marisa moved away.

They walked into the library and Marisa turned on them.

"How dare you humiliate me like this. How dare you treat me like a child."

"Now, Marisa, we only did what we thought was best for you," Richard said.

"Best for me!" She laughed, unable to keep the hysteria out of her voice. "That's a joke. You've never thought about me or my feelings. It's always what both of you want."

"Calm down, sweetheart, and we'll talk about this rationally," Richard urged.

"I'm not calming down or listening to anything else you have to say."

"Okay. Okay." Richard was trying to pacify her. "But, sweetheart, why would you go see that man?"

Marisa took a step closer to Vanessa and stared her straight in the eye. "Because I wanted to tell him about our son. He has a right to know."

Vanessa lifted her chin. "What did he say?"

"I never had a chance, with the storm and the electricity going out."

"So you never told him?" her father asked.

"No, but it's just a matter of time. Unless, of course, you have the police tail me everywhere I go."

"Doesn't he have a wife and a little girl?" Vanessa asked as if she hadn't spoken.

"He has a little girl, but the wife isn't there anymore. You probably know that, though, don't you?"

Vanessa's expression barely changed.

"He wasn't married when you told me he was. He married Shannon later. You only told me that so I'd get on with the wonderful life you had planned for me."

Vanessa lifted her chin again. "Yes, I lied. But the detective said Kincaid was involved with her. That didn't sound like a man deeply in love. I'd do it again to protect you."

"Protect me? From the man I love?"

Vanessa was obviously shocked.

"Don't worry, Mother. I'm so mixed up I don't know *what* I feel. But Colter hates me and he doesn't want me anywhere near his little girl. That should make you happy."

"What happened to his wife?"

"I'm not sure."

"But he has his daughter?"

"Yes, and she's adorable, bright and spunky—everything a child should be. So you see, Colter already has a child and he's not interested in hearing about the one we lost, but for my own peace of mind I have to tell him."

Richard spoke up. "Sweetheart, that's not wise. I thought you'd let the past go, but you're still clinging to unreal fantasies about this man."

Before Marisa could answer, Reed came in from the kitchen holding a cup of coffee. "Marisa, you're back," he said, coming over to her. "You okay?" he asked in a low voice.

"Yes, I am."

He gestured at her feet. "Where are your shoes?"

"I ruined them in the sleet." She wasn't telling them anything else.

"Other than that, you look fine." Reed took a sip of coffee.

"No, she isn't." Richard picked up the phone. "I'm calling a therapist and setting up some counseling sessions so you can get this man out of your system. Now, go upstairs and get some rest, and we'll discuss this again when you're in a better frame of mind."

Marisa was dumbstruck. They hadn't heard a word she'd said. This was the pattern of her life. They ordered and she obeyed. But not anymore. Not one minute more.

She raised her head, knowing her eyes were as dark as the secrets in her soul. "I'm going upstairs, but I'm not resting. I'm packing a few things, then I'm leaving for good."

Vanessa gasped.

Richard slammed down the receiver. "What are you talking about? This is your home."

"This is my prison," she said, her eyes not wavering for a second. "And everything here is for show, especially me. I'm a glorified puppet. You pull my strings, Father, and I entertain your business associates, decorate your stores and wear a made-up title. You parade eligible bachelors in front of me, in hopes that a marriage could benefit Dalton's. As a dutiful daughter, I keep trying to please, but you and Mother have broken me. I don't even know who I am anymore." She took a calming breath. "I have to find me."

"You're just upset," her mother said. "A lot of that's probably my fault, but Marisa, I'll be leaving tomorrow for a Christmas cruise to the Greek Isles on Niko's yacht. Please don't do anything drastic because you're angry with me."

"I was very angry," Marisa admitted. "Now I just want some peace, and I have to find that on my own. I hope you'll both try to understand." She turned toward the stairs, then stopped. "Have a good trip, Mother."

"I forbid this, Marisa," Richard said, his voice rising.

"Forbid all you want. I'm leaving." She ran up the stairs feeling light-headed.

RICHARD FROWNED at Reed. "Talk her out of this."

"How am I supposed to do that?"

"Any way you can. She's not leaving this house."

"I told you this would happen if you brought her back to Texas," Vanessa railed. "But no, you wouldn't listen. You wanted control of both our children, and now you've lost her. How does it feel, Richard?"

"Shut up, Vanessa."

"No, I won't." Vanessa pointed a finger at him. "*You're* the cause of this. If she'd just stayed in New York, like our separation stated, none of this would be happening."

"She was a zombie, and I wasn't leaving her in that condition."

"She'd just lost a child," Vanessa shouted. "That's a normal reaction for a woman. If you'd left her alone, she would have gone back to her career."

"Get out of my face, Vanessa, because I'm not listening to this."

"Both of you, take a deep breath," Reed said, intervening. "I'll go up and talk to Marisa, but only if you stop shouting."

Richard stormed off to his study, and Vanessa sat on the sofa, her lips tight.

Reed headed upstairs.

COLTER OPENED Ellie's door and walked into her room. She was lying on the bed, the shoes in her hand, Sooner at her feet.

He sat beside her, his back against the headboard. "We need to talk, angelface."

Ellie rose to her knees, her eyes red. "Why don't you like her, Daddy? She's nice and pretty and—"

"And what?"

Ellie fiddled with the shoes. "Nothing."

"And Santa might have sent her?"

Her eyes flew to his. "You know?"

"Yes." He touched her cheek. "Ellie, baby, you do understand that there's only one way you're going to have a new mother?"

"You have to get married." She hung her head.

"That's it, and I'm not doing that until I fall in love again."

"Like you were with my mother?"

"Yes."

"But you're getting old and it might not happen."

He suppressed a laugh. "Well, then, is it so bad with just you, Tulley and me?"

"No."

"Are you unhappy?"

"No. I'm happy all the time."

"So why do you want a mother?"

Ellie shrugged. "I could talk to her about things—girl things."

He'd heard some of this last night when she'd been whispering to Marisa. "You can talk to me about anything. You do know that, don't you?"

"Yeah. But sometimes it's embarrassing."

"If we talk about it, then it won't be embarrassing."

She smiled and dived into his arms. "I love you, Daddy."

"I love you, too, angelface." He kissed the top of her head. "I'll do the looking for a mother, okay?"

Ellie nodded against his chest. "I don't know why I want a mommy so much. I think about it all the time and I can't stop. Why do I do that, Daddy?"

"Oh, baby." He held her tight, his heart breaking. "I think it's normal for little girls who don't have mothers. And there's a club for kids who only have one parent. It's called Big Brothers and Big Sisters. How'd you like a Big Sister?"

A teacher at Ellie's school had told him about the program after Ellie had gotten several of her classmates involved in her matchmaking schemes. He'd told the teacher he'd think about it, but he hadn't—until now.

Ellie lifted her head. "But you said we didn't need to join."

"I've changed my mind."

"Cool! I'd like a Big Sister."

"Then we'll do it. Now, let's go have some breakfast."

Ellie stared at the shoes with a gloomy expression.

Colter's chest tightened. "You can keep the shoes."

Ellie threw her arms around his neck. "Thank you, Daddy, and I'm gonna give you lots of sugar this morning."

She kissed his face, and Colter knew he'd do whatever it took to keep her happy. Whatever.

MARISA GRABBED A SUITCASE and gathered an assortment of clothes, not knowing what she'd need. She didn't stop to think. She packed quickly before her parents could do something to prevent her from leaving.

Reed stood in the doorway. "You're determined about this?"

She paused for a moment to glance at her brother. "Yes."

Reed walked inside. "I've been sent to talk you out of it."

"I figured that." She zipped up the suitcase.

"They love you. They're just a little overprotective."

She set the case on the floor. "I don't feel loved," she told him. "They're smothering me and sometimes I can barely breathe. I don't want to live like that anymore. I'm going to get a job. I have to find out if I can survive in this world, away from the support of my parents."

"Get a job?" Reed echoed. "That's absurd. You have a trust fund and you can do whatever you want. Travel, do charity work, help the poor—but there's no need to join the workforce."

"You sound like Father." She pushed her hair back.

"Oh, God," Reed groaned, but quickly shook off the comparison.

"Marisa… You've been obsessed with this man, and now that you've seen him again, you're not thinking rationally. I'll admit Father went over the top calling the police, but we were all very worried. Please don't do something you'll regret."

She drew a long breath. "I haven't been 'obsessed' with Colter. I've been obsessed with the loss of our child. You've never experienced that, so you don't know the emptiness, the loneliness that never goes away. When I saw Colter again, I thought if I told him about our son, that feeling would leave. But he's not interested in anything I have to say. It made me realize, though, that he's moved on, and I have to do the same. I can't do that under the watchful eyes of our parents. I need time, space and my freedom. Please, Reed, help me."

He wavered, but not for long. "Go out the back and I'll stall them."

She kissed his cheek and grabbed her suitcase and clothes bag. "Thanks, Reed."

"Call and let me know you're okay."

"I will," she promised, and ran down the hall to the back stairs.

RICHARD PACED HIS STUDY, downing whiskey. He heard a noise and walked to the window in time to see Marisa driving away.

"Goddammit." He ran for the control panel to the gate.

Reed stood in front of it. "Let her go, Father."

"Get the hell out of my way." He pushed Reed aside and hurriedly punched in some numbers. He and Reed stood at the window and watched as the gate closed behind Marisa's car.

"Goddammit, Reed! Look what you've done. A split second more and the gate would've locked and she would've had to stay here, where she belongs."

"And what? Lock her in her room? She's not seventeen anymore."

"You don't know what the hell you're talking about," Richard yelled. "She's going straight to him and he'll destroy her—again."

"What's going on?" Vanessa asked, coming into the room. "Why are you yelling?"

"Marisa's gone and your son helped her leave."

Vanessa glared at Reed. "Why would you do that?"

"Because she needs some time and she needs her freedom. I see nothing wrong with that. You two act insane when it comes to Marisa. Let her live her own life, for a change." He stalked out of the room.

Vanessa stared at Richard. "She'll see him again. You know she will."

Richard nodded. "Yeah."

"Stop it before she gets hurt."

Richard reached for his whiskey. "I plan to."

Chapter Six

The weather had cleared and the ice had all melted, leaving the streets wet and slippery. Marisa drove very carefully. She knew that in a matter of minutes her father could have someone following her, so she had to think fast. She wouldn't let herself be brought back like a disobedient child. It didn't take her long to figure out a plan. She headed for Dalton's and parked in her usual spot, then called a cab using her cell phone. Once the driver had dropped her at a small café, she phoned Cari.

Marisa walked into the restaurant with her suitcase, clothes bag and purse, and found a booth in a corner facing the entrance. She ordered coffee, which she drank while she waited. Maybe she shouldn't have called Cari, but she desperately needed a friend right now.

Ten minutes later, Cari came through the door and hurried toward her. She wore jeans and a heavy sweater, although her dark hair was still damp. She'd obviously just showered.

"I'm sorry," Marisa apologized, getting up and hugging her. "But I need to talk."

"No problem."

"Has my father called?"

"Oh, yes, and I have strict orders to call him the instant you show up. What on earth is going on?"

Marisa heaved a sigh. "It's a long story."

"Where are your shoes?" Cari asked, staring down at Marisa's feet in her heavy socks.

In her haste to leave, she'd forgotten to put on shoes and hadn't even noticed. "Ah." Marisa smiled. "I gave them to the sweetest little girl you'd ever want to meet."

"You gave your shoes away?"

"Yes. I did."

Cari frowned. "Are you okay? You're acting a little… strange."

"I *feel* a little strange."

"Let me get some coffee, and you can tell me this long story. Do you want some more?"

"No, thanks." Marisa resumed her seat.

Cari signaled a waitress, ordered coffee and slid into the booth.

For the next thirty minutes, Marisa told Cari everything that had happened since she'd left Dalton's yesterday.

"Oh, my. Your father sent the police out there. That's unbelievable."

"The deputy arrived, and I never got the chance to tell Colter about our son."

"So all of this was for nothing?"

Marisa fingered her cup. "No, not really. It made me see that I have to change my life. My parents control me like the proverbial puppet—they always have and I've let them. I'm finally breaking free. I'm quitting Dalton's and finding my own place to live, and next week I'll be looking for a job."

"A job?" Cari asked in disbelief. "Your family's wealthy and you have what everyone thinks of as the American dream. You don't have to work."

"The American dream, I believe, is making it on your own in this land of opportunity, and that's what I plan to do."

Cari shook her head. "I don't understand. I've had to struggle for everything I've gotten and sometimes the struggle's exhausting."

"But you feel good about succeeding by yourself—you've told me many times."

"Yeah. I only have a high school education but I took some business courses. I was determined to be more than a sales-clerk."

"I want the same thing. To be a productive human being."

"So what's the plan?"

"I have to find a place to live."

"You can stay with me," Cari offered.

"If I did, you'd lose your job—the one you've worked so hard for."

"Hmm." Cari sipped her coffee.

"When you get back to your apartment, call my father. Tell him you saw me and that I refused to tell you where I was going." She smiled at her friend. "Because I'm not telling you. That way you won't have to lie."

"Marisa…"

"Sorry, no exceptions."

"But…"

"No," Marisa said, refusing to budge on that decision.

"Okay. You will call me from time to time to let me know how you're doing?"

Marisa nodded. "I'll do that."

Cari watched her for a moment. "So you gave your heels to Colter's daughter?"

"Yes. She's just a delight."

"You didn't feel any resentment toward her?"

"Not for a second. She has nothing to do with the past."

"Did you resent Colter?"

She gripped the cup more tightly. "At first I did. He and Shannon got married so quickly, and that hurt, but I have to take some responsibility there. That's what healing's about—admitting fault and taking responsibility." She pushed her cup away. "I'd better go before my father shows up."

"Marisa…"

"I'll be fine. Don't worry."

Marisa called a cab and left. She switched cabs several times, in case her father checked with the companies, then she bought a paper and checked into a motel. She didn't plan on being found too easily. After taking a shower, she scanned the want ads, looking for a place to stay. There were lots of apartments, but she felt the rents were too high. She wanted something she could afford on a working girl's salary. She was about to give up when she noticed a section describing rooms for rent. That would fit her requirement more closely; she wouldn't have to worry about furniture, and the rent would be lower.

She talked to a couple of the homeowners, but they didn't sound very appealing. The third one seemed pleasant, so she decided to have a look. The room was in an old Victorian house in an older part of Dallas. Getting out of the cab, she studied the house, which was attractive and well kept. The grounds, too, were nicely maintained, and the whole place had a warm, homey air.

She met Hazel Hackleberry, the owner, a short, plump friendly older woman whom Marisa liked the moment she shook her hand. Within minutes, Marisa had become her boarder. The room itself was white and pink with a lot of frills and lace, but Marisa didn't care. It would be her home for now.

The next day she moved in, and bought a used car because she couldn't continue to spend money on cabs. On Monday, she began searching for a job. She spent the entire week submitting applications and attending interviews, with no luck. She had a business degree, but once a firm became aware of her connection to Richard Preston, she was no longer considered a viable employee. Her father had put the word out—don't hire her.

Meanwhile she settled comfortably into Mrs. Hackleberry's house. Hazel was the motherly type, and although she'd told Marisa that meals weren't provided, she invited her to dinner almost every night. Hazel's only son had been killed in Vietnam and her sister lived next door. Other than that she had little family, and Marisa knew she was lonely.

There was a large Steinway in the living room. Every time Marisa passed it she itched to play. One evening, without really thinking about it, she sat down on the piano bench and ran her fingers across the keys. She hadn't touched a piano since her son's death. It felt so natural, though. So right. She played a Chopin piece, but the piano needed tuning. Still, she was lost in the music.

"Oh, my dear," Mrs. Hackleberry said, listening. "You play beautifully."

She turned on the bench. "Thank you. Do you play?"

Hazel shook her head. "Good Lord, no. My aunt left me the piano. Why, I don't know. I never played a day in my life."

"Do you mind if I play while I'm here?" Marisa couldn't believe the words coming out of her mouth. For years, she had ignored her training and avoided anything to do with music, but now she felt liberated. Maybe it was seeing Colter again. Maybe it was her bid for freedom. Or maybe she was finally letting go of the past.

"No. I'd enjoy it."

"Do you mind if I get it tuned?" she asked, then quickly added, "I'll pay for it."

"Go ahead," Hazel replied. "It's time someone used that old thing."

The next day Marisa had the piano tuned. On impulse, she stopped by the Dallas Symphony Orchestra. She was almost high with excitement when the conductor granted her an interview and then an audition. He seemed pleased with her work and said he'd be in touch after the winter season. She intended to pursue her music—her way this time. But now she had to find a job.

That night after dinner, Marisa played for Hazel, then sat at the table going through the want ads again, searching for a job.

"You can't find a job?" Hazel asked.

"No. My father's pretty well closed most doors." When she'd rented the room, she'd told Hazel some of the reasons she needed it. Later, she'd confided more. Hazel was easy to talk to, and Marisa felt she was lucky to find this place.

"I wish I could help, but I used to be a seamstress and that's all I know."

"Oh. Who did you work for?"

"Madame Hélèna."

Marisa's head jerked up. "You worked for Madame Hélèna, the designer?"

"Yes. Do you know her?"

"Just her work. She's very famous."

"We dressed some of the most important people in the world," Hazel said with pride. "When Hélèna first started, it was just the two of us sewing, but now she has factories full of workers turning out her designs."

"I love her work," Marisa said. "Her line is sleek yet simple."

"Would you like to meet her?"

"Oh, Hazel, no. I wasn't fishing for an invitation."

"It's not an invitation. It's an offer. Hélèna's always looking for good help."

"That would be wonderful. Do you think she's hiring?"

"I'll give her a call and find out."

Marisa waited, her heart in her throat, hardly able to believe her luck. She needed this. She needed a break.

Hazel wrote something on a piece of paper and laid it in front of Marisa. "That's the address. Be there at nine and don't be late. Hélèna likes a responsible person."

"I won't—and thank you." Marisa got up and hugged her. Marisa had trouble hugging her own mother, but with Hazel it was so easy. She knew the healing process had started now, and sometime soon she might be able to talk to her parents again. They had left her alone, which she found rather suspicious, but she was grateful for it. Marisa supposed they were waiting for her to fall on her face. She wouldn't, though. She was going to make it.

She *had* to get this job.

Later, she picked out clothes for the interview, took a shower, then crawled into bed. Excitement trickled through her and, try as she might, she couldn't keep thoughts of Colter at bay. All week she'd tried not to think about him and his little girl. At times she succeeded and at others she didn't. She'd had his sister's clothes cleaned, packaged and mailed to him, with a note that said simply, "Thanks for lending me those." No signature. Her own clothes were still at his place, and she was sure he'd probably thrown them out.

She turned over in bed and smiled, imagining Ellie in her heels. She hoped Colter let her keep them. Flipping onto her back, she wondered if Ellie was still searching for a mother; she'd never know, because she'd never see them again. Her excitement turned to sadness but she fought it. She had to. There was no other choice.

MARISA WAS AT Madame Hélèna's office at 8:45 a.m., and she couldn't believe how nervous she was. She straightened the jacket of her dark green suit three times before she forced herself to stop.

Madame Hélèna walked in promptly at 9:00 a.m. Marisa had only seen pictures of her and was surprised she was so petite. Barely five feet, she was slim and elegant, with auburn hair worn in a knot.

She stared at Marisa. "So you're Marisa Preston?" She spoke with a slight accent.

"Yes, ma'am," Marisa answered, and shook her hand.

Bracelets dangled from Hélèna's wrist, and she wore a beaded choker that complemented the sleek raw silk dress with its V-neck. Marisa recognized the style as one of Madame Hélèna's.

"Have a seat." Hélèna sat, too, putting on a pair of glasses, and looked through some papers on her desk. "Hazel says you're looking for a job."

"Yes."

Hélèna leaned back. "Why, *chérie?* Your father is rich."

"I've been pampered and smothered all my life. I need freedom and I need to make it on my own." Marisa tried to be as honest as she could.

"I understand that. I was born in Paris and I met an American GI and fell in love. He brought me to Dallas and I thought I was in hell. I hated it here, but I loved the man more. I gave birth to a son and became very domesticated—and then my husband died. I didn't know what to do. I could sew, so I started sewing for people—anything to feed my son and me. Dallas women were willing to spend extra money for an original dress. I tapped into that. Word got around and soon my business was flourishing. But there were a lot of people who tried to stop me." She paused. "Richard Preston was one of those people."

Marisa swallowed. "Oh."

"He resented that I was taking business away from Dalton's, but I stuck it out, and today I have shops here, in New York, Los Angeles and in my beloved Paris."

Marisa was unsure of how to respond, so she nodded. "Yes, I know. Your designs are very popular."

"Ten years ago, I would've hired you in a second to settle that score with Richard, but I don't have time for revenge anymore."

Marisa's heart sank. "Are you saying you're not hiring me?"

"I'm saying I won't indulge your whim to get back at your father."

Marisa slid forward, perching on the edge of her chair. "Madame Hélèna, this isn't about getting back at my father. It's about my independence. I have to work to pay my bills and, before you ask, I'm not taking money from my father. I have to find out who I am— All I'm asking for is a chance."

Hélèna studied her for a moment, then leaned forward. "What do you know about fashion?"

"I know what I like."

Hélèna stood. "Come with me." They went through a door into a large studio crowded with easels, rolls and rolls of fabric, mannequins and everything else a designer might need. Hélèna went to a drawing board. "This is a dress I'm working on. What do you think?"

Marisa looked over her shoulder at the drawing—a straight black dress with long sleeves and, again, a modified V-neck. "Very nice," she murmured. "Simple but classy—something that could be worn to almost any formal occasion. And that neckline works for practically every woman."

Hélèna picked up a pencil. "Yes. I'm debating whether to put the slit up the back of the skirt or on the side."

"The side. It shows off the leg and is more attractive." When she realized what she'd done, she immediately apologized. "I'm sorry—"

Hélèna turned to her. "Never be afraid to voice your opinion, *chérie*. You have good instincts about fashion. The slit up the side *is* better—makes a woman feel sexy, and we need that every once in a while." She laid the pencil down. "If you want a job," she said abruptly, "you've got it. Just be prepared to do whatever is asked of you. You might run errands, wait on customers, answer the phone, check in freight, whatever."

"Yes, ma'am. I'm willing to do anything."

"You'll start on Monday and I'll give you a week's trial run. If it works out, we'll talk about something permanent."

"Thank you, Madame Hélèna. Thank you so much."

Marisa left walking about six feet off the ground. She had a job and a place to live; things could only get better from here on.

She called Cari and told her the good news. Cari was genuinely happy for her, and said Richard had stopped pressuring her for information. Surely that meant he and her mother were finally going to let her live her life. She and Cari talked for a while, and Marisa told her where she was living, since it seemed her parents weren't going to bother Cari anymore.

Before she could end the call, Cari said, "I wanted to tell you the cradle's been sold."

"Oh." She felt a moment of sadness, as she did every year when it went. But some lucky couple had purchased it for their baby and that was the way it should be.

"Marisa?"

"Hmm?"

"I don't know why you don't buy it yourself. You love it."

"The cradle is meant for a couple waiting for the birth of their child."

"Marisa—"

"I'm all right," she said before Cari could ask. "I'm glad it has a home."

They talked for a few more minutes, then Marisa said goodbye and hung up. She stared at the phone, wondering why she was so attached to that cradle. But she knew. It represented all the happiness a baby was supposed to bring, and it spoke about the true meaning and joy of Christmas. She'd wanted all of that for her son and, yes, she'd wanted it for herself, too. But some things weren't meant to be.

She started to call Reed, but she'd talked to him yesterday and told him she was fine. That was all he needed to know. She didn't want to put him in the middle again.

Marisa went to bed feeling good about herself and her life. She was determined to work very hard for Madame Hélèna and she'd practice her music at night. For the first time in ages she looked forward to tomorrow.

COLTER RECEIVED THE PACKAGE of clothes from Marisa and went upstairs to put them in Becky's closet. He stopped short as he entered the room. Marisa's clothes were strewn across the bed. He hadn't even been up here since that night, and he'd forgotten about them. What was he supposed to do with her things?

He laid the package on the dresser, then picked up the linen dress. A faint scent of lilac drifted to his nostrils. She'd worn the same fragrance in Vegas, and it wrapped him in captivating memories.

No, no, no. He wouldn't do this to himself. Throwing the dress onto the bed, he left. He couldn't let himself get caught in that maelstrom of emotion. The whole week had been nerve-racking as he waited for a second impromptu visit, but she'd stayed away. He suspected her parents had something to do with that. He was just glad she wasn't going to disrupt his life again.

As he reached the bottom of the stairs, the phone rang. It was his sister, Becky.

"I've got bad news," she said without preamble. "Jen's having a problem with the pregnancy and the doctor's ordered complete bed rest."

"Is she okay? Is the baby okay?"

"Yes. The doctor said she and the baby are fine, but she has to stay off her feet until the delivery. The baby's due in February, so this makes it a little harder for Bart and me. Bart and I have the McKinney Western Stores on our schedule for next week. As you know, they'll be carrying your boots in their outlets in Austin, and I have it all set up for you to visit each store. The newspaper ads have all gone out."

"We'll just cancel. Jen and the baby are more important."

"No way are we canceling, big brother. It took Bart and me a year to arrange this. We're working out a routine with Jen. Bart's mom's going to help out while we're in Austin, then I'm taking two weeks off and Bart's taking two weeks at Christmas."

"Sounds as if you've got it all figured out."

"Not everything. Christmas does present a problem. We've always spent it together at the ranch, but since Jen can't travel, we were hoping that you, Ellie and Tulley would come to Jen's house."

"I don't know, Bec. Ellie's never been away from home at Christmas."

"Just think about it and we'll talk again."

"Okay. I'll give Jen a call, too."

Colter hung up, hoping Jen and the baby were okay. She and Bart had been trying for years to conceive, and he didn't want anything to go wrong. He wanted only happiness for both his sisters. The three of them had been so close since their mother's death, and then, when Shannon had left, his sisters had helped him with Ellie. Ellie was barely three months old at the time, and he'd hoped Shannon would come back, but when he got the divorce papers he knew that wasn't happening. He'd decided he would tell Ellie very little about Shannon. Maybe that had been a mistake. Maybe—

He yanked up the phone and called Jen. She seemed in good spirits, so he felt immeasurably better.

As he finished the call, Ellie and Sooner bounded into the room. Tulley followed at a leisurely pace.

"Hey, Daddy." Ellie propped her elbows on the table, her face in her hands, staring at him, and his pulse accelerated at the love he felt for his child. "You should've seen me! Dandy goes around the barrels so fast Tulley says all he sees is a streak. She's the best barrel racer we've ever had and I don't even have to guide her. She knows what to do. She's awesome."

He smiled. "*You're* awesome—and you're out of breath."

Ellie gulped in air. "I know. Dandy goes so fast."

Tulley removed his hat and sat down. "Shorty's right. Dandy's a good barrel-racing horse. Sassy's, too."

"When can I ride in the rodeo, Daddy? When?"

"When you're old enough."

"When's that?"

"When I say so." He'd ridden in rodeos, so Ellie wanted to do the same thing, but he tried to deter her in every way he could. He wanted a better life for her, one that included a good education, but she loved horses and she got that from him. She was good at it, too. And it didn't help that Tulley encouraged her. Or that Shannon had been a championship barrel racer.

"Aw, you always say that."

He changed the subject. "Aunt Becky just called."

Ellie's eyes grew big. "Is she coming here today?"

"No." Then he told them what Becky had said.

A sad expression came over Ellie's face and she crawled into Colter's lap. "Is the baby gonna be okay?"

"Sure, angelface, the baby's fine," he reassured her. "But Becky wanted to know if we'd come to Jen's for Christmas, because Jen can't travel."

Ellie jumped up, shaking her head. "No! We can't do that."

Colter frowned, not sure what this was about. "Why?"

"'Cause I *can't* leave. Santa knows where I live and I have to be here. If I go to Aunt Jen's, he won't know where I'm at and I won't get my wish."

"Ellie…"

"We can't go, Daddy," she said, turning and running to her room. Sooner sprinted after her.

Colter sighed in frustration. "I'm getting tired of this mother-Santa thing. I should just go in there and tell her there's no damn Santa Claus. What do you think?"

Tulley scratched his head. "I think I'm not going to be the one to break her heart."

"Dammit, Tulley. She doesn't want to leave because she's waiting for her mother to come back."

"Well, if you're going to tell her there's no Santa, then you'll have to tell her the truth about her mother. Are you ready to do that?"

"No," he replied in a wooden voice. He'd never be ready to do that. He'd never be ready to tell Ellie her mother didn't want her.

Not ever.

Chapter Seven

The week passed quickly for Marisa. She was at Madame Hélèna's early every day, and she stayed late. At first, she did everything from answering the phone to waiting on customers. Then Hélèna asked her to work in her private office, and she ran errands, reminded her of appointments, answered her mail and tried to calm her when she became enraged at a store or supplier. Marisa didn't mind any of it; she enjoyed the excitement and the challenge. It became very clear that the famous designer had a temper and none of her staff wanted to risk her ire.

On Thursday, as Marisa was getting ready to leave, Madame Hélèna asked to speak with her. It was after nine and Marisa was tired, but she didn't complain. This was what being in the workforce was like—long days, tired muscles and aching bones. She'd never felt like this in her life and she was exhilarated. Cari said she was crazy, but all the work and effort meant freedom and independence to Marisa.

"I know you're anxious to go home," Hélèna said, frowning over a sketch.

"Not if you need something." Marisa liked the fact that she could help someone instead of being waited on.

Hélèna took off her glasses. "I told you I'd give you a week's trial."

Marisa's stomach tensed. "Yes."

"I thought I'd tell you my decision tonight instead of waiting until tomorrow."

Marisa held her breath.

"You have a permanent job here and—"

"Oh, thank you!"

Hélèna held up a hand. "Let me finish. The job will be as my personal assistant. Very few people can work with me on a day-to-day basis. I'm told I have a temper and that I'm not nice sometimes, but you seem to take all my idiosyncrasies in stride. Besides, you have an eye for fashion and I appreciate that and the number of hours you're willing to put in. So what do you say?"

Marisa smiled. "I say yes."

"Good." Hélèna scribbled something on a piece of paper and handed it to her. "That will be your monthly salary, and you'll be paid every two weeks."

Marisa stared at the figure. "This is very generous."

"You'll earn every dime of it," Hélèna said. "Richard's a fool not to recognize your potential." Hélèna reached for her glasses. "My son, who's also my business manager, tells me it's not wise to hire Richard Preston's daughter, but I've always been a good judge of people—it's one of the assets that got me where I am today—and I trust you implicitly, Marisa."

"Oh, yes, ma'am, I know that everything is confidential."

Hélèna nodded. "All the information you see or hear in this office is extremely private and not to be discussed with anyone."

"I would never—"

"I know, *chérie*," Hélèna cut in, "and I wish you were going to be with me for a very long time."

Marisa frowned slightly. "Why wouldn't I be?"

"Like I said, I can read people, and you're searching for yourself, your place in the world. I hope it's here, but I feel your heart is somewhere else."

Colter's face flashed into her mind. Tears welled up in her eyes, and she was unable to stop them.

Hélèna got up and put an arm around her. "*Chérie,* what is it?"

In a few sentences, Marisa blurted out everything about Colter, their child and the past. She hadn't meant to but Hélèna's sympathy was her undoing.

Hélèna led her to a small settee and urged her to sit down. "Now I understand the sadness in your eyes," she said quietly.

Marisa wiped at the tears on her cheeks. "I'm sorry. I shouldn't be bothering you with this."

"*Chérie,* affairs of the heart can be so painful. I lost the love of my life and I never found anyone to replace him, so I threw myself into my work. That's what you're trying to do—lose yourself in something."

'That deep pain is always there, though."

"Ah, *chérie,* you have to face those demons from the past, and you've made a great start by striking out on your own. You've said you don't know who you are, but I do."

Marisa blinked away tears. "You do?"

"Yes, you're a warm, compassionate woman. A sweet woman. As a matter of fact, you're so sweet, I'm sure you bleed honey."

"Thank you." Marisa smiled.

"Now, go to Hazel's and you don't have to come in so early tomorrow morning."

"Oh, no. I'll be here at my usual time."

Hélèna smiled. "I failed to mention responsible, loyal and dedicated."

Marisa gave her a quick hug—she'd never done that before, but it felt completely natural. Then she drove home.

When she reached the house, Hazel came hurrying from the den.

"You're back. I was getting worried," she said.

"Hazel, you're not to worry about me," Marisa scolded in a gentle tone.

"I know, but you're so young and inexperienced and—"

She raised an eyebrow, and Hazel backpedaled. "Have you had anything to eat?"

Marisa held up the bag in her hand. "I bought something at a deli."

"I'll get you some tea."

"No." Marisa shook her head. "I'll get my own tea. You go to bed. It's past your bedtime."

"Okay. I am getting a little tired."

"Good night, Hazel—and, oh, I almost forgot. Madame Hélèna hired me as her personal assistant."

"That's wonderful. I'm so happy." Hazel smiled, then yawned. "I'd better go to bed. 'Night."

"'Night," she called.

Marisa was exhausted, and she could barely stay awake to eat her dinner. The exhaustion was very satisfying, though. She went to bed soon after, but dreams of Colter kept her tossing and turning.

COLTER SPENT THE WEEK driving back and forth to Dallas to check on Jen, whose good spirits had turned to boredom because she had to stay in bed. She and Bart lived close to the office and the factory that made Kincaid Boots. He tried to cheer her up with talk of Christmas, although they still hadn't made a decision about where to have their get-together. Jen's focus was now on the baby.

He hadn't spoken to Ellie about Christmas again, because he didn't want to trigger a scene. But he'd have to broach the subject, and soon. In his view, her obsession with Santa Claus was out of control.

On Friday, Becky had him scheduled to put in appearances at the stores in Austin that would be carrying Kincaid Boots. Ellie's last day of school was Thursday, so he had decided to take her with him. To his surprise, that plan was met with resistance.

"I can't, Daddy. I have to go to Lori's birthday party. She's my best friend."

He rubbed his temple. "I forgot about that." This presented a quandary. He didn't like leaving Ellie anywhere, but now that she was older it was getting increasingly harder to avoid.

"I can stay at Lori's. Her mommy said so."

"Tulley and I are flying to Austin. Aunt Becky and Uncle Bart are already there. You like meeting people and you've even signed a few autographs." He was trying to cajole her; he couldn't help himself. He wanted Ellie with him.

"I know." She twisted her feet, inner turmoil evident on her face, and he cursed himself for making her feel guilty.

He pulled her onto his lap, kissing her quickly. "Okay, Ellie. You go to Lori's, and I'll pick you up when I get back."

She covered his face with kisses. "Thank you, Daddy."

Ellie ran to her room, and he sighed. He didn't understand why he felt so reluctant about this. He just didn't like being away from her.

ELLIE SAT ON THE FLOOR in her room, rubbing Sooner's head. "We gotta have a plan," she said.

Sooner barked. "I *know* Daddy's gonna be mad, but I hafta do this. We might be going to Aunt Jen's for Christmas and I hafta see Santa. I really do."

Ellie thought for a minute. "We need money." She got up and opened a drawer and counted her savings. "Twelve dollars and fifty-two cents. That's not enough."

Sooner whined. "Okay, but I'm telling Daddy you told me to do it." She walked to the door and looked in the hall. "Bark if you see Daddy."

She hurried to her father's room. She knew where he kept extra cash—inside his sock drawer. Opening the drawer, she slipped her hand beneath the socks and pulled out a hundred-dollar bill. "That should do it," she murmured, stuffing it in her pocket. "Daddy, please don't be mad at me. I *hafta* do this."

THE NEXT MORNING Colter dropped Ellie at Lori's house. Ellie insisted on taking Sooner, which puzzled him, but Ellie said she'd promised Sooner he could go to the party. He called Gail, Lori's mom, to make sure it was okay; she told him it was fine, that all the kids loved the dog.

Colter still had misgivings, although he couldn't explain exactly what they were. Ellie was nervous and excited, and that was the way she should be, he told himself. She was going to a birthday party for her best friend.

But something wasn't right. He felt it in his gut.

He hugged Ellie tightly, hoping his fatherly instincts were wrong. On the drive to the airport and the flight into Austin, he kept thinking about it. He finally put it down to overprotectiveness. Ellie was growing up, and he had to let her—and he had to stop analyzing all her moods.

Their lives had been fine until Marisa showed up. Now he was on edge all the time. Why did he go to Dalton's that day? Why did he see her? And why couldn't he stop thinking about her?

THAT FRIDAY, Marisa had a busy day. Madame Hélèna was flying to her New York office, and Marisa had a list of things to do before she left. Her son was picking her up in an hour. Marisa packed the designs and swatches of fabric Hélèna had requested. In another case were various reports and sales figures she wanted to share with her New York staff.

Marisa had just finished when the phone rang. She picked it up as Hélèna walked into the room.

"Marisa, it's Cari. I have a problem."

Marisa glanced at Hélèna, hoping she didn't mind a personal call. "What is it?" Marisa felt sure it concerned her father, and she braced herself.

"I have someone here who wants to see you."

"Who?"

"Ellie Kincaid."

Marisa almost dropped the phone. "What...what's she doing there?"

"She said you promised her she could talk to Santa Claus."

"Oh, yes, I did, but I never dreamed Colter would bring her."

"I haven't seen him—just Ellie and a big dog who caused a scene downstairs. That's why they called me. I have her and the dog in my office. I think you need to get over here."

Marisa glanced at Hélèna again. She didn't want to jeopardize her job, but she'd made a promise to Ellie and she had to keep it.

"I'll get there as soon as I can."

"Your father's not in this afternoon, so you don't have to worry about running into him."

"Thanks, Cari."

She hung up, wondering how to explain this to Hélèna. Before she could find the words, Hélèna spoke up. "Where do you have to go, *chérie?*"

Marisa told her about Ellie and her promise.

"I see." Hélèna rummaged through the mail on her desk. "Have you finished everything I asked you to do today?"

"Yes ma'am, and your son should be here in about thirty minutes."

"Then go." Hélèna waved a hand. "Everyone should believe in Santa Claus."

Marisa grabbed her coat. "Thank you. I'll come in early tomorrow."

'Tomorrow is Saturday, *chérie,* so take the weekend off. I'll expect you back first thing Monday."

"Yes, ma'am," Marisa said. "Have a good trip," she added, hurrying out the door.

She parked in the customers' parking lot of Dalton's and went into the store, taking the escalator to Cari's office.

Opening the door slightly, she saw Ellie sitting in a chair, feet dangling. Sooner lay on the floor watching her. She didn't see Colter. *Where was he?*

When she stepped into the room, Ellie leaped up. "Ms. Preston, it's me! I came to see Santa Claus."

"Hi, Ellie."

"I'll wait outside," Cari said.

"Thanks," Marisa answered. "But could I speak with you first?"

"Sure."

"I'll be right back," she said to Ellie, following Cari into the hall. "What happened?"

"Like I said, I got a call from downstairs that a girl and a dog were in the children's department. The dog was barking his head off, and the little girl kept saying she had to see Ms. Preston. I brought them up here. Could've knocked me over with a feather when she told me her name. I paged Colter on the intercom and got no response."

"So he's not in the store?"

Cari shrugged. "He never answered the page."

Marisa nodded, frowning. "I wonder how she got here—and if Colter knows where she is."

"I'll let you find that out while I go get the man I hired to play Santa."

"Thanks, Cari."

Marisa went back into the room.

"Is he coming?" Ellie asked, her voice excited.

Marisa sat beside her. "Where's your father?"

"I can't tell you." Ellie stuck out her chin.

"I see," she said, knowing she'd have to be tough to get anything out of Ellie. "You can't see Santa until you tell me."

"Oh." Ellie's eyes widened.

"Where's your father?" Marisa asked again. If Colter didn't know where Ellie was, he must be extremely worried, and she had to notify him.

Marisa's serious tone obviously made an impact on Ellie, because she started talking. "He's in Austin."

"Austin!"

"Yeah. Some western stores are carrying Daddy's boots, and he goes there to meet people and sign autographs. I wanted to go, but I couldn't. I had to see Santa, and this was my only chance 'cause Daddy wouldn't let me come if he was home." Ellie looked at Marisa. "He doesn't like you."

"How did you get here?" she asked, trying not to show how those words affected her. Colter couldn't hide his hostility even from his child.

"My best friend had a birthday party, and her mom said Sooner and me could spend the day. When the party was over, Lori and I called a cab—we found it in the phone book—and it brought me here."

"Where's your friend now?"

"She didn't come. She was scared she'd get punished. Just Sooner and me came."

"Does your friend live in Dallas?"

"No. In Mesquite."

"You took a cab from Mesquite to Dallas?" She couldn't keep the shock out of her voice.

"Yeah, and I don't have any money left to get back to Lori's. The man said it was extra for Sooner."

"Where'd you get the money?"

The child squirmed.

"Ellie?"

"I took it out of Daddy's extra cash."

"Oh, Ellie."

"I know I did a bad thing and I'll probably be grounded for the rest of my life, but I *hafta* see Santa."

"Why is it so important that you see Santa?"

"Well, I wrote him a bunch of times asking for a mommy. I do that every Christmas, but I never got one. This year he could be sending me a mommy, and I have to tell him I might not be home for Christmas. I hafta be there when she comes." Her eyes searched Marisa's. "You *will* let me see him, won't you?"

Marisa's heart ached for this little girl who wanted a mother so badly, and she couldn't deny her wish. "Yes, but you have to give me your father's and Lori's phone numbers."

Marisa got a pencil and paper, and Ellie rattled off the numbers, along with Colter's cell.

"What's Lori's mother's name?"

"Gail Freeman."

Marisa called Colter's cell phone first, but there was no answer. She got Gail, who didn't even realize Ellie wasn't there. Lori and Ellie were supposed to be playing in Lori's room. She became agitated when she found out what Ellie and Lori had done. Marisa assured her Ellie was fine and that she'd continue to try to reach Colter.

Gail said that they were going to her mother's for Lori's family celebration in a little while, but she would come and get Ellie. Marisa told her there was no need, that she'd take Ellie home. Gail gave in reluctantly. Marisa hung up, wondering if she'd done the right thing. Colter was not going to appreciate her coming to his home again.

"Is she really mad?" Ellie asked, her face puckered in a frown.

Marisa sat beside her again. "Worried is more like it, and I have to continue trying to call your father."

"Okay," Ellie said in a quiet voice.

Marisa turned to her. "It was so dangerous to take a cab from Mesquite to Dallas by yourself."

"I know. Daddy talked to me about strangers, but I took Sooner. He protects me. Except when we got in the store, he got scared."

Sooner barked.

"You *were* scared, Sooner. So don't say you weren't."

Sooner barked more loudly.

"Be quiet." Ellie put a finger to her lips.

Marisa suppressed a smile. This was a serious situation, but it was delightful to be around Ellie and Sooner.

"Ellie." Marisa got her attention. "Promise you won't ever do anything like this again."

Ellie's face creased in thought. "You have to keep a promise, right?"

"Right."

Ellie shook her head. "Then I can't promise."

Marisa was stunned, and she couldn't hide her reaction.

"Daddy says not to lie and I don't want to lie," the child explained. "He says I think about a mommy too much, but I can't help it. Around Christmas it's all I think about. I knew coming today was wrong, but I *had* to. My mommy might come this Christmas, and I have to let her know I want her to. Santa will make it happen 'cause I believe."

Marisa's throat closed up. That was it. That was what Ellie's obsession was really about—wanting her mother to come home. Subconsciously, it had probably always been her desire, which was understandable in a child her age. She wondered if Shannon knew how much her daughter wanted her. Or if Colter had even told Shannon.

"Ellie, are you hoping your mother will come home?"

The child fidgeted in her chair. "Maybe I just want a mommy."

"Oh, Ellie." Marisa's heart broke and she wanted to comfort the little girl and— No! That was Colter's job. Still…

She didn't have time to consider that now, because there was a tap at the door. She opened the door to a man dressed completely in white: suit, shoes, shirt, tie—even his long hair and beard were white.

"I'm here to see Ellie Kincaid," he said, then added in a low voice, "I'm Santa Claus."

Marisa just stared at him. He was in his seventies and he fit the Santa persona to a tee, including the rounded stomach and red cheeks, except he didn't have on a red costume. But that was minor. Cari had done a great job in hiring someone so authentic.

She stepped aside, and as he entered the room, Ellie got to her feet. "Are you Santa?"

He nodded. "Yes. I'm Santa Claus."

"Where's your red suit?"

"I only wear it when I'm seeing children in the stores or riding in my sleigh. This is the suit I wear at home—and for seeing special little girls."

"Oh."

He sat in a chair and Ellie climbed onto his knee. "What did you want to see me about, little angel?"

"I wrote you a lot of letters asking for a mommy, and you never sent me one. This year we might have to go to my aunt Jen's for Christmas so I had to tell you I might not be at home. I didn't want you to send her if I'm not there."

"Don't worry. I know where you are at all times."

"You do?" Ellie's eyes grew enormous.

"Yes, and I'm not happy about what you did today. You're not ever to do that again."

"Yes, sir," Ellie answered, hanging her head.

For a moment, Marisa was perplexed. How did he know what Ellie had done? Oh, Cari must've told him. She'd almost believed he was the real thing.

"Am I ever gonna get my mommy?" Ellie twisted her hands.

"Don't fret, little one," he said. "You'll have your mommy before Christmas."

Ellie's head jerked up. "I will?"

"Yes. Now I have to go. I have lots to do before the twenty-fifth."

Ellie threw her arms around his neck. "Thank you." She leaned back and tugged on his beard.

"Why'd you do that?"

"My friend Lori says you're not real and that your beard is fake, but it *is* real, just like I told her."

He stood, setting Ellie on her feet. "Yes, little one, I'm real. Never be afraid to believe—belief is a very powerful thing."

"I won't," Ellie promised.

The man walked to the door and then stopped. He touched the back of his hand to Marisa's face. "You're never too old to believe, Marisa."

She was so surprised by his touch, and the sincerity in his eyes, that words eluded her.

"She believes," Ellie told him.

He exited the room and Marisa stared after him, feeling even more perplexed. *What did he mean? And how did he know my name?*

Chapter Eight

Marisa called Colter again in case he hadn't received the first message, then she took Ellie and Sooner home. Cari had a meeting, so she didn't have a chance to talk to her about the Santa Claus, which she planned to do later.

Today the weather was much nicer than the last time she'd made the trip out to the ranch. The temperature was in the fifties and a pale sun shone. Ellie sat in the front seat, Sooner in the back, and Ellie chatted nonstop. She was in a very good mood, thanks to Santa, but Marisa felt sure Colter would change all that the minute he got home.

Ellie knew where the key was and let them into the house. Sooner whined plaintively.

"Okay. Okay," Ellie said, and ran into the kitchen. "I gotta feed Sooner."

Marisa took a seat at the table, wondering why Colter hadn't called.

COLTER HURRIED TO HIS TRUCK at the airport, cursing that he'd left his cell phone inside. He always kept it with him when he was away from Ellie, but this morning he'd been in such a state over leaving that he'd placed it on the seat and forgotten it.

He'd called Gail once from a store and she had said everything was fine. When he tried again, he didn't get an answer. That worried him.

In the truck, he picked up the phone. "Dammit."

"What?" Tulley asked, closing the door.

"There are two messages from Gail and two from Marisa."

"Marisa?" Tulley's eyebrow shot up.

"There's only way she could have gotten my cell number."

"Ellie," they said in unison.

"What the hell's going on?"

"Listen to the messages," Tulley suggested.

All of them were the same: *call as soon as possible.* He called Gail's cell first and his blood ran cold at the story she told him. As he relayed it to Tulley, he gripped the steering wheel until his knuckles turned white.

"She took a cab from Lori's to see Santa?" Tulley asked in a horrified tone. "What in the world possessed her to do such a thing?"

"Marisa," Colter said from between clenched teeth. "She told Ellie she could have a private sitting with him."

"Lordy, lordy, this is getting out of hand."

"I'm putting a stop to it once and for all." He punched in Marisa's cell number.

He heard her soft, tantalizing voice and it made him that much angrier. "Where's my daughter?"

"I brought her home to the ranch," Marisa answered.

"You're at my house?" he asked, taken aback.

"Yes. I didn't know where else to take her."

"This is all your fault." He couldn't stop the angry words. "If you hadn't encouraged her, none of this would've happened."

"I didn't—"

"Listen," he snapped. "Stay with her until I get there. Don't you dare leave her by herself."

"I would never do such a thing."

"Yeah, right." He clicked off before his anger completely overtook him.

ONCE AGAIN MARISA felt the brunt of his anger, but she tried not to let it upset her. Turning to Ellie, she noticed the little girl had removed her coat and was standing on a chair pulled up to the cabinet, busily applying butter to a pile of toast.

"What are you doing?" she asked as she watched her continue to toast bread, four slices at a time, butter it and stack the toast higher.

"This is for Sooner."

"You're making toast for the *dog?*"

"Yep," she said, jumping down from the chair. "Sooner's real mad at me 'cause I got him in trouble. So I'm making his favorite food. When he eats all this toast, he won't be mad at me anymore."

"Oh," Marisa said for lack of anything better to reply. Somehow she felt that Colter would not approve.

"Is Daddy mad?" Ellie asked.

Mad was a mild word for Colter's reaction, and she hoped he'd be patient and understanding with Ellie.

"Let's just say he's not happy," Marisa replied.

Ellie's face crumpled, and she picked up the plate of toast and quickly ran out the back door, Sooner whining at her heels.

Marisa was caught in the middle and she didn't understand how that had happened. Colter had said it was her fault. Maybe it was, maybe she'd been too eager to help Ellie see Santa Claus. She'd made such a mistake in coming here that first day, but it was a little late to change that. It was too late to change anything.

Ellie came back and settled in a chair. "I'm sorry I upset everybody."

"You scared me by taking such a risk, and I'm sure your father feels the same way. I'm just happy you're all right."

"You're nice. You're pretty, too," Ellie said, studying Marisa's face.

The compliment took Marisa by surprise, but she smiled. "Thank you. And you're a very pretty little girl."

"Daddy says I'm going to be beautiful, just like my mother."

Colter thought Shannon was beautiful. She experienced a pang of jealousy and forcefully pushed it away. Why hadn't they stayed together? Why hadn't they made a home for Ellie?

"Of course, I've never seen her, so I don't know what she looks like." Ellie's words cut through her thoughts.

"You've never seen your mother?" The words charged out of their own volition.

Ellie shook her head. "No, she left after I was born."

Marisa could hear the wistfulness in the tiny voice and felt an intense dislike for Shannon. How could she do this to Ellie?

As if reading her mind, the girls murmured, "Daddy said she left 'cause she was unhappy. It wasn't 'cause she didn't love me. She lives way off on a ranch and she's a champion barrel racer. I'm gonna be one, too."

Ellie was silent for a moment, and Marisa was unsure of what to say.

Ellie squirmed in her chair. "Santa's sending my mommy."

"Please don't get your hopes up." Marisa had to say it. She would also have a talk with Cari about Mr. Santa promising children things he couldn't deliver.

Ellie looked into her eyes. "I believe, Ms. Preston. Don't you?"

"Call me Marisa," she invited, hoping Colter wouldn't mind.

"Okay," Ellie said. "She'll come back. I know it."

"Ellie—"

The sound of a truck stopped her.

"Uh-oh. Daddy's home."

TULLEY CAUGHT COLTER'S ARM before he could get out. "Take a deep breath and calm down."

He exhaled deeply. "I am so angry."

"I know, and anger never solves anything. Ellie's a little girl searching for answers and it's time you told her the truth about her mother. That's the only way all of this is going to stop."

"None of this would've started if Marisa hadn't put ideas in her head."

"Stop blaming Marisa for everything," Tulley said. "Ellie had these ideas before Marisa ever showed up."

Colter glared at him. "You're taking *her* side?"

"I'm stoutly on your side—always have been—always will be, but it's time to lay the past on the table and sort through all the painful stuff. You blame Marisa for everything that happened to you after she left, so tell her. Tell her the whole damn story. That's the only way you're ever going to get over your feelings for her."

Colter began to speak, but Tulley held up his hand. "Don't say you feel nothing for her. I see it in your eyes every time you look at her and I see it in her eyes, too. You have Ellie, and she and Marisa seem to have a connection. So tell Marisa about Ellie and Shannon, and take it from there."

"You're asking the impossible," Colter muttered, but his anger was easing.

"Maybe. You do best, though, when the odds are stacked against you."

Colter got out of the truck without another word. On the walk into the house, Tulley added, "Go easy on Ellie. And you might think about going easy on Marisa."

COLTER APPEARED IN THE DOORWAY dressed in jeans, boots and a leather jacket. Marisa's stomach tightened. His eyes were worried and rimmed with shadows of resentment.

Ellie got out of her chair and stood facing her father. Colter removed his hat, placed it on the table. He was taking his time, making Ellie sweat, and it was working. Ellie shifted from one foot to the other.

"Are you gonna spank me, Daddy?"

Tulley cleared his throat and walked into the den.

All of Colter's anger evaporated with those nervous words.

He didn't want Ellie to be afraid of him under any circumstances. "Have I ever spanked you?"

"No, sir, but I did something really bad, and Lori said when you're really bad you get spanked. So I'm ready for my spanking."

Colter reached down and picked Ellie up, held her tightly in his arms.

Ellie started to cry. "I'm sorry, Daddy. I'm sorry."

He smoothed her hair. "I know, baby. Now go to your room while I talk to Ms. Preston."

Ellie slid to the floor. "Don't be mad at her. She didn't know what I was doing, and she was real nice and helped me."

"Wait in your room and think about what you did. I'll be there in a little bit and we'll discuss it thoroughly."

"Yes, sir," Ellie muttered, her head bent as she went toward the back door.

"No." Colter stopped her. "Go to your room without Sooner."

Ellie's bottom lip trembled and she ran toward the hall. Marisa noticed that Tulley quickly followed.

Ellie had been spared her father's wrath, but from the glitter in his eyes Marisa had a feeling she wasn't going to fare as well.

Her nerves were stretched to the breaking point as she watched him. His dark hair curled against the collar of his leather jacket and his expression was resentful. She waited.

"What happened?" he asked in a voice so low she could barely hear him.

Marisa did a double take. Those weren't the words she was expecting and she could see he had a tight rein on his temper. But he was willing to listen—that was the important thing.

"I got a call at Madame Hélèna's that Ellie was at Dalton's asking for me."

His eyes swept over her in the slim-fitting champagne-silk Madame Hélèna's creation. Hélèna insisted that her staff wear her clothes to show them off to customers. Marisa was glad to do so; the dresses were fabulous and offered at a considerable discount.

"You buy your clothes at Madame Hélèna's?" he asked in disbelief.

"Yes. I work there."

He shook his head. "You said you worked at Dalton's."

"I did until my father sent the police out here. I knew then that my parents were still controlling my life, so I left. I found a place to live and I got a job with Madame Hélèna. I'm out on my own, which I should've done years ago."

He shook his head again. "We're getting off track. Tell me about Ellie."

She told him what Ellie had told her, and Colter sank into a chair.

"God, I get cold chills every time I think about her taking a cab by herself. Anything could have happened…."

"But she found me and I brought her home. She's okay."

His eyes flashed. "Why did you have to come back into my life?"

She chewed on the inside of her lip. This might not be the time or place, but she had to do it. She knew that now beyond any doubt. "I came here to tell you something—something important. But you wouldn't listen."

He sighed with fatigue. "I'm tired, upset, my head's pounding and I'm not in a mood to listen to any more lies."

"I haven't lied to you."

He stared at her, his eyes matching the challenge she knew was blazing in hers. "Okay." He gave in with a hint of anger. "You've got five minutes."

She glanced toward Ellie's room.

"Don't worry," he said. "Tulley can't stand to see her cry and he'll pacify her for a while. You've already told me you were seventeen instead of twenty-one and your mother forced you to leave by threatening to have me arrested. What else is there?"

His tone offended her, but she had to follow through. She took a steadying breath. "When I left, I had plans to find you again, but that never happened. Then I discovered one fact that changed everything."

"What?"

She counted to three, then said, "I discovered I was pregnant."

Nothing. Not even a flicker of surprise. For a second she was thrown, but she quickly recovered. "I had to find you, so I hired the private investigator. Then my mother found out and everything came to a head. I told her I was pregnant and she told me what the PI had discovered—that you were married. I know that's a lie now, but back then I was devastated."

She paused, waiting. No response. Nothing. She went on. "Mother insisted I have an abortion, but I refused."

A distressed sound left his throat, but he didn't say anything.

"She then demanded I give up the baby for adoption and I still refused. I wanted my baby. The stress caused a lot of problems with the pregnancy, and Mother put me in a clinic in upstate New York. I didn't realize it was an adoption clinic until later. Then I became so upset that I went into early labor." She swallowed. "After thirty long hours, the baby was born dead."

His glare was chilling. "What did you say?"

She made herself repeat the words. "Our son was born dead."

"We had a son?" he asked.

"Yes. I never got to see him or hold him…but I heard him crying. Though the doctor said I only imagined it, because he was stillborn."

"You and I had a son?" he asked again.

"Yes," she replied. "That's why I came out here—to tell you about him. I wanted you to know he existed."

"Did you give him a name?"

"Yes. James Colter—after you."

Colter didn't react. "Where's he buried?"

"What?" She blinked in confusion.

"If he was full-term, then he'd be buried somewhere. All I'm asking is where."

She put a hand to her temple, which was beginning to throb painfully. "Mother took care of all that."

"You've never been to your son's grave?"

"No."

"Every year during the holidays, Ellie, Tulley and I put flowers on my parents' graves and Tulley's wife's grave. That's what you do when someone's important to you." His eyes narrowed "Did you think I wouldn't ask?"

"I…uh…" Words jumbled in her head. She didn't know where her own son was buried. Her mother had said it would be too traumatic for her, and she'd been in such an emotional state that she'd adhered to her mother's wishes. Then her father brought her to Texas and she never went back to New York—never went back to her son…

Colter stood abruptly. "Get out of my home and don't come back."

She shivered at the cold hostility in his voice. She'd expected a lot of reactions, but not this rage. He was acting as if he didn't believe her. Did he think she hadn't wanted their child?

Fear made her feel shaky. *He didn't believe her.* The reality of that overwhelmed her and she had nothing to say, no words to defend herself. Callously she'd never asked to go to her son's gravesite. That made her an awful mother. Oh God, she had to get away from him.

But how could she get away from herself?

"The truth has your tongue tied?" he asked, his voice ripping through her. "Our child might be dead to you but not to me, and if you cared anything about that child you wouldn't sit there so selfishly and expect me to understand. Just leave and stay out of my life."

Despair, swift and strong, swept over her and she stood on legs that felt like rubber. She gripped the table for support, but Colter didn't offer any help. Numbly she grabbed her coat and purse and headed for the door.

Running to her car, she gulped in the chilly evening air, but it didn't cool the heated emotions churning through her. As she drove away, tears streamed down her face. For years she'd agonized over the death of her son—not able to really live again. She'd thought it had to do with Colter and his not knowing, but it had to do with *her* and a deep-seated guilt she hadn't even known was there. The guilt of never going to her son's grave.

Her mother had convinced her of the trauma of such an act, and she'd acquiesced—as always. Where was their child buried? That was the first thing Colter had wanted to know, as a good parent would. A sob left her throat. She had to find out what cemetery they'd put her son in, and she'd be on the first plane to New York.

Her mother was on a cruise, but her father would have information on how to reach her. Since they both owned Dalton's, it was imperative that they know each other's whereabouts.

She could be in New York by morning. And she'd touch her son's grave, feel his presence and apologize. Then maybe she could find that measure of peace she'd been searching for.

And she didn't need to see Colter again. Not ever.

Chapter Nine

Her inner turmoil drove her thirty minutes later as she sped down the street leading to her father's home. The brown brick was a Greek Revival mansion with classic white columns that framed the front portico. Built by her grandfather, it boasted spiral staircases, hardwood floors and stone fireplaces, echoing Texas style both past and present.

Seeing the familiar house didn't make her feel better. She'd been a prisoner behind those wrought-iron gates and brick walls—sheltered, protected and suffocated. Coming back wasn't easy and facing her father wouldn't be easy, either. But she had to know where her son was buried.

COLTER SAT IN A STUPOR, hardly able to believe what Marisa had told him. They had a son? *A son.* James Colter. He was still grappling with that.

"Colt, boy."

He jerked up his head to see Tulley staring at him.

"What's wrong?" Tulley glanced around. "Where's Marisa?"

"Gone—for good."

Tulley took a seat. "What happened?"

He jammed his hands through his hair. "You won't believe what she tried to tell me. Lies. Why does she keep lying to me? She stuck a knife in my heart eight years ago, and she keeps on twisting it."

"What did she say?"

Colter told him what Marisa had said.

Tulley frowned. "A son? She said you had a son?"

"She sat there, her voice so sincere, her eyes sad, and she was pulling me in like she always did. God, Tulley, I *wanted* to believe her—and that makes me the biggest fool that ever lived." He took a quick breath. "But you should've seen her face when I asked where he was buried. She was speechless and she could see that I knew she was lying."

"Colt, boy, I've said this before and I'll say it again. You two need to have an honest-to-God talk. Put the past on the table, call an ace an ace and a spade a spade. You have to get at the truth. Marisa doesn't seem the type to tell lies but then, I don't suppose either one of us really knew her."

"I sure didn't. But you're right. I thought I could let this go, but—"

The phone rang, interrupting him, and he got up to answer it.

"This is Cari Michaels with Dalton Department Stores. I'm calling to check if Ellie made it home okay."

"Yes," he said. "Ellie's fine."

There was a pause.

"May I speak with Marisa? She left a message that she'd be there."

"She's left."

"Oh, well, I'm glad Ellie's okay. Thank you."

"Ms. Michaels," he said before she could hang up. He had to sort out the truth, and to do that he had to see Marisa again. "Could you please tell me where I can find Marisa? I'd like to speak with her."

This pause was longer. "Normally she'd be at home with her family in Highland Park, but she rented a room recently and that's probably where she'll be." She rattled off the address, and he scribbled it on a pad.

"Thank you," he said, hanging up and stuffing the paper into his shirt pocket.

"Before you blast out of here, you'd better talk to your daughter," Tulley informed him. "She's about to cry herself to sleep."

"I wouldn't go anywhere without talking to Ellie. She's my first priority and always will be."

HE FOUND ELLIE lying on her bed clutching a pillow. Her hair had come out of its ponytail and her face was red from crying. His heart twisted at the sight, but he forced himself not to take her in his arms and say all was forgiven. They had rules and she'd broken a big one today. As a father he had to make her understand he loved her, but she still had to obey the rules— rules that existed for her benefit, whether she saw that or not.

He sat in the old wooden rocker that had belonged to his mother. Becky had put pink and white floral cushions on it to match Ellie's room. He'd rocked Ellie in this chair since she was a baby: when she had colic, when she was teething and when she was sick. Raising a child alone had been rough, but Ellie made it a pleasure. She was a smiling, happy baby and her bubbly personality had quickly surfaced. She took after her mother—a mother she wanted in her life. His heart twisted a little more.

Ellie sat up and wiped her eyes. "Are you mad at me, Daddy?"

"No, Ellie, I'm not mad," he told her. "I'm troubled. Troubled that you'd take such a risk. Troubled that you'd take money out of my drawer without permission. And troubled that you couldn't talk to me."

Her bottom lip quivered and she dived off the bed into his arms. He held her tight. "I'm sorry, Daddy."

He stroked her hair. "I know, baby. Tell me why you did it."

"You said…you said we might have to go to Aunt Jen's for Christmas, and I had to tell Santa Claus. He had to know where I'd be when he sends my mommy."

"Ellie." He tried not to show his frustration. "We've had

this talk before, but obviously we're not communicating. Is all this Santa stuff about your real mother coming back?"

Ellie nodded against his shoulder.

"Oh, baby." How did he explain that her mother didn't want her?

She raised her head. "It's okay, Daddy. Santa said I'll have a mommy by Christmas, and he told me not to worry about being at Aunt Jen's. He knows where I'm all the time."

"Santa told you that you'd have a mommy by Christmas?" Why would the man tell her that? Now he had to undo the damage.

"Yep." Ellie nodded. "So all I have to do is wait."

"Ellie…"

She placed her fingers over his lips. "Don't say it, Daddy. I believe."

He could see that she did, and he just couldn't break her heart. He'd deal with it later. That was the coward's way out, but he couldn't hurt his daughter. Still, he had to talk about her trip to Dalton's.

"Do you understand that what you did today was very dangerous for someone your age?"

She hung her head. "Yes, sir."

"Promise me you won't ever do anything like that again."

She lifted her head, her eyes watery. "I promise, and you can spank me if you want."

He gently pinched her cheek. "Ellie, I've never spanked you and I never will. Hitting doesn't solve anything. However, you will not talk on the phone or watch TV for a week. And you will not get your allowance for a month."

"Okay." She clenched her hands. "Can Sooner come back in the house?"

It would hurt Ellie far more if he kept Sooner away from her, but he couldn't do that. He hesitated, though, just so she'd think it was a possibility.

"Yes. Sooner can come back in."

Her arms crept around his neck and she whispered, "I love you, Daddy."

He swallowed. "I love you, angelface." He held her for an extra moment. "Daddy has to go out for a little while, so help Tulley feed the horses, take your bath and read one of the books you brought home from school."

"Okay. Can I go get Sooner now?"

"Yes. Go get Sooner."

Like a whirlwind she was gone. He drew a long breath at what lay ahead of him. He had to see Marisa, though; that was the only way to settle this.

HE STOPPED AT A GAS STATION to buy a map of Dallas. He spread it out over the steering wheel and searched for the street Ms. Michaels had given him. The Highland Park area caught his eye. When he'd started his boot business, he, Tulley Becky, Jen and Bart had dinner with a business lawyer who'd given them his advice. He was a man Becky had met in college and he lived in Highland Park.

Colter knew exactly where Richard Preston lived. He remembered the sprawling estate and the large security gates with the Dalton logo. Marisa was probably there at the time and he hadn't known. So close, yet…

He folded the map. If he wanted the truth, he'd have to get it from Richard and Vanessa Preston. They would know what Marisa was talking about.

MARISA PARKED IN FRONT and ran up the steps to the double doors. Instead of ringing the bell, she went in. Winston, the butler, was instantly at her side.

"Ms. Preston, it's so good to see you," he said in surprise. "I'll tell your father you're here."

"No." She stopped him. "There's no need."

"Yes, ma'am."

She made her way through the living room to the library.

She heard loud voices and paused, frowning. *It can't be,* she told herself, as she listened to the high-pitched voice that sounded like her mother's. What was Vanessa doing here? She was supposed to be on a cruise.

She walked uneasily toward the closed doors. Yes, it was definitely her mother's voice—shouting angrily at her father.

"Leave her alone, Richard."

"She's working as Madame Hélèna's gopher and making us the laughingstock of Dallas. I won't have it."

"I can't take any more." Her mother's voice was no longer angry, just resigned.

"Then why the hell didn't you go on your cruise? I can take care of Marisa. I can take care of both my children."

"Marisa belongs to me." Vanessa's voice rose an octave. "That was in the agreement, Richard. You would raise Reed and I'd raise Marisa—without interference."

"You're the one who called me, Vanessa."

"I never should have listened to you. You said Marisa would come back to New York, but she hasn't."

"Texas is her home and this is where she belongs," her father bellowed. "If *he* hadn't shown up, everything would be fine."

"But he has, and now…"

There was a moment of silence, and the chill inside Marisa turned to an icy foreboding. Then she heard her mother's voice.

"Yes. We'll lose her. We will lose her forever."

What was her mother talking about? Marisa restrained herself from charging into the room. Her heart pounded painfully, and she tried to steady her erratic pulse as she waited for her mother's next words.

"It wasn't easy having full responsibility for Marisa when she was seventeen and pregnant. I handled things badly and I wish…"

Unable to stand still for one more minute, she opened the door. "You wished what?" she asked.

Her parents stared at her, shock on both their faces. Her mother was the first to recover. Dressed in a fashionable cream-colored suit, she rushed over to greet Marisa, giving her a quick hug. "Darling, you're back."

"What were you talking about?" she asked again.

Her mother looked nervously at her father, and it was clear that Vanessa didn't want to answer. Marisa was about to insist when her father spoke up.

"Your mother is dramatizing everything as usual."

It was more than that and, for a change, she was getting some straight answers. "Mother said she never should've let you talk her into something. What did she mean?"

Richard shoved his hands into the pockets of his suit slacks. "She was talking about our decision to call the police when you were stranded on *his* ranch. It was probably the wrong move, but I couldn't tolerate the thought of that man hurting you again. You almost didn't survive the last time, and when I think of the pain he put you through—well, I did what I figured was best."

Normally she would have accepted that explanation, but not now—not after what she'd heard. "His name is Colter Kincaid, and it was *my* decision to go to his ranch. He didn't force me."

"Of course not, darling. We're just glad you're home," her mother put in.

"Yes," Richard added. "I'm very glad you're home. Your room's waiting for you and so is your job at Dalton's."

"I have a job, Father, and I get paid for the work I do, not for being Richard Preston's daughter."

Her father bristled. "You are a Dalton and a Preston, and you belong here and at Dalton's."

"Really?" She lifted an eyebrow as she remembered parts of the conversation she'd overheard. "I thought I belonged to Mother."

Her father was speechless, and suddenly she could see the past for what it was. "That's it, isn't it? You brought me to

Texas to get me away from Mother. I'm like a prized object, and neither of you has ever thought about *my* feelings. It's just you and this tug-of-war for dominance of your children."

"Darling, please, let's not argue," her mother begged.

Marisa turned to Vanessa. "Why aren't you on your cruise?"

"I couldn't leave with you running off like that. I had to know you were okay."

"Surely Father's PI told you I was."

"All right, Marisa," Richard said, his words sharp. "This rebellion isn't like you, and I've had enough. It's time for you to come home."

In the past she'd always submitted to that tone of voice, but not today. Not anymore. "Sorry, Father. I'm not seventeen and I've earned the right to live my life the way I choose."

"Fine, you want more control at Dalton's, you've got it. You want an apartment somewhere, you've got it. Just tell me what the hell you want."

"Peace, Father. That's what I want."

He scowled, looking perplexed. "What are you talking about?"

"I need peace about the past. I've never recovered from losing my son."

Richard's features softened. "Sweetheart, no woman ever truly recovers from something like that."

"I know what my problem is."

"What?" Richard asked.

She turned to her mother. "Where's he buried?"

Vanessa turned a pasty white. "Darling, why are you putting yourself through this?"

"Because a mother should know where her child is buried." She swallowed visibly. "When Colter asked me, I couldn't answer, and I realized that I left my baby behind and I never visited his grave. I was emotionally traumatized by his death, but—"

"You told Kincaid about the baby?" her father asked.

"Yes." She glanced at Vanessa. "Where did you bury him?"

Raised voices interrupted them, and Marisa turned to see Colter and Reed walk into the room.

What was Colter doing here? Had he followed her? A new hope lightened her heart. Was he ready to listen? Was he ready to hear about their son?

He looked tired and angry—just as he had earlier. He wasn't wearing a hat and his dark hair had been tumbled by the wind. There was a disturbing glint in his eyes.

Richard confronted Colter. "How did you get in here, Kincaid? You're not welcome— Winston!" he shouted.

"I let him in," Reed said. "He asked to see Marisa and I didn't see any harm in that."

"You know what this man did to your sister. Can't you use some common sense?"

"I am," Reed replied, undaunted by their father's temper. Then he looked at Marisa. "Do you want to see him?"

"Yes," she answered in a low voice.

Winston rushed into the room. "Yes, sir."

"Remove this man immediately," Richard ordered.

Colter stood almost six feet tall, broad shouldered and whipcord lean. Winston was five foot six, thin and almost effeminate. The thought of Winston bodily removing Colter was ludicrous.

"Come this way, sir," Winston said.

"I'm not going anywhere until I speak with Marisa."

"I'll call the police," Richard threatened.

"Go ahead," Colter said.

Richard stepped toward the phone.

"No," Marisa insisted. "Colter's here for the same reason I am. We want to know where our son is buried. Just tell us and we'll leave."

Colter stared at her blankly. "I deserve more than your lies," he said coldly.

Marisa stared back at him. Lies? What was he talking

about? She'd been as open and honest as she could. What else did he want from her?

His gaze swung to her mother. "We meet again, Mrs. Preston."

Marisa's eyes widened in disbelief. "You've met my mother?"

"Of course," he answered, as if that should make sense.

"But how?" she asked, her voice like a film of ice that threatened to crack at any moment.

"Come on, Marisa, stop playing games," Colter warned.

"Games?" she choked out. "Do I look like I'm playing games? I feel I'm going insane and everyone around me is talking in riddles! I tried to tell you how much I wanted our son, how I fought to keep him, how he died before I could even hold him, but you wouldn't listen. Now, you're accusing me of lying. Please tell me what—" Her voice cracked as a sob rose up in her throat.

Colter took in the pallor of her skin, her harassed appearance and the desperate look in her brown eyes. She wasn't acting or lying. She *believed* everything she was saying. That realization fueled his anger and resentment, and he turned to face Vanessa Preston with a look bordering on suppressed violence.

"You didn't!" he demanded, begging to hear a denial.

Vanessa remained silent, studying her long pink fingernails.

Her refusal to speak gave Colter his answer. "OhmyGod, you did," he groaned. "OhmyGod."

His body stiffened and he clenched and unclenched his hands, fighting for control. "Tell her the truth, dammit—tell her!"

Chapter Ten

Vanessa looked at her daughter, her eyes filled with torment, then she shook her head. "Don't do this, Mr. Kincaid," she begged. "It'll destroy her."

"There's no choice. She has to know."

A vein in her mother's neck jerked erratically. "I can't, I can't," she sobbed, wiping tears from her cheeks.

Marisa had never seen her mother cry. She was always so strong, so in control, and Marisa knew that her mother was confronting something she couldn't handle. The thought scorched her nerve endings, but could do nothing to stop the panic.

Richard grabbed Colter by the arm. "We'll take care of it from here. You can leave."

Colter pulled his arm away. "I'm not going anywhere until the truth is said out loud."

Vanessa appealed to Marisa. "Darling, please ask him to leave."

"Why?" she asked, more confused than ever. Vanessa didn't answer, and Marisa felt questions beating at her, but she wouldn't acknowledge them. She had one goal and she focused on that. "Just tell us where our son is buried." That was the only thing that made sense to her at the moment.

"Tell her!" Colter shouted. "Tell her, or I will."

Vanessa flinched. "You were so young and I didn't know

what else to do. You had your whole life, a brilliant career, ahead of you, and I couldn't…couldn't let you throw it all away."

"What are you talking about?" Marisa asked, her voice sounding unfamiliar to her ears. "Tell me," she demanded.

Vanessa took a jagged breath, but before she could speak, Richard broke in. "Don't, Vanessa."

It was clear that her parents had some information she needed, and Colter knew what it was. She glanced at him. "What don't they want me to find out?"

He opened his mouth, but there was no sound. He tried again. "You…didn't have a…son."

The words ran through her head like the shrill of a whistle alerting her to danger, and she tried to rid herself of that sense of foreboding.

"Yes, I did," she said. "I carried him for almost nine months and I felt him kick and move and I talked to him. I named him James Colter, and he weighed five pounds, two ounces. He was stillborn."

Colter closed his eyes briefly. "Yes, except—"

"Except what?" she asked, wondering how he knew all this. She had the urge to put her hands over her ears to block out his next words.

"Except your baby wasn't a boy and he wasn't stillborn."

Marisa turned to her mother. "Tell him about my son, Mother. Please."

Vanessa hung her head, and Marisa turned to her father next—and what she saw in his eyes chilled her to the bone. "Father, you know what happened. Tell him."

Silence became a deafening sound that echoed through her heart.

She looked at Colter and braced herself for his next words.

"You had a daughter…and she was born alive."

"What!"

"It's true," he said.

"No, no, no." She flung her head from side to side. "Why are you saying that? Why are you lying to me?"

"It's true, Marisa," he repeated.

She stared at Vanessa, mouth dry. "Mother, please, tell me he's wrong."

Vanessa raised her head. "He's not," she said in a low, defeated voice. "Your baby didn't…didn't die at birth."

A black fog settled over Marisa. Her first reaction was to laugh, then cry, then scream, but of course, she did none of those things. Her mother's words rendered her immobile as the full implication drove into her.

She swallowed convulsively, and her body began to tremble. She was dangerously close to the breaking point and she tried to calm herself, but all she could do was continue to stare at her mother as if she was some diabolic stranger.

"You're lying! Why are you lying?" Marisa choked out. She closed her eyes against the shock, the truth, only to hear her baby cry once again. It was so clear, so real, just as it had been years ago. Everything began to fall into place: the crying, the dreams, Colter's hostility, her mother's nervousness. As her mind began to clear, she knew her mother wasn't lying. Not this time.

"Your daughter is alive," her mother said.

The words bounced in Marisa's head like lead marbles, each one making an indention she could feel. "How?" she breathed, not knowing if she had enough strength to face the truth.

Vanessa took a breath. "When you wouldn't sign the adoption papers, I didn't know what to do, so I called Richard."

Her eyes moved to her father. "You were there?"

"I came when your mother called, and we decided what was best for your future."

"*You* decided. *You* decided," she cried, almost hysterical. "I loved my baby and I wanted him—her, but you decided…you decided…" She had to take a breath before she could continue. "You took my baby from me! You told me he…I mean, she was dead and you let me live with that lie. How could you think *that* was best for me? I'll never forgive you for this. Never!"

A gasp of pain left her throat. Her baby was alive. Fast on that thought, a more agonizing one followed. *Where was she?*

She fought the fear rising in her. "Where's my daughter? Did you give her to strangers?"

"No," Vanessa said.

"No?" Marisa echoed. "What does that mean? Who did you give her to? I demand to know."

There was a slight pause, then her mother glanced at Colter and said slowly, "We gave…gave her to…her father."

A tense silence followed the announcement. Marisa turned to Colter as the truth began to sink in. That meant…that meant… She couldn't even formulate the thought that tortured her mind.

"Ellie is our daughter." Colter said the words for her.

"No!" she cried, her hands against her mouth. "No! She's Shannon's daughter." As she denied it, Ellie's face flashed before her eyes—the delicate features so like her own, the blond hair. Why hadn't she recognized her own daughter? "Oh God," she moaned. She didn't want to be the woman who'd given away that adorable child.

She could see how things had happened. Her mother had told her she'd had a son and that Colter had married—all lies to keep her away from him.

Colter took a step toward her, his face etched with pain. "Your parents found me and told me you didn't want the baby, so I gladly took her."

Another lie. Another deception.

Ellie wasn't Shannon's. Ellie was her daughter.

The reality was too much to endure, and she felt herself shattering into a million pieces. Through the pain and numbness, she held onto one fact. Ellie was her daughter…her precious baby. *She was alive!*

She backed away from her parents, muttering incoherently, "No, no, no." She knew she was shaking her head and the denial burned her throat, but she was only aware of grappling with the facts, striving desperately to comprehend and accept them. Backing into Reed, she clutched at him for support.

"Reed, is this real or am I dreaming?" she asked in a feeble voice.

"You're not dreaming," he said, his voice touching a chord of reality.

It was true, then. Colter had their daughter and had raised her for over seven years, since the day she was born. That was why he hated her so much—he believed she'd willingly given their baby away.

"Darling, listen," her mother appealed.

"No! I don't want to hear anything you have to say. Being my parents didn't give you the right to do this."

She could feel the pressure building inside her head, the sharp throbbing, and she sensed the walls closing in. She felt faint, but she fought back, needing to explain. She had to make Colter believe how much she'd wanted their baby.

"Colter, I…" she began to say in a shaky voice as the dizziness consumed her. The room swayed and blackness engulfed her—and two strong arms reached out to catch her as she crumpled to the floor.

MARISA AWOKE to a strange numbness, a numbness of mind, body and soul. It was several moments before she realized she was lying on the sofa in the library. The events of the last hours started to come back. Was it true? she asked herself. Was Ellie really her daughter? Yes, she was. The truth resounded in her head like chimes in the wind. Ellie… Ellie…Ellie.

With that name secure in her heart, she slowly sat up, pushing her tumbled hair away from her face. She tried to calm her shakiness as her eyes strayed to Colter.

He sat in a chair, his lean body hunched forward, his elbows resting on his knees, hands clasped tightly together. He was white as a sheet, and his eyes reflected a sorrow that broke her heart.

What must he think of her? For years he'd believed that she hadn't wanted their child—that she'd given her away. And she'd thought he was being hostile for no reason, when all the time... A whimper left her throat.

At the pained sound, Colter glanced at her, his eyes full of worry and concern, but he didn't come to her. He watched her with a troubled gaze as if he didn't know what to say or do. He seemed disillusioned with the whole situation. She couldn't blame him.

She hadn't realized Reed was sitting beside her until he asked, "Sis, are you okay?"

"Yes," she muttered through dry, stiff lips, but she knew her answer belied the grief that must show in her face.

"Good," he said. "I know you're still shaken up, but Mother and Father have some things to say that you need to hear. It's important. Okay?" He patted her hands to reassure her.

"I have nothing to say to them."

"I empathize with the feeling, and after they're done, you and I will walk out of here and never come back."

Her eyes narrowed on his face. "You're leaving?"

"You and I will not be puppets anymore, but I feel you need to hear the details before you can completely accept what happened. Okay?"

She nodded. Everything in her rejected the idea, but she didn't have the strength to resist.

Colter got slowly to his feet. Their eyes met and intense emotions flowed between them, but neither said a word. They didn't need to. Their eyes were conversing in a way their voices never could. There were so many feelings written on his face, but the one that she saw most clearly was "I'm sorry," and she was sure the same message was written on hers.

Vanessa and Richard moved forward, and Marisa gripped

her hands as they lay in her lap, waiting for the appeals and the pleading to start. But the silence stretched until she thought they weren't going to speak at all.

"I don't expect you to forgive us," Vanessa said. "I'm not sure I can forgive myself, but I hope you'll listen…and try to understand."

Understand? They wanted her to understand. No woman on earth could be that understanding.

"When I met your father, I had a promising career as a ballerina in front of me—a dream I'd had since I was a child. There was a strong sexual attraction between us and we had a brief, passionate affair while I was visiting my parents in Texas. I returned to New York to continue my dancing and then discovered I was pregnant. I was nineteen years old and faced with becoming a mother and losing everything I'd ever dreamed about." She paused.

"My parents forced me to marry your father. It was the only option for a young lady in those days. The marriage was a disaster, of course. I had to give up my dream of becoming a dancer, and I've regretted it every day since."

She'd always thought her parents had an arranged marriage. She didn't know her mother was pregnant at the time. Vanessa had never talked about that part of her life.

"Don't you see, Marisa?" her mother begged. "As much as I love you, I couldn't let history repeat itself. You deserved the career I never had. I didn't want anything to take that away from you."

Marisa got to her feet, surprised she could actually stand; something inside was giving her strength she hadn't known she possessed. She began to see her mother in a whole new light—a woman tormented by her own past, trying to protect her daughter from the same fate she'd suffered. She had allowed her own shattered dreams to become entwined with her daughter's. In effect, she'd done the very thing she had tried to prevent—she'd taken drastic measures to force Marisa onto the path she deemed best for her and had not considered Marisa's own desires.

"I never wanted that kind of career, Mother," she said, her voice weak but very clear. "*You* wanted it, but you can't live your life through me. I have feelings and dreams of my own. You never gave me a choice. You just demanded and manipulated until I gave in. And I was desperate to please you. I wanted your love."

Her mother closed her eyes as if she was in pain, then opened them again. "Oh, darling, I do love you. You've been my whole life since the day you were born. Reed was always so independent, your father's son, but you—you always seemed to need me."

Marisa realized that was true. She'd been very attached to her mother as a child. Leaving her father and brother had been a traumatic experience, and she had clung to her mother even more, afraid of losing her, too. She'd been eager to do everything her mother had asked of her, even playing the piano for long periods of time, trying to gain the expertise she needed to achieve the goals Vanessa had set for her. She'd never had the courage to tell her mother that those goals weren't hers.

She could see now that as a teenager looking for freedom, she'd probably used Colter as a means of escape. It didn't diminish the love she'd felt for him; it only helped explain how everything had gotten so out of control. If she'd been open and honest and able to talk to Vanessa, she would've saved everyone so much heartache.

Her mother thought she'd done the right thing. She had wanted Marisa to be happy and she'd believed that happiness was in her career. It showed just how little they knew each other.

Her eyes darkened. "I'll never understand that kind of love. The kind that hurts and destroys other people."

A spasm of pain crossed Vanessa's face. "I have a hard time understanding it myself. All I can say is that I wanted to save you from the mistakes I'd made. I was sure the infatuation you had for this man would burn itself out, and you were so young, so ill-equipped to raise a child on your own. Adoption seemed the only choice, but I couldn't get you to agree. I was at my wits' end and finally I called your father. He agreed that you were too young to be a mother." She looked down at her hands. "We decided the best solution was for the child to be with her father. We contacted Mr. Kincaid, and he came immediately and took the baby. Richard paid the doctor to lie to you. It was the perfect solution. The child would be with her natural father and you could get on with your wonderful life."

Wonderful life echoed through Marisa's mind, resounding in the hollow places of her heart left by the empty years.

"But your feelings went deeper than we ever imagined. You didn't get over losing the baby. You were close to a nervous breakdown and you seemed to use your father as a sort of lifeline to get away from me. By then I knew we'd made a terrible mistake, but I didn't know how to correct it."

"You could have told me the truth," she said with force.

"Don't you think I tried? As the months turned into years, you seemed determined not to come back to New York and your training, and I knew I should tell you. But I couldn't. I tried so many times, but I didn't want you to hate me."

"Now I've lost seven years of my daughter's life. Seven years I can never get back."

"I'm so sorry, my darling."

Marisa didn't respond to the heartfelt words, but she saw the past with much greater clarity. She'd been the focal point of her mother's life—a way to fulfill the dream she'd wanted so badly. And Marisa, in awe of her beautiful mother and wanting her approval, had been a willing victim. But not anymore.

New strength pumped through her veins. She could get through this. She wasn't going to sink down into that valley of despair. A younger Marisa might have, but not the adult

Marisa. In her determination she felt as if she'd emerged from shadows into sunshine.

"When I overheard you and Father talking earlier, you said if I ever found out, you'd lose me forever. You were right. You have hurt me beyond belief, and no parent has the right to do that. I will never forgive you."

"Marisa, please," Richard begged. "You're a Dalton, a Preston. We're bound by blood—we're family."

She drew a deep breath. "Ellie's a Dalton, a Preston, and you gave her away like unwanted garbage."

Richard paled.

"You should see her, Father. She's bright, funny, adventurous, strong-willed—everything a Preston should be."

"Marisa…"

"You want me to understand, to forgive, but some things just aren't forgivable." She turned toward the door. "I'm leaving. Please don't try to contact me." She walked out, and Reed and Colter followed.

Outside, she leaned against her car, trembling severely.

"You can't drive in this condition," Reed said.

"Please take me to Cari's."

Cari's? Colter frowned, wondering why she didn't want to go to Ellie. That should be her first reaction. Maybe she needed time. He didn't want to judge her, but he had a little girl who desperately wanted her mommy.

He was still reeling from the impact of everything he'd heard tonight. Marisa was, too. He had to give her a chance to adjust. He didn't know what Marisa had in mind.

One thing he knew for certain, though: Ellie wasn't leaving the ranch or him. He'd lost Marisa, but he would not lose his daughter.

Chapter Eleven

"Please follow us in your car," Marisa said. "We have to talk."

Colter nodded. There wasn't much he could say. They would now decide what was best for Ellie, and his gut tightened at the thought of his daughter getting hurt. Marisa had been hurt too much, though, and she deserved to know their child. But he wasn't sure where that left him—somewhere in the middle, fighting for a future for Ellie...and himself.

He followed them through the busy Dallas traffic to an apartment complex and parked beside them. A dark-haired woman ran out to the car; this must be Cari, and obviously Marisa had called her. Colter took a moment to call Tulley. Ellie was in bed, and he told Tulley he'd get back as soon as he could. He'd tell him later about everything he'd learned tonight. It wasn't something he wanted to discuss on the phone. He grabbed his hat from the seat and made his way toward the group.

Marisa and Cari hugged while Reed stood some distance away. "My baby's alive, Cari. My baby's alive."

"This is so wonderful," Cari said, studying Marisa's face with a big smile.

"What?" Marisa asked, brushing away an errant tear.

"I'm just so relieved. I was afraid this last blow might be too much for you. But looking at you now, I know you're made of much stronger stuff. I also know you can handle anything—including Colter Kincaid."

"Oh, Cari, what am I going to say to him? He's lived with as many lies during the past few years as I have."

"Just tell him what's in your heart."

She tried to remember those words as he walked up, and they climbed the stairs to Cari's apartment with its stunning view of the Dallas skyline. No one was looking at it, though, or commenting on Cari's Christmas decorations. Marisa saw only Colter. His hat was in his hand, his eyes filmed with anguish.

She realized she'd never truly known this man. He had stirred her emotions, filled her heart with girlish fantasies and made her body yearn in a wanton fashion that had left her wanting more, but she'd never really known the person he was inside. How many men would give up so much to raise a child? He was probably more of a man than she'd ever meet again.

She moistened her dry lips with the tip of her tongue. "Colter." Her voice came out a mere whisper.

Uncertainty mingled with disbelief in his eyes. She could see that he was having difficulty adjusting to the truth. Oh God, how were they ever going to get through this?

"Marisa," he murmured, taking a step toward her. "Are you all right?"

She took a stilted breath. "I don't think I'll ever be the same again."

Running a hand through his hair, he admitted, "I know what you mean. I feel as if I've been kicked in the gut and I'm still trying to catch my breath."

Silence took hold, and no one seemed inclined to speak.

Cari stepped forward and held out her hand to Colter. "Nice to meet you in person, Mr. Kincaid."

Colter shook her hand, dragging his eyes away from Marisa. "Thank you for taking care of Ellie today."

Cari smiled. "She wanted to see Marisa, and I found Marisa for her. She's a very determined little girl."

"Yeah. She can be headstrong."

She didn't get that from me, Marisa thought. She'd always been the dutiful daughter…until she met Colter.

Silence prevailed again.

"Junior," Cari said, "there's a nightclub around the corner. Why don't you buy me a drink?"

"I don't—"

"Sure you do." Cari grabbed her purse and linked her arm through Reed's. "We'll see you two later."

Cari pulled Reed out the door, but Marisa and Colter hardly noticed. His eyes held hers, and it was just the two of them, needing answers, reassurance and, most of all, forgiveness.

"Have a seat," Marisa invited, sitting on the sofa before her legs gave way.

He sat beside her.

"I—" They spoke at the same time.

She pushed her hair nervously behind her ear. "I'm not sure what to say to you. Words seem insufficient."

He placed his hat on the coffee table. "I feel the same way." He stared at his hands. "I'm so sorry for all the cruel things I've said to you."

"It doesn't matter now," she murmured. "I understand."

"I just keep thinking that if I'd demanded to see you the day Ellie was born, none of this would've happened." He paused. "When the PI gave me the address and I discovered the kind of clinic you were in, I felt like I'd been sucker punched. Not only did you not want *me*—you also didn't want our child."

As he talked, tears streamed down her cheeks. He turned to look at her, his eyes darkened by the emotions he was feeling.

"God, Marisa, why did you let your mother take you there?"

She felt a familiar stab of guilt. "I think I told you I had a lot of problems with the pregnancy. Mother suggested it would be easier for me in a private clinic, where I could get constant medical attention. I didn't object because I knew she was ashamed that her daughter was another statistic, an unwed pregnant teenager, and I also knew she wanted to get me away from her circle of friends and the impending gossip. But I didn't realize it was an adoption clinic until I arrived. By then I was very depressed that you'd married someone else. Nothing seemed to matter anymore. I just wanted peace and quiet." Her eyes held his. "I adamantly refused to sign any adoption papers. I intended to keep my baby. I…" A sob escaped her and she couldn't speak.

He waited, clenching and unclenching his fingers.

She quickly brushed the tears away with the back of her hand. "I yearned and prayed for you to be with me when he— I mean, she—was born. And all the time you were there, thinking…" She stopped, fighting for control, then added, "I wanted our baby."

"I know," he assured her. "Believe me, I know…now."

Struggling with her tears, she whispered, "Tell me about Ellie."

His eyes took on a soft glow. "Let's see, you know how much she weighed. She had these blond curls, and her eyes were a bluish green, and the first time I saw her she was crying at the top of her lungs."

Crying? She closed her eyes and she could hear the sound. It *had* been real; Ellie was real.

"I heard her crying," she said. "The labor was so long and they medicated me. I don't remember much afterward, but I do remember hearing a baby cry. Mother said it was my imagination. Afterward, I continued to hear that cry in my dreams. The sound has haunted me for years. Somehow, my subconscious must've known my baby wasn't dead."

After a pause he said, "Don't you think it's time Ellie met her mother?"

Yes instantly hovered in her throat, then fear consumed her. What was she going to say to Ellie? Could the child cope with the situation?

"Don't you?" he asked, obviously noticing her indecision.

"Yes." She gulped in air, trying to explain. "I want to be

in control of my emotions when I see her so I can handle her reaction. I don't want her to hate me."

"You've met Ellie, and you're well aware of her desire for a mother."

"Everything in me wants to drive straight to the ranch and take her in my arms, hold her, tell her I'm her mother, but I'm afraid I'll fall apart if I do that. I have to——"

"I can't even imagine the pain you're going through, and when I think of your parents all I feel is anger. But I'm tired of all the anger and resentment, and it's time to focus on Ellie."

"Santa said she'd have a mother by Christmas and he was right. I just never dreamed it would be me." She took a deep breath. "How do we tell her what happened?"

"Very carefully——with the truth. And we need to do it together."

"Yes. But I need tonight to prepare myself."

"Okay," he said, and stood. "It won't be easy for you or for her, but it has to be done."

"I'll be there first thing in the morning," she replied, knowing she couldn't stay away any longer than that.

He moved to her side and gently stroked her cheek. A familiar flutter started in the pit of her stomach, making it difficult to think coherently. He slipped his arm around her waist and pulled her close to him. Resting her head against his chest, she felt his heart beat out a message, a message she understood, a message of forgiveness. They stood there holding each other, letting the pain and misunderstandings of the past slowly ebb away.

"I've got to go," he murmured into her hair. "I don't like leaving Ellie this long."

She drew back, feeling deprived of his warmth, his closeness, but Ellie came first.

"Yes." She smiled through her tears. "Tomorrow her real mother's coming home."

Colter picked up his hat. "See you in the morning." He turned and left.

ALMOST ON CUE, Cari and Reed walked into the apartment.

"You okay?" Reed asked, giving her a hug.

"I'm better than I've been in the past eight years. I have a daughter, and tomorrow I'll see her as her mother for the first time."

"I'm proud of the way you're handling this."

"Me, too," Cari said. "Now, let's have some pizza."

Marisa noticed she had a big pizza carton in her hand. "I'm not very hungry."

"You're eating," Cari insisted. "You'll need your strength for tomorrow."

Marisa gave in, and as she nibbled on the food, Cari and Reed's bantering kept her amused. Then the three of them discussed sleeping arrangements. Marisa tried to talk Reed into going home, but he was adamant in his decision to leave Dalton's and their parents behind. Like her, he was tired of the manipulation and control.

In the end, they all slept in the den. They talked until the wee hours, then Reed fell asleep in a recliner and Cari on the sofa. Marisa curled up on the love seat with thoughts of Ellie…her baby.

She went over and over every detail of their short time together, especially the conversation about Ellie's mother. "She's very beautiful, and Daddy say I'm gonna look just like her." There was much more meaning behind those words now; Ellie hadn't been talking about Shannon, but about her. *Colter thought she was beautiful.* That was what he'd told Ellie—probably to satisfy her curiosity. She wasn't sure why Colter had married Shannon, but she would find out in the days ahead.

It must have been very painful for him to talk about Ellie's al mother, believing what he had. She was just grateful he hadn't poisoned Ellie's mind against her. But he wasn't that kind of man. He loved his daughter; he would never hurt her.

What was she going to say to Ellie? She pushed those troubling thoughts from her mind. For now, she'd just savor the knowledge that her baby was alive. If someone had asked her to draw a mental picture of her daughter, the child would have looked exactly like Ellie. She was perfect with her big green eyes and that enchanting smile. Marisa felt a deep sadness for all the years she'd missed, but she couldn't let herself dwell on that. The fact that Ellie was her daughter gave her the strength to face what lay ahead.

COLTER WALKED THROUGH the back door feeling tired and drained. When he'd left here earlier, he'd just wanted answers. Now he was wondering if he could deal with everything he'd learned tonight.

Tulley was in the recliner watching TV, half asleep. When Colter sank onto the sofa, Tulley sat up straight, blinking.

"You've been gone a long time. What happened?"

Colter rubbed his hands over his face. "It's unbelievable and nothing like I imagined—nothing." He went on to tell him the events of the night.

"What! She didn't know Ellie was her daughter?"

He shook his head. "Thanks to her parents she thought her baby was dead…and Ellie was mine and Shannon's."

"Lordy, lordy, what kind of parents would do something like that?"

"I don't know, but you should've seen Marisa. Her pain was heart-wrenching and she actually passed out from the shock. But she came back with a strength that surprised me. She told them exactly how she felt and broke all ties with them. She's staying at a friend's."

"Why didn't she come here with you?"

He didn't have an answer, but Tulley had plenty to say. "*This* is where she belongs—with Ellie…and you."

"We can't just turn back the damn clock," he snapped. "Too much has happened and the good emotions have gotten lost in all the senseless pain. I'm not even sure how I feel about her anymore."

"Well, then, you need to buy yourself a mirror."

"What are you talking about?"

"Whenever you look at Marisa, all those good emotions are in your eyes for the world to see. They're not lost. They're right there inside you."

Colter jumped to his feet. "I'm not ready to talk about this."

Tulley rose more slowly. "You know how sometimes we put blinders on a horse to keep him from getting skittish?"

He didn't respond.

"Well, Colt, boy. You're wearing the blinders now."

"I'm checking on Ellie." He headed for the hall.

"Tripp called. Said he and Brodie would come by tomorrow to pick up those horses," Tulley called after him.

"Fine," he muttered.

He walked into Ellie's room, clearing his mind of everything but thoughts of his precious child. She lay on her stomach, arms and legs in all directions. Sooner was curled at her feet, and raised his head when Colter entered.

Colter patted Sooner and drew the covers over Ellie. As he did, she stirred and murmured, "Daddy?"

"Yes, angelface, it's Daddy."

"Hug me."

He gathered her in his arms and she laid her face on his shoulder. "I did something bad and I thought you weren't coming back. I waited and waited and…"

His throat closed for a second. "You can never do anything bad enough that I wouldn't come back. I will always be here for you. Always."

She rubbed her face against him. "I love you, Daddy, and tried to stay awake so I could give you kisses. You can't sleep I don't give you kisses."

"No, J can't. I have to have my angelface kisses."

She kissed his cheek and was asleep almost instantly. He held her for a moment longer, then gently put her down and pulled the blanket over her. He stared down at this little girl he loved more than life itself. For now it was just the two of them. Tomorrow would be different.

Tomorrow she'd meet her mother.

Tomorrow.

MARISA DOZED on and off and woke before dawn, feeling an anticipation, an exhilaration she hadn't experienced in a long time. She was going to see her daughter, her baby, she told herself. A chorus of nervous jitters followed this, but nothing and no one would keep her away from Ellie.

Reed and Cari were sleeping soundly. They'd been up late comforting her, and she didn't wake them. She scribbled a quick note, which she placed on the table, then left. She knew Cari would drive Reed wherever he wanted to go.

Within minutes, she was at Mrs. Hackleberry's. It was 5:00 a.m. and, not surprisingly, the house was dark. Marisa let herself in and tiptoed up to her room. She quickly showered and changed.

She went through everything in her closet, unable to decide what to wear. Finally she chose rust-colored slacks and a matching jacket with a cream-colored silk blouse. It wasn't too dressy or casual; it was just right. Or was it? She wavered, then realized she was only procrastinating. She brushed her hair one final time, checked her makeup and hurried to the front door.

The kitchen light was on, so she stopped to speak with Hazel, who offered her a cup of coffee. The aroma alone gave her a jolt of energy, and Marisa happily accepted the cup Hazel handed her. She told Hazel about her daughter, and fo▪ the first time actually let herself feel an incredible joy.

"Oh, my dear." Hazel hugged her. "This is so unbelieva▪ And your baby's a girl instead of a boy?"

"Yes. My parents weren't taking any chances," she said, unable to keep the bitterness out of her voice. "If I ever met Colter again, they wanted to make sure I'd never suspect Ellie was mine. And I didn't."

Hazel clicked her tongue. "I don't understand how your parents could do such a thing."

"I'm having a hard time with that myself," she admitted. "But can't dwell on it. I have to go see my daughter." She slipped her purse over her shoulder. "I'm not sure when I'll be back, so don't worry about me."

"Oh, my dear, I don't think I can help doing that."

Marisa gave her a hug and left, her thoughts totally on Ellie…and Colter.

THE DRIVE OUT TO THE RANCH was similar to the one she'd made yesterday. Had it only been yesterday? It seemed like decades ago. So much had changed; her whole life had changed.

Today she had a child—a daughter. It all felt so unreal, so ethereal, and she knew it would be quite a while before it became real to her.

Her nerves were taut by the time she reached the ranch. She drove to the back and parked beside a truck pulling a horse trailer with horses inside. Two men were standing by the truck talking to Colter. She recognized them immediately—Brodie Hayes and Tripp Daniels. They were cowboys just like Colter and had been in Vegas all those years ago.

She sat for a few moments, gathering strength, as she stared out at the cold December day. There was a slight breeze and the air seemed to crackle with excitement.

She took several deep breaths and finally climbed out. She was nervous enough about seeing Ellie, and she didn't want to have to make small talk with these men. She had liked them years ago because they were close friends of Colter's, but she hadn't expected to see them today.

Colter came over to her, and her heart fluttered anxiously at the sight of him. He was dressed in jeans and a white shirt that emphasized the broadness of his shoulders.

"Hi," she said, her voice husky.

"Hi," he replied.

She sensed a tension in him and knew that he was nervous, too. It was there in the steady gaze of his brilliant eyes, in the vein that beat fitfully in his neck, and in the way he shoved his hands into his pockets. They'd been through so much, but they still had one hurdle to get over, and it was clearly on both their minds.

Colter turned to his friends. "You remember Brodie and Tripp?"

"Yes," she replied with a slight smile. "Nice to see you again."

Brodie removed his hat, revealing dark wavy hair. "The pleasure's all ours. You're more beautiful than ever, Marisa." Brodie was a born flirt and a charmer, and Marisa never knew quite how to take him. He and Colter had been friends for a long time, so she merely smiled.

"That goes for me, too," Tripp put in.

So many memories came back at the sound of his voice. Tripp didn't talk much, but she remembered when he'd told her about his estrangement from his family; there was a sadness in him she could identify with. She liked Tripp. He and Colter had been the best of friends, competing together, and Marisa was glad they'd remained friends over the years. This wasn't the day to reminisce, though.

The message must have gotten through, because Brodie said, "Catch you later, Colt." Tripp tipped his hat and they climbed into the pickup.

She and Colter walked into the house. "Sit down," he invited as they entered the den.

She was glad of the invitation, fearful her legs wouldn't support her much longer.

Tulley stood in the doorway to the kitchen. "Good morning, Marisa."

"Good morning." She tried to smile and failed miserably.

"I'm so sorry, girl. Colter and I never dreamed anything like this had happened."

"I know." She sat on the sofa. "Colter thought I didn't want our baby."

"Yep." Tulley nodded. "That pretty much sums it up." He grabbed his hat. "I'll mosey outside before the person in question makes an appearance."

"Where is Ellie?" she asked, gripping her hands. She wanted to see her daughter so badly that the anticipation was almost unbearable.

"She's not up yet," Colter said, sitting down in a recliner.

"Have you told her anything?"

"No," he replied. "She was half-asleep last night when I got home. In any case, we agreed to tell her together."

"Yes," she muttered, trying to control the spasmodic trembling within her.

He eyed her strangely. "You're not having second thoughts, are you?"

"Of course not," she said. "I'm scared. I don't know how she's going to react."

"Just relax and everything will be fine," he told her, his voice softening.

She was starting to relax, but her whole body tensed at his next words.

"We haven't discussed Ellie yet, but she's been my whole world for the last seven years and her home is here on the ranch. I want her to stay here."

He was worried she might try to take Ellie away from him; she could see it in his eyes and hear it in his voice. She had to reassure him.

"I would never do anything to disrupt Ellie's life. I'm just hoping you'll allow me to be a part of it."

They stared at each other. Colter started to speak, then stopped when he heard Ellie calling, "Daddy, where are you?"

"In the den, angelface," Colter called, his eyes holding Marisa's.

Everything in Marisa seemed to tighten, and she had trouble breathing as she waited for her daughter to enter the room.

Chapter Twelve

Ellie came racing into the room in her pajamas, Sooner behind her. She slid to a halt when she saw Marisa. "You're back," she exclaimed, and climbed onto Colter's lap. She wrapped her arms around his neck and gave him several loud kisses.

Marisa's breath solidified in her throat as she watched her daughter. This was the baby she'd created in her womb, the baby she'd nourished for almost nine months. She remembered the joy of hearing her first heartbeat and of feeling that first kick. Her hand strayed to her stomach, and she remembered the months she'd lovingly stroked her swelling abdomen, talked to her baby. The baby was now in front of her. *Ellie.*

She'd given Ellie life, fought for thirty long hours to bring her into the world—but did that make her a mother? A mother's title was earned by getting up in the middle of the night, walking the floor during bouts of colic, changing diapers, being there to hear the first sound, the first laugh and to applaud the first step. She'd missed all that, and at that thought, an intense pain filled her heart.

"Did you come to see me?" Ellie asked Marisa, resting against Colter.

"Yes." Marisa clenched her hands until her nails dug into her palms, but she didn't feel it. All she felt was the anxiety in her stomach.

Noticing her difficulty, Colter came to her aid. "Angelface, I want to talk to you."

Ellie swung her gaze to her father's, eyes wary, as if she knew what was on his mind. Raising her hands in a palms-up gesture, she declared, "I won't be bad anymore, Daddy."

"This isn't about yesterday," Colter said calmly. "This is about something else."

"Okay." Ellie gave Colter a little smile.

She was so adorable, it took every ounce of strength Marisa had not to grab her and cover her pixie face with kisses. Instead, she bit her lip and watched as Ellie looked up at Colter with trusting eyes.

"You've been wanting a mother…"

"Yep." Ellie nodded. "Santa said she'd be here by Christmas."

He swallowed, glanced at Marisa, and said, "She's here now."

Ellie sat up, clapping her hands in excitement. "Here at our house?"

"Yes."

Ellie bounced off his lap like a rubber ball, jumping up and down at his feet. "Is she outside with Tulley? Is she? Is she?"

Colter was a bit taken aback by the quick response, but didn't falter in his answer. "No. She's in this room."

"Where?" Ellie looked around as if she expected her mother to pop up from some hiding place. Then her eyes settled on Marisa. "There's nobody here but Marisa."

Colter cleared his throat. "Marisa's your mother… your real mother."

"No, she isn't." Ellie leaned against Colter's knee. "Why are you saying that, Daddy?"

"Because she is."

"No," Ellie said adamantly. "My mommy raced barrels. I heard Brodie say so."

Colter's heart kicked against his ribs. "That was Shannon—your stepmother. Marisa is your real mother."

Ellie stared at Marisa as if she were seeing her for the first time. A sense of inadequacy swept over her as Ellie inspected her from the top of her blond head down to her shoes. She didn't miss a thing, her eyes finally resting on Marisa's face. Marisa wondered what she was thinking, but all she could see in the child's expression was a deep curiosity. Then her face puckered into a frown.

"How come you didn't tell me you were my mommy."

Marisa tried to speak, but the words were trapped in her throat.

Ellie's pucker deepened. "You lied to me. I don't want a mommy who lies. And I don't want you." Saying that, she ran for the bedroom.

"Ellie," Colter shouted, but she didn't stop. She kept running.

Marisa bit her hand to keep from crying out. Her worst fears had come true. Ellie had rejected her. She felt as if she'd been hit by an eighteen wheeler and there was nothing left of her. Nothing.

She wasn't even aware of Colter sitting down beside her until he took her into his arms. Her arms went convulsively around his waist, and she found herself clinging to him, needing his support and comfort more than she'd ever needed anything in her life.

He held her, gently rocking her. "She didn't mean it, Marisa. We'll give her a minute, then talk to her again. She's just a child. She'll change her mind. I promise."

"No, she won't," she sobbed against his chest. "She hates me. I knew it. Somehow I knew it. That's why I was so afraid."

His hand idly caressed the nape of her neck, his breath on her hair. "She's just upset right now. In a few minutes it'll be a completely different story. She's wanted a mommy for so long, and at the moment she's angry that you didn't tell her immediately. Ellie doesn't stay angry for long, though. Trust me."

His voice soothed and caressed her, lulling her fears and her pain. Her body began to react to him, and she became aware of other sensations, like the hardness of his chest pressed against hers, the muscles in his back, the clean tangy scent that emanated from him. Desire began to curl in her stomach, sending her emotions off in an entirely different direction.

Those feelings consumed her and she drew back to look at him. His eyes were glazed, and his head came down, his lips lightly touching hers. It was a comforting, soothing kiss. He pulled her closer, and she formed herself against him, enjoying the feel of his body. She didn't know when the kiss changed, but her lips opened under the sensual pressure of his, returning an ardor she'd almost forgotten. The blood that had lain lifeless in her body started to pump hard through her veins.

It felt good and right, and one kind of tension was replaced with another. But this *wasn't* right. They should be thinking about Ellie.

Pushing herself away from him, she self-consciously brushed her hair back from her face. "Please, let's not cloud the issue."

He studied her, his face unreadable. "Yes. I'm sorry."

Marisa didn't want an apology. She wanted…she couldn't put into words what she wanted from Colter. What she'd felt in his arms was only a remnant of the past and it was simply a result of their heightened emotions. She certainly didn't want to complicate things by getting involved with Colter. Ellie was her only concern.

Before she could think of a suitable reply, Tulley came in. "What's wrong with Ellie?"

Colter got to his feet. "Why?"

"I was checking to make sure all the gates were closed after Brodie and Tripp left and I saw her running toward the creek in nothing but her pajamas. It's forty degrees outside. I hollered at her but she wouldn't stop."

"Damn. She must've sneaked out." Colter said. "We told her and she didn't take the news well. I'll go get her. First, I'd better get her some clothes." He hurried away to Ellie's bedroom.

Tulley squinted. "I don't understand this. She's wanted a mother ever since she realized other kids had mommies and she didn't."

Marisa stood on unsteady legs. "She thinks I lied to her."

"Oh."

Colter came back with a jacket, socks and slippers, and they went outside into the cool December morning.

"Aries is saddled if you want to take him," Tulley said.

"Thanks." Colter looked at Marisa. "I'll bring Ellie back and we'll talk this through. Don't worry."

That wasn't so easily done, but she concentrated on Ellie and not on the pain in her heart. Colter ran toward the barn, and she watched as he led a horse outside and swung effortlessly into the saddle. She remembered that about him; he was magnificent on a horse.

"Why don't you go inside where it's warmer?" Tulley suggested.

"I'm not going anywhere until I know my—" she wiped away a tear "—daughter is okay." The word was so new to her that she had a hard time saying it, believing it.

She caught Tulley's worried expression. "I'm not going to fall apart," she told him. "I'm not the weak young girl I used to be."

"I can see that." He folded his arms across his chest. "I've hated you a lot of years for what you did to him and to Ellie. Now I'm not sure what to say to you."

"Just be understanding. That's all I ask."

"I can do that," he answered, buttoning his jacket. "Why don't I get you a chair."

"No, I'm fine. Thanks," she replied. "I couldn't sit anyway. I'm standing right here until I see her again."

"Then I'm standing with you."

They stood together, waiting, and Marisa wrapped both arms around her waist to still her nerves. Ellie *had* to forgive her. How could she explain to a seven-year-old child what had happened? How could she expect a child to understand?

Those questions tore at her, but she was confident that Colter would have the answers. He knew Ellie better than anyone, and she'd listen to him.

Ellie, baby, please listen to your daddy.

COLTER SAW HER not far from the barn, sitting in the winter grass by a small creek that ran through the property. Her arms were tight around Sooner, her face buried against him. His heart lurched at the sight, and he dismounted and walked over to her, searching for the words to ease her pain. He squatted beside her and handed her the socks and fuzzy slippers.

She grabbed them. "Sooner and me are running away," she announced, shoving a foot into a sock. "Don't try to stop us."

He laid her jacket in her lap. "Where are you going?"

"Don't know." She poked her arms into the sleeves. "We might live in the woods. Tulley said you can live on berries, bark and other stuff, but I forget." She shrugged. "Doesn't matter. Sooner and me will figure it out."

"I see." He sat on the grass and drew his knees up. "That makes me very sad. Who's going to give me angelface kisses?"

There was silence for a moment, then her bottom lip trembled and she flew into Colter's arms. "I will, Daddy. I will," she cried against his face. "Why did she lie to me? Didn't she want me?"

He smoothed her hair with a shaky hand, praying for strength to tell her the truth without hurting her. "She didn't lie to you, baby."

Ellie stuck out her chin. "Yes, she did. She knew she was my mommy and she didn't tell me. She even let me talk to Santa and she *knew*."

Colter settled her in the crook of his arm. "I'm going to tell you a story and I want you to listen carefully."

"Okay." She held his hand tightly.

"When I met your mother, she was seventeen, shy and very beautiful. The moment our eyes met, it was like—" he thought for a second "—like spontaneous combustion. Do you know what that means?"

"No."

How could he explain so she could understand? "We fell in love instantly, and we spent every moment we could together."

"Oh," Ellie said. "It was real love, Daddy?"

"Hmm." He'd believed it was, hoped it was. Now he wasn't sure. He wasn't sure about anything.

"What happened next?" she asked, playing with his fingers.

"We were so busy being in love that we ignored the problems in our relationship."

"What problems?"

"Remember how when you asked about your mother, I told you she left because she was unhappy?"

Ellie nodded.

"That was partly true. Marisa lived in New York and was a gifted pianist, and it was her mother's dream that one day Marisa would be a world-renowned musician. But that wasn't Marisa's dream. She was tired of the long hours of training. That's why she and some of her friends came to Vegas that year for the National Rodeo Finals. Her mother was away and she wanted some freedom, some fun. But when she told me she loved me as much as I loved her, I asked her to marry me and she said yes."

Ellie was quiet, so he continued. "The next morning, I rushed out to buy her a ring. When I got back, she was gone."

"Where did she go?"

"Her mother found out where she was and came after her and made her leave."

"Why?"

"Marisa was only seventeen, and her mother had control of her. She was still considered a minor."

"Like you have control of me?"

"Yes. Like I have control of you." He rested his chin on the top of her head and prayed for strength to finish the story.

"Back in New York, your mother soon realized she was pregnant, but she didn't know how to get in touch with me. I hadn't told her exactly where I lived when I wasn't riding on the circuit. So she hired a private investigator to find me, and he told her I was already married to someone else."

"Oh." Ellie looked up at him. "Were you, Daddy?"

"Not then, but later I married Shannon," he said. "The detective was paid to lie to her, and Marisa became very upset and started having problems with the pregnancy. The problems became so severe, her mother put her in a clinic."

Ellie was absorbing every word, and he was glad she didn't ask who'd paid the detective.

He had to finish the story. His courage wavered for a second, then he resumed. "Marisa's mother felt Marisa was too young to be a mommy and planned to put the baby up for adoption, but Marisa refused to sign the papers. She wanted her baby, and she intended to keep you."

"Did she really want me, Daddy?"

"Oh, yes, she wanted you." He was certain of that now.

"What happened?"

"Her parents decided that you belonged with your father, so they contacted me and I went to New York to get you. They told me Marisa didn't want the baby and she didn't want to see me."

"No, Daddy, no," Ellie whimpered, squeezing his hand.

"They were wrong about that, but I didn't know it then." His arm tightened around her. "Three days later, I flew back to Texas with my brand-new daughter."

"What happened to Marisa?"

He noticed she couldn't say "Mommy" just yet, and he took a long breath. The next part would be hard, but he had to tell her. "Your mother was under a lot of medication for the delivery, so she doesn't remember too much. She heard a baby crying, though, and she's been haunted by that sound for the past seven years." He turned her face up to his. "You see, baby, they told her you were stillborn."

"What does that mean?"

He breathed in deeply. "That you were born dead."

She shook her head. "No, I wasn't."

"I know, but your mother's believed that for all these years. She's been very sad. That's the reason she came out here the first day, when we had the storm. She wanted to tell me about you—that you were born—but I was so angry because I still believed she'd given you away."

"But she didn't?"

"No, baby. She didn't even know you were alive until last night. It's been quite a shock to her."

Ellie threw her arms around his neck.

"You've been wanting a mommy and she's been grieving for her baby. Both of you have been searching for the same thing— each other. She loves you, angelface. Give her a chance."

"I want my mommy," she sniffled into his shoulder.

He stood with her in his arms. "Let's go tell her that."

He placed her in the saddle, then mounted behind her. It had been a while since they'd ridden like this. Ellie was fiercely independent, and by the age of three she was riding by herself. People changed, just like the seasons, and he hoped he was ready for the changes that were about to occur in his life and Ellie's.

THEY RODE UP TO THE BARN and Ellie swung her leg over the saddle horn and slid to the ground. Marisa stood in the spot where Colter had left her. Her arms were wrapped around her waist as if to brace herself. He dismounted and watched Ellie.

Marisa watched her, too. She held her breath as she waited for her daughter's next move. Ellie's hair was disheveled and she looked a sight in the fuzzy pink slippers and heavy jacket—the best sight Marisa had ever seen.

Forgive me. Forgive me. Forgive me echoed back through the years, through all the pain, all the heartache. And every-thing came down to this child's reaction, her understanding and acceptance.

Ellie kept staring at her.

Marisa licked parched lips. "Remember when we were waiting to see Santa, you told me your mommy wanted to come home and you had to let her know you wanted her to. That's why you had to see Santa. That's why you believe." She dragged in a breath. "You were right. I'm here, Ellie. I'm your mother."

Ellie flung out her arms and sprinted toward Marisa. The pain inside Marisa abated and she ran to meet her daughter. She lifted her up in her arms, holding her in a fierce grip.

"I'm sorry, Mommy," Ellie cried against her neck.

The sound of that word tripped every emotional breaker in her, and she struggled for composure. "No, baby, no." Marisa caressed her hair, her face. "You have nothing to be sorry for."

"Mommy, Mommy, Mommy" was Ellie's sad refrain.

The emotional current took its toll and Marisa sank to her knees under the impact. Tears flowed unheeded and she held tight to her daughter, kissing her face over and over.

Colter watched from a distance, his stomach churning with the same emotions.

Tulley walked up to him. "I can't take this. I'll unsaddle Aries."

Colter couldn't take it, either, but he had to. Mother and daughter had found each other. He was happy about that, but deep inside a worry stabbed at him. It had been just the two of them, he and Ellie, for so long. Where did this leave him? He had no desire to question or to deny Marisa's right to Ellie. He just wished he knew her plans for the future. At this point, he suspected she didn't have any. Later, though, it would be different. *How* different was what he wondered.

He remembered the way they'd kissed earlier. The fire, the passion was still there for him. For Marisa he wasn't sure. She'd responded, but seemed to hate herself for that reaction. He shouldn't have kissed her in the first place. It was spontaneous, as he'd told Ellie—like it always had been between them.

He had never been more aware of the differences in their

two worlds than he was today. She was imported wine and vacations on the Riviera. He was beer and a drive to the lake. How did he ever think two such different people could make a marriage work? They had nothing in common except a simmering passion, and they'd both learned the hard way that it wasn't enough.

Where did they go from here? *To an uncertain future* was his only answer. He'd take it one day at a time and make this transition as easy as possible for Marisa and Ellie…and pray that he wouldn't get his heart broken again. Hell, it had never even been repaired after the last time, so the best he could hope for was a friendship with Marisa to build a stable future for Ellie.

It wouldn't be easy being friends with a woman he'd loved and hated more than anyone in his life, but he had to find some kind of compromise with Marisa—for all of them.

Chapter Thirteen

Colter walked over and clasped Marisa by the elbows, lifting her to her feet. He tried to take Ellie from her, but her arms tightened around the girl.

"Let's go into the house," he suggested. "It's much warmer."

He went ahead and held the door open. Marisa followed him, then settled on the sofa with Ellie on her lap. She helped Ellie off with her coat and cupped her face in both hands. "I love you," she said in a hoarse voice. "I have always loved you."

"I know. Daddy told me."

Marisa glanced at Colter, sending him a silent thank-you. He sat beside her, his leg brushing against hers.

"I told her the whole story. The time for lies and secrets is over."

"I don't like your mommy," Ellie said. "Why didn't she want me?"

Marisa stroked her face. "Oh, baby. It wasn't that." She kissed Ellie's cheek. "She just thought I was too young to be a mother."

It seemed odd to be defending her mother, but she had to protect Ellie to ensure she didn't grow up with any hatred or bitterness. Ellie deserved complete happiness. For a paralyzing moment she wondered if her mother had experienced those same feelings about her.

"Daddy said you play the piano really good."

"Yes," she admitted, surprised he'd told Ellie that.

"I take piano lessons, and my teacher says I'm really good, too."

This time she couldn't hide her surprise, and she looked at Colter for confirmation.

"I thought it might be something she'd enjoy," he explained.

She stared at him, seeing a different side to this man she'd once loved so deeply. Back then, their relationship had been mostly physical. Now she was getting a glimpse of the loving, caring man he really was.

"I do," Ellie said, "but I like riding better. I race barrels, and Tulley says I'm getting faster. You got to be fast to win and I'm gonna be a winner like my daddy."

Marisa stroked Ellie's face again, loving the confidence in that tiny voice. She'd never been that way, and she envied that strong spirit. "There's no doubt in my mind you will be."

"I can play the piano, too," Ellie told her again.

Marisa sensed that Ellie wanted to please her, and she had to make something clear. "You never have to do anything to please me. I love you just the way you are." She wouldn't pressure Ellie or set goals for her that weren't her own.

"Okay, but I can play sometimes, except Sooner said it hurts his ears."

Marisa smiled, hardly able to believe this adorable child was hers—and Colter's. She held Ellie's face. "Do you know how many times I've wondered what you looked like?"

"Bunches?"

"Yes, bunches, and in all my wondering you had those beautiful green eyes." In her dreams her baby was a boy, and she realized Colter hadn't told Ellie that part of the story. She was glad—it would only confuse the child more.

"Daddy's eyes."

"Oh, yes, you have your daddy's eyes. I wish I'd seen you

as a baby, as a toddler, as a—" Her voice cracked and she had to stop.

"But you can see me now," Ellie said, her eyes bright.

"Yes. I can see you now, and I'm so grateful for that. I meant when you were first born."

"Me, too." She jumped off Marisa's lap and pointed to the built-in entertainment center, its rows of bookshelves filled with videos. "Daddy took tons of videos of me. Let's show her, Daddy."

Colter got to his feet and joined Ellie.

"Get the first one," Ellie instructed. "The very first one."

"Okay, angelface," Colter said. "Have a seat and I'll pop it in the VCR."

Ellie ran back to Marisa and sat on her lap. Colter got the remote and clicked it on, then returned to his seat by Marisa.

Soon images flashed on the screen and Marisa caught her breath. There was Colter, a younger Colter, the man she'd known, and he was holding a baby wrapped in a pink blanket.

"I'd like to introduce Ellen Kincaid." Colter's voice came from the TV. "I named her after my mother, but I think I'll call her Ellie. With that angel face, she looks like an Ellie to me." The camera zoomed in on the precious little face. Ellie was asleep, and her features were perfect—bow mouth, pert nose and blond hair with a pink ribbon in it. Marisa's arms ached to hold that baby. Instead she hugged the little girl in her arms.

"There's Tulley, Aunt Becky and Aunt Jen." Ellie pointed out the people hovering around the newborn. "There's Brodie and Tripp and a friend of Daddy's."

It was Shannon Wells—the woman Colter had married, the woman who had taken her place. She wondered about that relationship, but she didn't have time to speculate on it as she watched her child.

She was mesmerized by the videos. Her baby grew right before her eyes; she heard the first gurgles. She saw her smile, roll over, rock on all fours and then crawl. Ellie pulled herself up on furniture and took tottering steps toward Colter. He was there to catch her when she fell, just like he'd been since the day she was born.

Marisa didn't even realize she was crying until Colter thrust a wad of tissues into her hands. She wiped at her eyes, unable to take them from the screen. *Dada* was Ellie's first word and she said it over and over, trailing behind Colter. Every birthday, holiday and special occasion was there for Marisa to see, and her heart broke a little more at each one she'd missed.

Tulley made sandwiches for lunch, and they continued to watch Ellie's life. There were so many videos, but Marisa never grew tired of them. She needed to see them all, and Ellie was excited to show her everything.

Marisa lost track of the time. She was enthralled with the wonderful gift she'd been given—the gift of her daughter's life. They ate supper around the TV, and her eyes didn't move from the screen as Ellie got ready for her first day of school. In the video Colter was trying to reassure her, but it was clear that Colter was the one who was nervous, not Ellie. Later she saw Ellie lose her first tooth and wake up to find money from the tooth fairy under her pillow. The last video was of this past Thanksgiving with the Kincaid family; she could clearly see that Ellie was the center of attention in a loving home.

The screen went blank; the videos were over and Ellie was asleep in her arms.

She looked at Colter. "What time is it?"

"Almost midnight." He stood. "Let me take Ellie. I'll put her to bed."

"No." Her arms tightened around the child. "Please, let me do it."

"Okay." As he stepped back, Marisa rose to her feet with Ellie and carried her to her room. Colter pulled the covers back and she gently laid her down. Ellie still had her pajamas on.

"Should we change her pajamas?" Marisa asked.

"No, she's fine." He tucked her in.

Ellie squirmed. "Daddy?"

"Yes, angelface?"

"Gotta…gotta give you kisses," she mumbled.

He bent down to kiss her, and Marisa wondered if Ellie would ever need her the way she needed her father. Anger threatened to overwhelm her—anger at her mother, her father, at what had been taken from her—but those were emotions that could destroy her. She wouldn't let them. She had too much to be happy about and that was what she'd concentrate on.

"Mommy," Ellie whimpered, and hearing that one word made all the grief and rage disappear.

"I'm right here, baby," she answered, kissing her softly. She rearranged the covers around her, and Sooner jumped on the bed. "'Night," she whispered as she and Colter left the room.

In the hallway she asked Colter, "Do you mind if I stay the night? I'd like to be here when she wakes up."

"No," he replied. "It'll save me answering a million questions in the morning."

She wanted to hug or touch him, but she didn't. "Thank you," she said instead.

"You can use Becky's room. Take whatever clothes you need."

"Thank you," she said again. "And thanks for explaining everything to Ellie."

He nodded and she could feel a tension building between them, an unbearable tension that neither knew how to end.

He turned toward his room, then swung back. "Tulley said your friend Cari called. He told her you were watching videos of Ellie and she said not to disturb you. She asked if you were okay, so you might want to give her a call."

"I will, thanks."

"Good night."

"'Night," she called as he walked down the hall.

She hurried upstairs to Becky's room and picked up the phone. It was twelve-fifteen, but since it was a Saturday, Cari was probably still awake.

"Cari, it's me," Marisa said when she answered.

"Marisa, are you okay? What's going on?"

She told her about Ellie and what they'd done that day.

"Wow. So you're spending the night?"

"Yes, and I don't want ever to leave my daughter."

"Maybe Colter will let you stay there for a while."

"I don't know." She hesitated. "He's been very kind under the circumstances, but I can feel the distance he keeps between us. I'm not sure I want it any other way."

"Marisa, you're kidding yourself," Cari said. "You've been in love with him ever since I've known you. You can't just turn off that kind of love."

She drew a jagged breath. "But that kind of love hurts, and I don't want to experience it again. All I want is my daughter."

"Are you saying you're going to try and get custody of Ellie?"

"God, no. I'd never do that to Ellie or Colter. But I intend to be a part of her life."

"Well, Marisa, you may not have noticed, but they come as a package deal."

"Yes," she mumbled, suddenly feeling tired. She had to ask Cari a question, though. "Where did you find the Santa with the white suit and beard who talked to Ellie?"

There was a slight pause. "I didn't hire anyone like that."

"Sure you did. He came to your office and spoke with Ellie."

"Oh, good. I'm glad he finally made it. I rushed all over the place and never could find the Santa who was scheduled that day. They said he was taking a break, and I told everyone to send him to my office, so I guess he got the message."

"Cari, this man was round, with red cheeks and his long hair and beard were white and obviously real."

"I didn't hire anyone who looked remotely like that."

"Did you tell Santa about Ellie or me?"

"No. I never had a chance to speak with him, but as I said, I left messages all over the place."

"That's so weird," Marisa mused. "He knew Ellie had taken a cab to Dalton's and he also knew my name."

"Maybe it *was* Santa Claus," Cari teased.

"At this point I'd believe just about anything—the toy shop, flying reindeer, the works."

Cari laughed. "I'll ask around to see if anyone's seen this man."

"Please do. I'm very curious now, since he told Ellie she'd have a mother by Christmas." She paused, then asked, "Do you know where Reed is?"

"He checked into a hotel." Cari gave her the number.

"I'll call him tomorrow."

"Marisa, are you okay?"

"No, I'm not." She didn't lie. "I'm worried and scared, yet I feel a strength I've never felt before. I'm not sure about the future, but one thing I do know—I will not let go of my daughter again."

Another long pause. "Your father's called several times."

"Please, Cari, I can't talk about them. I'll call you later. Bye."

Overpowering feelings returned in full force. "No," she said aloud to stop the turmoil inside her. She wouldn't think about them today—not today, when she had all these wonderful new memories of Ellie.

She took a quick shower and found an oversize T-shirt to sleep in. The lonely bed wasn't all that appealing. She was too far away from Ellie…and Colter. She grabbed a terrycloth robe and went downstairs, intending to sleep with Ellie. That was the only way she'd get any rest tonight.

As she walked down the hall, she noticed Colter's light was on, and without thinking, went toward his room. He was sitting on the side of the bed, his face in his hands, his shoulders stooped, as if the weight of the world had crashed down upon him. In that moment, she realized how all of this had affected him. She had broken his heart once before and now she was doing it again by disrupting everything he'd built with Ellie. She wasn't sure how to make any of this right—there probably *wasn't* a way—but she had to talk to him.

"Colter."

His head jerked up. "I thought you were in bed."

"I came down to sleep with Ellie."

"She has a twin bed," he told her.

"Doesn't matter. I just need to be near her." Her eyes held his. "You do understand that, don't you?"

"Yes, Marisa, I understand that." His voice was cool, belying those words.

She sat on the bed beside him. "Could we talk?"

"Sure." He moved a space away from her, which didn't escape her notice.

"I feel as if I should apologize, but I'm not sure for what. Maybe for being young, stupid and gullible."

"Do you regret what happened between us?"

"No," she admitted in a strangled voice. "I just regret what happened afterward."

"But that wasn't your fault."

She linked her fingers. "It was. Don't you see? I was looking for freedom…and excitement. I found all of that with you, and I never considered any consequences. And later when I discovered I was pregnant, I was too scared and weak to stand up to my mother. I let her make all the decisions for me, just like she always had." There, she'd said the words that had tormented her during the long hours of the previous night.

"You didn't sign the adoption papers," he reminded her. "That took strength."

"But look what happened. I kept thinking I heard Ellie crying, and yet I believed everything I was told. If I'd just—"

"Marisa, you can't live your life on *ifs*. It happened, and we can't go back and change a thing. We have to move forward."

"I know, but I just feel so responsible, so helpless."

"Don't you think I've been feeling the same way? I lay awake last night wondering how I could've let this happen. I was old enough—and experienced enough—to think about the consequences, but when I was with you all rational thought went right out of my head. Placing blame isn't going to help either of us, though."

It wasn't that she wanted to place blame. She just had to voice these feelings that were clamoring inside her—and she had to know how he really felt about her.

"What comes next?" she asked. "For us, I mean."

"What do you expect me to tell you?"

"The truth," she said.

"I don't want to hurt you. You've been hurt enough."

His poignant words touched her, and for a moment she hesitated. Maybe she should let him keep his feelings to himself, but she couldn't. They had to be honest with each other to get through this.

"Don't worry about me. I can take care of myself," she told him with more confidence than she felt.

He glanced at her. "You've changed in so many ways."

"Yes," she agreed.

"But I can't help wondering if maybe everything worked out for the best."

Color drained from her face. "How can you say that?"

"I don't mean about Ellie," he hastened to explain. "You and she will never get back those lost years. I'm talking about you and me."

"What *about* us?" she asked, suspecting she wouldn't really like the answer.

"I don't think we were ever meant to be together."

To Marisa each word was like a blow.

"Looking back, can you honestly see yourself traveling the

country in a small trailer? The rodeo life was stressful for you. The animals frightened you, and you were uncomfortable with the crowds, the injuries, the day-to-day existence. Within a month, the gypsy lifestyle would've gotten to you and you would've gone back to New York, to your mother."

The truth of his words lay between them, and as much as she wanted to, she couldn't deny what he'd said. "Maybe," she had to admit. "I was so young, so out of touch with reality, but I…I really loved you."

"You were seventeen years old. You knew nothing about love. I was the first man you'd ever slept with."

"Does that diminish my feelings?"

"No, of course not, but—"

"I was unsure about a lot of things back then, but not of that. I loved you."

He swallowed. "I loved you more than I'll ever love anyone again."

"So what happened to all that love?"

He took a deep breath. "It's like ashes after a fire. It's too late to revive the flames."

She gripped her fingers until they were numb. "I probably would've made you a terrible wife anyway." She'd meant to be lighthearted, but the words came out sounding hurt.

"We'll never know, will we?" was his only reply.

"No," she said, feeling an acute pain for losing more than seven years of her daughter's life.

"We're two totally different people. In certain ways, you're still that young girl whose life is so completely unlike mine." He ran a hand through his hair. "Your life is the city, your career, your family. My life is here on this ranch, tending to my horses, looking after my daughter. My idea of a good time is saddling up and camping out under the stars. Your idea of a good time is going to New York—shopping, dining out and spending the evening at the opera."

She remembered telling him how much she loved the

opera, and she did love New York. But that was so many years ago, a lifetime ago, and it wasn't who she was today.

"I'm *not* that same girl." She tightened the belt of her robe. "I'm estranged from my family and I have a nine-to-five job. I can't even remember the last time I went to the opera."

His eyes clung to hers. "Yes, you've changed—you've matured, but…" His voice trailed off, leaving them with visions of a life they were never going to share.

"Did you love Shannon?" The words emerged before she could stop them. He and Shannon shared the same kind of life, the same interests, but their marriage had failed, and she was curious—very curious.

He got up and shoved his hands into his pockets. "Not the way I loved you."

"Then why did you marry her?"

For a second, she thought he wasn't going to answer, then his words came.

"After you left, I tried to lose your memory in a bottle. I took risks I shouldn't have and got several cracked ribs and a broken collarbone. Tulley talked until he was blue in the face, but I wasn't listening. I was set on a course of self-destruction. Shannon made me her own personal cause, and eventually I started to listen to her. I saw her differently than I had in all the years I'd known her. She was an attractive, caring woman. I knew she wanted us to have a future, but I couldn't do that until I got you out of my system."

He sucked air into his lungs. "Neither one of us was prepared for the shock of finding out about Ellie. Shannon said it didn't matter—that she wanted to try and be Ellie's mother. *Try* was the operative word. Ellie was my baby and I wanted to do everything for her and, in truth, I never really gave Shannon much of a chance. I regret that, but after a few months we both knew the marriage was over. She returned to Wyoming, then filed for divorce. She continued to ride the circuit and I stayed in Texas to raise my daughter."

"I see," she murmured, staring down at her white knuckles. So much heartache and pain, and a little girl caught in the middle.

"I apologize for kissing you earlier. I was entirely out of line."

Her eyes flew to his.

"As much as we might want to, we can't rekindle feelings from the past. Those ashes have been scattered to hell and back, and there's nothing left. Right now our concern is Ellie and her future, and that should be our total focus. She's at the age where she needs her mother."

Tears stung her eyes. She willed herself not to cry. He was only echoing her feelings. Then why did his words hurt so much?

"She's out of school for the holidays, and it's only seven days before Christmas, so why don't you plan on spending that time with her."

Her pulse quickened. "You mean stay here?"

"Yes. I think it's what Ellie needs."

"I need it, too," she said, getting to her feet. Still, she had the impression that it was the last thing Colter wanted. She wasn't questioning his reasons, though.

"You can use Becky's room. She won't be here for the holidays. In her off time, she's helping our sister Jennifer, who's having a difficult pregnancy."

"Thank you. I appreciate that, but I have a job with Madame Hélèna and I'll have to check with her about my schedule."

His lips thinned. "When you can fit Ellie into your schedule, let me know."

He began to walk past her and she grabbed his arm. All the years of being manipulated and controlled came down to this moment, and strength born from the lessons learned surged through her.

"How dare you!" she said fiercely. "Everything else has been taken away from me, but you're not taking my pride.

Madame Hélèna was gracious enough to give me a job when no one else would. Out of respect, I feel I owe her an explanation. On Monday I plan to tell her about Ellie and I'm hoping she'll give me the time I need. If not, I'll have to quit. My daughter comes first."

He removed her hand from his arm and his touch sent pinpoints of warmth along her skin.

"Let's be clear on one thing. As I said before, Ellie stays here with me. This is her home."

"What are you saying?"

"I'm saying Ellie's not to go *anywhere* without my permission."

"Oh," she whispered, seeing fear in his eyes and recognizing it for what it was. He was afraid she'd try to leave with Ellie and never come back.

"Let *me* be clear on one thing," she said, her anger subsiding. "I will never hurt Ellie or take her away from you. If you want me to ask permission to go places with her, then I will—to set your mind at ease."

He seemed dumbstruck. Finally he said, "Thank you."

"You're welcome. All I'm asking is that you not judge me as the weak young girl I used to be. Judge me for the woman I am today and trust me a little."

"I'll try," he muttered, but she could see that she'd have to earn that trust. And she would.

She stalked toward the door. "Now I'm going to my daughter."

Ellie was sprawled across the bed, and Marisa stood there for a moment, watching her. Then she pulled back the covers and crawled in. Sooner whined in protest and moved to the foot of the bed. She gathered Ellie in her arms.

She didn't know how she and Colter had arrived at such an angry standoff, but she knew their difficult situation would invoke many disagreements, possibly even arguments. She just hoped they could continue to talk them out.

She drifted into a beautiful dream, and she held the dream in her arms.

COLTER WALKED into his closet, pushing back clothes to reveal a safe. He turned the knob to the correct numbers and opened it. He took out three objects—a small box, a certificate and a piece of paper—and carried them into the bedroom. Sitting on the bed again, he opened the box. A diamond ring sparkled up at him, as bright as all the lights in Vegas. He'd bought it for Marisa and he still had it. Why? He wasn't sure. He just hadn't been able to get rid of it.

Picking up Ellie's birth certificate, he stared at the name: *Marisa Ellen Kincaid.* He and Tulley were the only ones who knew he'd put Marisa's name on it. At the time, he wasn't sure why he'd done that, either. He just wanted Ellie to have something of her mother's.

Later he'd regretted that impulse. He didn't want Ellie to have *anything* of Marisa's, so he told everyone her name was just Ellen. No one ever questioned him, not even when he registered her for school.

He reached for the single sheet of paper and forced himself to read the words on it: Colter, I've changed my mind. I can't marry a rodeo rider. Our worlds are too different. I'm sorry. Marisa.

He'd told Marisa their love was like ashes after a fire. Then why did these three objects have such power over him?

Quickly, he left the house and headed for the corrals. Within minutes, he'd saddled up and headed out into the cold December night. He spurred the horse on, feeling as if demons were chasing him, knowing that the only way to escape them was to ride hard and long until exhaustion overtook him.

Chapter Fourteen

Colter woke up the next morning and quickly dressed. He wasn't sure what this day was going to bring, but as long as Ellie was happy, that was all that mattered to him. He stopped at her doorway, glancing in. Ellie was cradled in Marisa's arms and both their faces looked content. *You have your mother, baby girl. And Daddy's feeling a lot of conflicting emotions.*

He'd been hard on Marisa last night, but she'd asked what he was thinking and feeling. A lot of his inner turmoil had spilled out, and he'd said things he hadn't meant to.

The sight of the two of them was mesmerizing. They'd kicked the covers away, and Marisa's T-shirt had ridden up to reveal her long, slim legs. An unwelcome jolt of awareness centered in his lower abdomen. She was a restless sleeper. He remembered that about her—and so many other things that continued to haunt him.

Tearing his eyes away, he went to the kitchen. Tulley was sitting at the table drinking coffee and reading the paper.

"Morning," he said, pouring himself a cup.

"Morning, boy." Tulley put down the paper. "Marisa's car is still here. Is she in Becky's room?"

"No." He sat across from Tulley. "She slept with Ellie."

"Should've guessed that." Tulley peered at him. "Why are you so down in the mouth?"

He shook his head. "I'm not sure. I'm glad we finally

know the truth. Ellie has her mother and Marisa has her daughter, but I keep wondering where we go from here."

"To the future...together," Tulley answered without hesitation.

"I wish it was that simple."

"Why isn't it?"

"Because it isn't," he snapped. "Marisa's life has been torn apart and she's not sure *what* she wants."

"Her daughter," Tulley replied. "She wants her daughter."

"Yeah." He shifted uncomfortably.

"What are you worried about?"

He gripped the cup. "This is Ellie's home, I want her to stay here, but as she gets to know her mother she might feel differently."

"You mean she might prefer to live with her mother."

"Yeah and...and that would kill me." He took a big swallow of coffee.

Tulley clicked his tongue.

"What?" he asked when Tulley didn't say anything.

"Colt, boy, you have to trust Marisa to do the right thing."

"I don't think I can ever trust her completely again."

"That's the problem," Tulley said. "You're hiding behind the past and all the pain—pain you don't want to feel a second time. But you're going to have to step forward now and see Marisa for the woman she is today. The woman I see would never hurt Ellie—or you. So give her a chance. For Ellie, give her a chance."

Marisa had said almost the same words last night. He gazed out the window, knowing Tulley was right, but that trust would not come easy. "I invited her to stay here during the holidays."

"That's good. I'm proud of you."

His eyes slid to Tulley. "How long do you think she'll hang around the ranch? It's not what she's used to."

"I don't think she cares where she is as long as she's with Ellie—and you."

"No. I'm not even in the picture."

Tulley clicked his tongue again, and it irritated him.

"Will you stop that?"

"Now we're getting to the crux of what's really bothering you. It has nothing to do with how long she'll stay here or if she'll take Ellie away. It's how she feels about you."

"That's nonsense. What we had is over—has been for a very long time."

"Has it?" Tulley raised an eyebrow.

Colter glared at him and opened his mouth to speak, but then they heard voices and he knew Marisa and Ellie were awake. His concentration was now on them.

Tulley got to his feet. "I'll start feeding the horses."

"I'm going to Dallas to tell Becky and Jen about Marisa, so I'll be gone most of the day."

"Leaving the wicked mother alone with your child, huh?"

Colter stood. "That's not funny."

"Lighten up, boy, or you're gonna explode with all those emotions inside you."

He took a deep breath. "Just keep an eye on them while I'm out."

"Okay. Tell everyone hi." He reached for his hat and ambled out the door.

"Daddy, Daddy, Daddy," Ellie called, racing into the room with Marisa and Sooner behind her. She flew into Colter's arms and he held her tight. "Daddy." Ellie smothered his face with kisses. "When I woke up, Mommy was in my bed."

"Really?" He met Marisa's eyes.

"Yeah. That's cool, huh?"

"Very cool."

He sat with Ellie on his lap and watched Marisa pour a cup of coffee. He should've asked if she wanted some, but when he was around her his brain didn't function too well.

"Listen up, angelface." He pushed back Ellie's hair. "Daddy's going to Aunt Jen's, so you and your mother are on your own today."

"Okay. I'll show her my horses and how good I can ride."

He tweaked her nose. "No showing off."

Ellie made a face.

He stroked her hair, needing to hold her for a moment longer. "We have to get a Christmas tree. We've never left it this late."

"When can we, Daddy? When?"

He rose and stood her on her feet. "Maybe tomorrow. You be good for your mother, okay?"

"I will," Ellie chirped.

His eyes met Marisa's again. "She usually has cereal and fruit for breakfast."

"I'll fix whatever she wants."

He grimaced. "Please don't say that. She'll have you jumping through hoops."

"What's that mean, Daddy?" Ellie asked.

"It means, don't take advantage of your mother."

"Okay." She pulled a chair up to the cabinet. "I'll fix toast. Sooner likes toast."

"Ellie…"

"Don't worry," Marisa said. "I'll make sure she doesn't give Sooner a loaf of bread."

"You're beginning to know her." They stared at each other for endless seconds, then Colter turned away and grabbed his hat. "I'll see you both later."

Outside he drew a couple of deep breaths. He hadn't planned to leave this early, but he had to get away to sort through what he was feeling.

THE DAY WAS ONE OF THE HAPPIEST of Marisa's life. She was grateful to Colter for giving her this time with Ellie, although she wished he hadn't felt he had to leave. After last night she wasn't sure where she stood with him. He didn't trust her— that was very clear. In the days and weeks ahead she resolved to regain his trust. *And his love.* Those words hovered in her mind and she pushed them away. She couldn't be in love with

Colter after all these years. But sometimes, in her weaker moments, she wondered if she'd ever fallen *out* of love with him. Colter was right, though; their love was like ashes after a fire, never to be rekindled again. Today she chose to believe that.

After breakfast, Ellie took a bath and they got dressed, then Ellie showed her every nook and cranny of the house. Marisa hadn't really looked at Colter's home before. It was quite large, with three bedrooms upstairs and three downstairs. Tulley's room was off the kitchen. She loved the country charm, the baby grand piano and especially the attention lavished on Ellie's room.

The room that really caught her eye, though, was Colter's study. It suggested masculinity, from the dark mahogany walls to the oversize desk. Large windows gave a breathtaking view of the ranch, but that scene wasn't what really held her. It was the trophies, belt buckles, hats, pictures and memorabilia from his rodeo days. There were so many things, even a silver saddle, that she could hardly take them in.

Later they went to the barn. Ellie wanted to show her how well she could ride. Marisa sat on the fence, her heart in her throat, as Ellie raced around the barrels, but the little girl handled her horse magnificently. Just like her father...

"Did I do good?" Ellie asked Tulley, who was timing her. He nodded. "Gettin' better."

"You were marvelous." Marisa clapped from the fence.

Ellie rode up, dismounted and gave the horse some sugar cubes. "Wanna pet her?"

Marisa's pulse quickened, but she slid to the ground, trying to hide her fear.

"She won't hurt you, see?" Ellie patted the horse's head, sensing Marisa's nervousness. "Touch her," she said, as if instructing a child, and Marisa reached out and stroked the reddish brown face. If Ellie had asked her to walk on hot coals, she probably would've done that, too.

"Her name is Dandelion, but I call her Dandy."

"Hi, Dandy." Marisa smiled and the horse nuzzled her. Her whole body froze.

"She just wants sugar," Ellie said, handing her a couple of cubes. "Usually I give her carrots 'cause Daddy says it's better, but Dandy loves sugar." Marisa relaxed and held the cubes out to the horse. She gobbled them up.

Surprising herself, Marisa stroked Dandy's neck. It was so easy. The horse was gentle and affectionate, and she responded to that.

"Time to feed Dandy," Tulley said.

"Okay," Ellie answered, and Marisa followed them into the barn.

Ellie unsaddled the horse with the ease of someone much older and then led Dandy to a pasture, where she removed the bridle. She hurried back for a bucket of feed and dumped it in a trough.

Marisa noticed a red stallion, the horse that had thrown Colter, in another corral, pawing the ground in anger.

"That's Red Devil," Ellie told her. "He's a mean old horse, but when Daddy gets through training him he won't be so mean. Daddy knows all about horses."

There was pride in every word, and it reinforced what Marisa already knew—how much Ellie loved her father. Marisa had no intention of changing that.

They sat on a wooden swing on the patio, and Ellie talked about her friends, her school and the ranch. Marisa listened avidly. She soaked up every nuance of her daughter's life and personality, and for the first time in years she felt at peace.

When Colter returned, they had a quiet supper. He seemed distant, and she wondered what his sisters had said about her. He announced that everyone was fine and looking forward to Christmas, with no further comment or details.

Later Marisa explained to Ellie that she'd be gone in the morning, assuring the child she'd be back as soon as she could.

"You *will* come back?" Ellie asked with a tremor in her voice.

Marisa cupped her face. "Now that I know about you, I'll always come back. No matter what, you can count on that."

"Okay." Ellie shuffled her feet, and Marisa wanted to call Madame Hélèna and quit on the spot.

She couldn't do that, though. She had to be a responsible adult and she had to set an example for Ellie.

"When I get back, maybe we can talk your dad into getting that Christmas tree."

"Oh boy." Ellie brightened. "A big one?"

"Yes," Marisa said with a grin. "A really big one."

"Time for bath and bed," Colter interrupted.

"Aw, Daddy."

"Ellie." There was a note of warning in his voice.

Ellie stomped off to her room. "When I get big, I'm *never* going to bed."

As Ellie left the room, Marisa glanced at Colter and noticed something in his eyes she couldn't describe. Was it sadness? No, it couldn't be. He had no reason to feel sad unless…unless he was regretting his decision to invite her for the holidays.

Marisa and Colter tucked Ellie into bed, and Marisa assured her again that she'd be back. They made their way to the den. Tulley had already gone to bed. Marisa sat staring into a roaring fire, watching the flames dueling with each other, just as her emotions were. She was intensely happy, yet deeply saddened by all that had happened. The child she'd thought dead had been returned to her. What more could she ask? Why was there still a void deep inside? She had to admit there was a place in her that Ellie couldn't reach.

She looked over at Colter, recognizing that he was the reason for the void. Until he forgave her and trusted her, she would never have complete peace.

"I can't believe she accepted me so easily," she said, studying him closely. "I expected it would take weeks, months even."

He smiled. "She's been wanting her mother for a long time."

That smile leaped out at her, touched her.... No, she couldn't.... It would only complicate things. She forced her thoughts down a less dangerous path.

"It must've been hard for you with a small baby," she said, thinking that Ellie had probably changed his life drastically.

"It wasn't easy," he said, easing into his recliner. "The first week of her life, I sat by her bassinet just to make sure she was still breathing. I was paranoid about her—Shannon pointed that out to me numerous times. I tried to continue riding the circuit, but found that she required all my attention, especially when Shannon left. Luckily, I was at a point in my career where I could retire and concentrate on the business end. Becky and Jen were already here, handling the construction of the house. Ellie, Tulley and I lived in a trailer until the house was finished. Becky had all these business ideas and we worked on them. I designed a boot like the one I'd specially made for myself, and the girls and Bart, Jen's husband, did all the rest. Kincaid Boots is a corporation of five people—Tulley, Becky, Jen, Bart and me."

"I'm glad it all worked out for you," she said. "You've done very well, and you have a beautiful home."

"Thank you. I had a lot of help with the business end, but Ellie was solely my responsibility. That was a big problem between Shannon and me. I diapered her, fed her, took her everywhere with me. Shannon was very fond of Ellie, and I should've let her step into the role of mother, but—well, I handled it badly."

She closed her eyes, listening, having no difficulty envisioning a younger Colter being fiercely protective of his child. He was that type of person. She couldn't even bring herself to imagine Shannon as Ellie's mother. That would hurt too much.

Opening her eyes, she dispelled the image. "You've done

a great job. She's energetic, spirited and caring, and not in the least spoiled. She's very special."

He raised an eyebrow. "And you might be slightly prejudiced."

When he looked at her like that, it did crazy things to her and she remembered how he'd held and kissed her yesterday. So many emotions struggled for dominance. Emotions she wasn't ready to face.

"I'd better get some sleep." She got unsteadily to her feet. "I plan to leave before dawn." Taking a step, she turned back. "You haven't mentioned what your sisters said." It was none of her business, but she couldn't leave it alone.

"Like everyone else, they were shocked," he said. "Being women, they're trying to see this from your point of view, but it might take them a while."

She swallowed, knowing Colter's family had a right to dislike her, but she hoped they wouldn't judge her too harshly.

"Tulley, Ellie and I will be spending Christmas Day with my family at Jen's house. You're welcome to come, but that's up to you."

She nodded. "Thanks, but I wouldn't want to intrude." That was how she felt—like an intruder. She hurried from the room before tears defeated her.

Her abrupt departure left his mind in turmoil—once again. He'd hurt her, and he didn't like that, but he couldn't seem to stop. He was still struggling to accept this situation.

Tulley was right. He was bound to the pain of the past; it was easier. It was safer. Opening himself up to more heartache seemed too much of a risk. And that was the coward in him. A man who'd ridden wild bucking horses was a coward. He'd never seen himself that way until now, and he hated the feeling.

He trudged to his room and went to sleep, still seeing the pain in her brown eyes.

MARISA CURLED UP in Becky's bed, unable to get Colter out of her mind. He'd been so gracious, allowing her time with Ellie, but why did he have to be wary of her? Why did he continue to hurt her? At times she could feel a softening, but almost instantly his guard would go back up, as if he needed to protect himself. Why? She'd never hurt him again. Didn't he believe that? Couldn't he see how much she'd changed?

THE NEXT MORNING, Marisa was up and dressed at 5:00 a.m. She tiptoed into Ellie's room and gave her a kiss, then headed for Dallas. Forty-five minutes later, she arrived at Mrs. Hackleberry's, where she quickly packed her clothes. With her suitcases in the hall, she went to the kitchen to tell Hazel about her plans. The older woman was very understanding, as Marisa had known she'd be.

She got to Madame Hélèna's before seven. When she unlocked the door, she noticed the lights already on and was surprised to find Hélèna at her desk.

She glanced up as Marisa entered. "You're very early."

Marisa sat in a chair opposite the desk. "Yes. I need to talk to you."

Hélèna nodded, removing her glasses. "I've already spoken with your father."

"What!"

"There were three messages on my machine from him. He finally got me last night, wanting news of you."

"I'm so sorry, Madame Hélèna. He had no right to bother you." Why couldn't her father stay out of her life?

"Yes, and I told him that." She picked up a swatch of fabric from her desk. "But he's used to getting his own way and at the moment he wants to talk to you."

She shook her head. "No. I'm not ready to see my parents." She looked directly at Hélèna. "Did he tell you the whole story?"

"Yes, *chérie,* and I'm so happy you have your daughter."

"Thank you."

"I suppose you're here to quit your job."

"Not exactly," she said. "It's presumptuous of me after working here for such a short while, but I was hoping you'd let me have the holidays to spend with my daughter."

Hélèna caressed the fabric. "Yes, that's presumptuous."

"I need this time, but I also need this job."

Hélèna laid the fabric down and stared at Marisa. "The reason I'm here so early is that my son and I have decided to spend Christmas in Paris, and we're leaving tomorrow."

"Oh."

"So take the time you need, but when I return after New Year's I expect you back in this office."

"Oh, yes, ma'am. Thank you!"

"Under other circumstances, I would fire you."

Marisa stood. "Thank you for understanding."

"*Chérie,* I see a lot more than you do, and as I've said before, your heart is not in this job. You're good at it, but your future is not in fashion."

"Do you read tarot cards or something?"

Hélèna waved a hand. "Go be with your daughter and find the happiness you deserve."

"Why are you being so kind?" She had to ask.

Hélèna leaned forward. "It's not kindness, *chérie.* That's what you don't see." Her smile was flimsy. "I've waited a lot of years to stick it to Richard Preston, if you will forgive the vulgarity, and this is about as sweet as it gets."

Marisa stiffened. "You said you didn't have time for revenge."

"Sometimes an opportunity's too good to pass up."

Marisa couldn't keep the disappointment from showing on her face.

"I like you. I have from the beginning, but old hurts are hard to forget."

Marisa knew someone else who felt like that. Colter couldn't forget, either.

"I like working with you, and I appreciate your letting me keep my job. I'll see you in January."

"Ah, *chérie,* don't sound so wounded."

She slipped her purse over her shoulder. "I guess I'm naive about the business world."

"No. You just don't have that cutthroat instinct."

She didn't see that kind of instinct as a plus. She saw it as deceitful and conniving, and she knew her father's world and Hélèna's wasn't a place she wanted to live in. It was a world where they took innocent babies from their mothers and—

"Have a wonderful Christmas, Madame Hélèna."

"You, too, *chérie.*"

She walked away, feeling thoroughly inducted into the world of business. She didn't like it—but she had a job. Suddenly she didn't see that as a plus, either. Her parents were still controlling her life behind the scenes. Right now, though, her focus was on Ellie.

As she drove back to the ranch, she called Cari and then Reed.

"Marisa, I'm glad you phoned," Reed said as soon as he heard her voice. "How are things going?"

She told him about Ellie.

"That's great. And I'm glad Colter asked you to stay."

He paused, then said, "I saw our parents yesterday."

"Oh?"

"I felt I had to make my position clear. I told them I was disgusted with what they'd done to your life and said I'd no longer be working for Dalton's."

"Reed, your whole life is Dalton's! You've been trained to take over one day. Think about it."

"I have."

"Don't do this out of some misguided loyalty to me. This is your *life.*"

"That's what I've finally figured out," he said. "I'm almost thirty-one years old and my father still dictates my decisions—but not anymore. I'm going away for the holidays, but I'll call every now and then."

"Reed…"

"Be happy, Marisa. You deserve it, and maybe one of these days, I'll find happiness, too."

"Merry Christmas, Reed." She hung up, feeling lonely and alone. Then she saw the sign for the Kincaid Ranch and her spirits lifted. Ellie was waiting—and maybe Colter was, too.

Chapter Fifteen

As she drove up, she saw Ellie and Sooner sitting on the front step. Her heart lodged in her throat. She hadn't expected this.

She pulled up to the garages and they both came running. Marisa opened the door and got out, catching Ellie as she flew into her arms.

"You came back," Ellie cried. "You came back."

Marisa kissed her face. "Baby, I will always come back. Remember? I told you."

"I know," Ellie said, resting her face on Marisa's shoulder. Marisa felt so vulnerable, so… She held on to Ellie, fighting tears. But she was tired of crying. It was time for smiling, laughing and happiness.

"Want to help me get my things out of the car?"

Ellie raised her head. "Sure. Sooner and me can help. Can't we, Sooner?"

Sooner barked.

"That's very thoughtful." Marisa smiled, trying to act normal when what she felt was ecstatic, excited.

Marisa handed Ellie a small suitcase and took the larger one and a clothes bag herself. Together they made their way into the house.

Inside Sooner whined, then barked several times.

"He wants to stay outside," Ellie told her. "Okay, okay,"

she said to Sooner. He trotted to the back door and disappeared through the doggie flap.

Marisa smiled inwardly. Maybe they did understand each other on a level that only they knew.

Dragging the bag upstairs, Ellie said, "You can stay in the same room." She talked as if Marisa had stayed there many times before.

As Ellie helped her to unpack, Marisa wondered where Colter was, but didn't ask. She enjoyed having Ellie to herself

"Wanda, the cleaning lady, put the clothes you left in the closet," Ellie said.

"That's fine," Marisa replied, realizing she'd forgotten all about them.

Ellie picked up a pair of high-heeled shoes. "How do you walk in these?"

"Very carefully." She laughed.

"Can I try?" Ellie asked. "I still got the ones you gave me, but I keep falling."

"Sure. Just walk slowly."

Ellie was sitting down to take off her sneakers when they heard Colter calling, "Ellie, where are you?"

Ellie jumped up, ran to the door. "Upstairs, Daddy."

A few seconds later, Colter appeared in the doorway. "Sooner is chasing Mr. Squirrel again," he said to Ellie.

"Oh no, that bad dog," Ellie cried, running from the room, completely forgetting about the high-heeled shoes.

"Mr. Squirrel?" Marisa lifted an eyebrow.

"He's a squirrel that lives in the backyard. Ellie feeds him, so he's become more or less a pet. But Sooner's jealous and chases him every chance he gets."

"She loves animals, doesn't she."

"She takes after me in that," he said, walking into the room.

As he drew near, her stomach fluttered nervously. Looking away, she put some clothes in a drawer, hoping her face had revealed nothing.

She turned around. "Ellie was waiting for me when I got here."

"She's been waiting out there ever since breakfast. I think she was afraid you wouldn't be coming back."

Her heart ached with a new pain—the pain of knowing Ellie felt insecure about her. She sank onto the bed. "How do I make her understand that I'm never going to leave her again?"

He shoved his hands into the pockets of his jeans. "By loving her and never letting her down."

Her eyes met his. "I won't."

"That's all she wants. To be able to trust you."

A message hovered behind the words and she didn't miss it. *I want to trust you, too.* She'd have to prove herself; that was the only way to show them she was sincere.

"I promised Ellie we'd get the Christmas tree," he said, breaking into her thoughts. "So if you're ready, we'll go."

"Yes." She'd finish unpacking later. "Where do you buy trees?"

"We go to a tree farm not far away."

She remembered Christmases past. A decorator did the trees in her mother's home and in her father's. She had never had anything to do with it, not even as a child. The tree was just there, beautifully decorated, but that personal touch was lacking.

"This will be a new experience for me," she said, then added without thinking, "I seem to experience a lot of firsts when I'm with you."

As soon as the words left her mouth, she wished them back. Colter knew exactly what she'd meant. She could see it in his eyes. He was remembering their first night together; she'd been a virgin.

"Something else you lied about." His words weren't harsh. He was just stating a fact.

"I didn't lie—you never asked me," she said defending herself. She had tried to appear experienced, like the other women he'd known. She'd wanted to be with him so much, but that omission *was* the same as a lie.

"You let me assume you had experience, and later, well…it was much too late."

She hung the clothes bag in the closet. Yes, it had been too late. She remembered that night as if it were yesterday. She'd been so naive. Everything she knew about sex she'd learned from books and from the other girls. She'd always heard that the first time would hurt. But Colter had been so gentle and had carried her to such heights of pleasure that there'd been very little pain.

Later, his eyes had blazed with anger at her lie about her virginity, but using feminine instincts she hadn't known she possessed, she'd been able to coax him into a better mood. Their second time had been even more satisfying. Her body had come alive under his tutelage.

From then on, a look, a touch, a caress could send their bodies up in flames. They had lived in their own private world, full of intimacy and sensual delight. But outside, the real world had been waiting.

"I don't see any point in rehashing the past," she said, steeling herself against the onslaught of memories.

He observed her closely. "Does it make you uncomfortable to talk about that night?"

She shut the closet door. "Of course not. As I told you, I just regret what happened afterward."

"We keep coming back to that," he retorted.

"Yes, and it's something that will always haunt me."

He stared at her, seeing the young girl she'd been at seventeen, completely dominated by her mother. The fact that she'd ignored her mother's wishes and gone out with him, made love with him, agreed to marry him, must mean that she'd felt something for him at the time. He desperately needed to believe she hadn't used him merely as a means of escape.

He saw the sadness that touched her face and wanted to ease her pain. "Let's go get that tree with Ellie."

"Okay." She smiled slightly.

They walked out the door, but Marisa suddenly stopped. "Oh, I forgot my jacket," she told him. "I'll be right with you." She hurried back into her room.

"We'll be waiting outside," he said.

She grabbed her jacket, slipping into it as she ran down the stairs. She found Colter leaning against a pillar on the patio, smiling at Ellie. He was wearing a sheepskin coat and a Stetson. He stirred her senses. She quickly followed his gaze to Ellie, trying to forget how he made her feel.

Ellie had Sooner by the collar and was leading him to his doghouse. "Naughty, naughty dog," she scolded. "You have to stay in your house until you learn you can't eat Mr. Squirrel." Tucking his tail between his legs, Sooner ran into his house in disgrace.

Colter looked at Marisa, then wished he hadn't. His muscles tightened with a sexual need that shocked him as his eyes roamed over her tight-fitting jeans and settled on the blond hair that hung around her face. Her brown eyes were so deep, so sensual, so—oh God, where was his strength? This woman could wreck his whole life; he had to remember that.

They stared at each other in silence for several seconds before he forced himself to break the contact and shifted his attention to Ellie. "Come on, angelface. Let's go get the Christmas tree."

They started for the garage, with Ellie marching ahead. A woeful whining stopped them in their tracks. All three turned simultaneously to see Sooner's pitiful face peeking out from the doghouse.

Ellie glanced up at her father, and Colter nodded.

"Okay, you can come," Ellie called, and Sooner bounded out of his house. He ran to her, jumping up to put both paws on her shoulders while licking her face, nearly knocking her over in the process. Ellie gave him a big hug, laughing. "You crazy dog."

Colter rolled his eyes, and Marisa smiled.

They got into a silver four-door pickup. Ellie and Sooner climbed into the back, while Colter and Marisa sat in front. They traveled several miles from the ranch to the tree farm and, not surprisingly, the place was busy.

Ellie had to personally inspect each and every tree, occasionally asking for their opinion—and Sooner's. Every time Sooner barked, Ellie shook her head and moved on to another tree.

"Remind me to strangle that dog," Colter whispered to Marisa.

Although she laughed, his low voice and the warmth of his breath caused a tremor of excitement to course through her.

After much deliberation, Ellie decided on the right tree. Colter looked up at the tall Virginia pine. "That's about twelve feet. It's going to touch the ceiling."

"I don't care," Ellie said, looking defiantly at Marisa. "Do you care, Mommy?"

"Not in the slightest," she answered, and received a frown from Colter. But he accepted defeat graciously.

A man at the farm helped cut the tree down, and within minutes they had it in the bed of the truck. As they headed for home, Ellie kept a watchful eye on it through the back window.

Decorating a Christmas tree with Ellie was unlike anything Marisa had experienced. She'd thought the tree had to be perfect, with the ornaments and decorations coordinated like they'd been in her parents' homes. Ellie, however, had a very different view. Everything had to be done with the greatest speed, using as many bright colors as possible. Marisa followed Ellie's lead until it came to the icicles. Ellie made short work of those by throwing them all on at once.

Marisa glanced at Colter, smiling, and he returned the smile, amused at the antics of their child. The sincerity of his smile flowed through her like good wine, soothing and relaxing.

"Oh, Daddy, we forgot the star," Ellie cried, rummaging in a box and lifting the ornament into the air.

Colter placed the star on the tree, which required a ladder, since the top brushed the ceiling. Everything completed, Ellie stood back admiringly.

"Oh, it's the most beautiful tree in the whole world," she exclaimed, walking over and putting her arms around Marisa's waist. "I'm glad you're here, Mommy."

At those precious words and the tiny arms around her, Marisa fought back tears. Ellie had called her Mommy several times, but suddenly she *felt* it—felt it deeply. She bent down and held her child. She was a mother. Ellie's mother.

"I didn't mean it when I said I didn't want you for a mommy," Ellie mumbled into her neck.

Marisa stroked her hair. "I know, baby. I know."

Colter's had a lump in his throat. Mother and daughter were forming a bond. He only hoped Marisa would live up to Ellie's expectations.

THE DAYS BEFORE CHRISTMAS were busy and happy. Every morning Marisa found Ellie sitting on her bed, waiting for her to wake up. As soon as Marisa opened her eyes, Ellie would start chattering, planning their day.

Colter was cool and distant at times; at others, he was warm and friendly. He obviously still had doubts, but he'd put them aside for Ellie. Both were determined to make this a special time. But she wondered if Colter was ever going to see her as the woman she was now, if he'd ever trust her with his daughter's heart—or his own.

As Christmas drew near, Ellie could hardly contain herself. Her excitement was infectious, and Marisa was looking forward to Christmas in a way she never had before.

Every day Ellie thought of something new that had to go on the tree. Today it was popcorn, so that evening, Marisa and Ellie sat on the den floor, stringing strands of popcorn.

Tulley was half asleep in his chair, while Colter lazed on the sofa with his legs stretched out in front of him, eating popcorn.

Colter was in a good mood as he observed Marisa with Ellie. Her eyes sparkled, her skin glowed, and there was an air of anticipation about her that he remembered from long ago. An excitement that charged his senses—which was something he would do well to forget.

Ellie giggled, and moved closer to her mother. It seemed as if they'd known each other all their lives, and that was how it should be. A girl needed her mother. There were so many things that Marisa could share with Ellie that he couldn't—makeup, boys and feminine things he hadn't a clue about.

He felt as if Ellie was slowly taking steps away from him. He shouldn't think like that, but he couldn't keep the doubts from torturing him. *He had to trust Marisa. He had to trust her. He had to trust her.*

"Daddy, you're eating the decorations," Ellie scolded, shaking him out of his reverie.

"Well, pardon me." He pretended to be affronted. "I'm just trying to help. If you put anything else on that tree, it's going to collapse." Some branches were actually beginning to sag.

"The tree's *supposed* to look like that," Ellie informed him.

"Oh, excuse me, I didn't know." Colter grinned. His amused glance swung to Marisa, and when she smiled back at him he couldn't look away. *Admit it,* he challenged himself. *You want to make love to her as badly as you did eight years ago.* His gaze slid over the tight jeans, her breasts pressing against her blouse and the soft blond hair. She was beautiful. More beautiful than ever. She was a mature woman now, and he wondered what it would be like to make love to her….

Although Colter tried to stop his thoughts, he couldn't. He had to acknowledge that she fit into his household well. He'd expected the city lady to be completely out of place when it came to the everyday routine of a working ranch. And yet the other day he'd found her helping Tulley feed the horses in the corral. Of course, Ellie was there helping, too, but it shocked him to see Marisa handling the feed. And then he'd seen her making supper alongside Tulley, which was another shock to his system. He would've sworn she didn't even know what a stove was. Maybe she *had* changed. She certainly seemed able to take care of herself these days.

She'd become strong and independent, but he had to wonder how deep that strength went. Years ago, she hadn't been strong enough to fight for their love, but now he felt she was capable of fighting for whatever she wanted. And she wanted Ellie….

Colter's penetrating gaze heated Marisa's skin and she immediately looked away. One glance from him had the power to make her feel giddy and breathless, like that seventeen-year-old who'd fallen in love with him. But there wasn't any chance of that happening again. His feelings toward her had hardened, and the only reason he tolerated her presence was Ellie.

She knew he'd been watching her, judging her actions, making sure she had Ellie's best interests at heart. At times it made her angry, and at other times she understood, but she wished he didn't feel as if he had to protect Ellie from her.

It would make things a lot easier if she wasn't so *aware* of him. Even knowing the way he felt about her, she was still intensely attracted to him. Her pulse pounded as her eyes found the taut muscles of his legs and the dark curls of hair that peeped out from the V of his shirt. She could remember winding her fingers through them and tugging gently, initiating a response that ended with them making slow, passionate love. Why was she torturing herself by recalling every detail, especially when the man in question seemed to distrust her.

Marisa and Ellie hung the strands of popcorn on the tree. "Gosh, that looks great, huh, Mommy?"

"Just great," Marisa answered.

"Wanna hear me play the piano?" Ellie asked eagerly.

"Sure."

Ellie and Sooner charged off to the living room where the piano was, and Marisa followed more slowly. Ellie ran her fingers across the keys and Marisa sat beside her on the bench. She could see herself at that age, and felt a bitter sadness for all the tireless hours she'd spent on a piano bench.

Ellie played through a chorus of "Jingle Bells" and "Frosty The Snowman." Marisa thought she was brilliant.

As the last note died away, Ellie said, "Now you play."

After her baby's birth, she hadn't been able to bring herself to play, no matter how much pressure her mother had applied. It'd been so easy at Mrs. Hackleberry's, though—and Marisa felt she knew why. She'd met Ellie, and subconsciously must have known that this child was her baby.

Lightly she touched the keys, and her fingers moved as if of their own volition. She played Rimsky-Korsakov's "Flight of the Bumble Bee," then went into a spirited Chopin piece and ended with Gershwin's "Rhapsody in Blue." The lovely sounds consumed her, and she was unaware of anything but the music.

When her fingers stopped, the room became very quiet.

"Golly," Ellie said, her eyes round. "I never heard music like that. That's awesome."

"I agree," Colter said from the doorway. "I'd never heard you play before."

Marisa looked at him and realized again how little they'd known about each other back then. They only knew they were in love, but there was so much more to a relationship. Things like responsibility and commitment, which were concepts that had been virtually unfamiliar to her as a teenager.

Colter stood transfixed, suddenly understanding just how talented she was. And she'd been willing to give it all up for him. That was a sobering thought.

If Ellie had that kind of talent, he wasn't sure what he'd do. Would he pressure her like Vanessa had pressured Marisa? And if Ellie got pregnant at seventeen, what measures would he take to ensure that she reached her full potential? He didn't have an answer, but he had a very chilling look at the other side of Marisa's life.

"Time for bed," he said to Ellie.

"Daddy," Ellie groaned.

"Christmas is still three days away," he reminded her.

Ellie pulled a face, but obediently slid off the bench. "Remember to come and tuck me in," she called, running from the room. Sooner barked as he loped behind her.

Marisa stared down at the piano keys.

He noticed her tearful brown eyes and he wanted to take her in his arms and kiss her, to feel the softness of her lips against his. Instead he sat down beside her.

She clenched her hands in her lap and he wondered if his nearness bothered her.

"I never realized your great talent," he said, needing to tell her that.

"Thank you," she replied, head down. "It feels good to actually be playing again. I just couldn't play after I lost my child. I didn't have the drive anymore. The lady I live with in Dallas has an old piano, and I've been playing it. I even stopped by the Dallas Symphony Orchestra to try out."

"Do you regret giving up your music?"

"No. But I have missed it." She looked at him. "I plan to continue playing."

"With a talent like yours, I think you have to."

"Thank you," she said, her eyes holding his.

"As I was listening to you, I wondered what I'd do if Ellie had that kind of talent."

She frowned. "What do you mean?"

"I mean—would I force her to play?"

"Oh."

"And more important, I wondered what I'd do if she got pregnant at seventeen."

The question gnawed at her, and she was unable to answer.

"This isn't easy for me to say—but if I'm completely honest—I know I'd want to kill the boy who did that to her—to her future."

"But you'd listen to Ellie, wouldn't you?"

"I hope I would, but I'd probably be so angry I couldn't say that for sure."

She had no response, and silence fell between them.

"I never imagined I'd see this from your parents' point of view."

"Me, neither," she said in a quiet voice.

"Sometimes it's easier to hate than to understand and forgive."

She pushed back her hair with a trembling hand.

"I didn't mean to upset you."

"You haven't," she assured him. "I'm just staggered by the view I'm seeing as a parent. It's one I never considered before."

"Yeah," he murmured.

She got to her feet. "We'd better tuck Ellie in."

Later, as she lay in bed, Colter's words returned to her. She had thought she'd never forgive her parents and she wasn't sure she could. But now she was able to see the reasons behind their actions. They did what they believed was best for her, as any parent would. As she'd do for Ellie.

Some of the sadness in her eased, and she was grateful to Colter for opening her eyes. Now she wondered if he'd ever forgive her.

And if she could forgive herself.

Chapter Sixteen

The next day Marisa and Colter went Christmas shopping. Since Ellie wasn't grounded anymore, they dropped her off at Lori's so the girls could exchange presents.

Ellie wanted a red bicycle and they searched until they found the perfect one in a large sporting goods store.

Marisa told Colter she'd like to give Ellie the jeans she'd wanted that day in Dalton's. He said that was fine, so she called Cari and met her in the children's department. She knew she wouldn't run into her father; he was never on the floor unless it was a special occasion.

Colter browsed in the store while she shopped with Cari, and she tried to hurry because she didn't want him to wait too long. She bought Ellie a complete outfit—jeans, a matching jacket, blouse, socks and headband. Then she found something for Colter and Tulley, and a pen-and-pencil set for the brother-in-law. Shopping for Colter's sisters was more difficult. She decided on a purse mirror that folded into a decorative case for Becky and a photo album for Jen.

"So, how are you?" Cari asked as they waited for the items to be gift-wrapped.

"Great." She smiled.

"I can see that."

"I wanted to wish you a Merry Christmas because I won't see you on Christmas Day." Marisa hugged her. Colter had left it up to her, and she didn't want to be away from Ellie, so she'd decided to spend Christmas with Colter's family.

She handed Cari an envelope.

"What's this?"

"It's your Christmas present—a day at the spa. The works, from a facial to a massage to a pedicure."

"Marisa! You didn't have to do that."

"Yes. I did. You're my best friend."

"Thank you. Wait right here," Cari said, hurrying over to a counter. She came back with a package, which she gave to Marisa.

Marisa opened it then and there. It was a small, beautifully produced book on the Christmas Cradle and how it was made and it included the illustrations of the Twelve Days of Christmas that were etched on the cradle itself.

"Oh, Cari. Thank you."

"In the back is the man's name and address, in case you'd like one of your own."

Marisa hugged her again. "My baby is seven years old, so I don't think I'll need one, but I love the book and I've always loved that cradle." Over Cari's shoulder, she saw Santa Claus handing out candy to children, and it jogged her memory about the Santa in the white suit. She drew back. "Any news on the Santa who spoke with Ellie?"

"Yes. I've been meaning to call you. My assistant talked with him, and he was an older gentleman filling out an application in her office, which is across the hall. I called him and he said he'd heard everything that was going on between you and Ellie, and he decided to play Santa. So he told Ellie everything she wanted to hear. I informed him that we like our Santas to use a little more discretion and not promise children things that are unrealistic."

"What did he say?"

"He apologized and said he hoped there was a happy ending. He also said anyone who believes that strongly should get his or her wish."

"I knew there had to be a reasonable explanation," Marisa murmured.

Cari lifted an eyebrow. "You sound disappointed."

"Maybe, like my daughter, I want to believe." And she did. Not in Santa Claus, but in the power of love.

"Well, then, believe." Cari laughed. "It's Christmas, after all."

"Have a wonderful one." She hugged Cari once more and soon joined Colter, who'd been wandering through the store.

They'd been gone two hours, and Marisa couldn't wait to see her daughter. She met Lori and her mother when they collected Ellie. The child bounced up and down with excitement, and that excitement lasted all the way home. Ellie couldn't stop talking.

Colter grinned at Marisa. "I think she's had too many sweets."

Marisa smiled, feeling truly a part of this family for the first time.

CHRISTMAS EVE DAWNED bright and sunny, but cold. Brodie and Tripp came by to bring presents for Ellie, and she proudly introduced Marisa as her mother. Brodie and Tripp were both friendly, and she enjoyed visiting with them.

The men saddled up and galloped to the pasture to look at a horse Tripp wanted to buy from Colter, and Marisa and Ellie fed Dandy. Walking back to the barn, Marisa noticed a young Mexican man holding something in his arms. He was one of several ranch hands, but she hadn't met any of them.

"Let's go see what José's got," Ellie said, running toward him, Marisa close behind.

"It's a baby deer," Ellie cried as José carried the animal into the barn and laid it on some loose hay.

The little animal was limp and trembling and had sores all over its body. Ellie touched it gently, and Marisa wanted to grab her hand, afraid she might catch something.

"Where's Tulley and the boss?" José asked.

"They're looking at a horse with Brodie and Tripp," Ellie said.

"Ain't nothin' the boss don't know about animals. He fix this little one up in no time."

A moment later, they heard the clatter of hooves as Tulley and Colter rode in. Colter swung out of the saddle in one easy movement, then handed the reins to Tulley, who guided the horses through the barn into the corral. Obviously Brodie and Tripp had left.

"Look what I found, boss." José pointed to the bundle in the hay. "I was feeding in the south pasture and there it was, Thought it was dead, but no, it's still alive."

Colter knelt down in the hay and ran his hands over the small animal. "Fire ants almost got her. She's weak and de-hydrated. Her mother must've been killed or she'd never have left her alone."

"Killed," Marisa breathed, unable to keep the horror out of her voice.

Three pairs of eyes turned to her. "Yeah," Colter answered, "it's deer season around here."

"But surely it's not legal to kill a mother!"

"'fraid so, ma'am," José said.

"That's terrible! How could someone kill a mother?"

Colter pushed back his hat, noting the painful emotions on her face. "Does are plentiful, so permits are issued every year. Most of the time it's sport, but a lot of people hunt to feed their families."

"Still—" Her eyes flashed with outrage. "It's not right."

Colter got up and went into the stockroom, and soon he was back with two syringes, a bottle, some ointment and rubber gloves.

He handed Ellie the bottle and gloves. "Start cleaning the sores with peroxide, then rub ointment into them."

"Okay, Daddy," Ellie said, slipping on a glove.

Goose bumps rose on Marisa's skin as Colter gave the animal two injections in its hip. Ellie meticulously cleaned the wounds, then rubbed the ointment into them. Marisa didn't think this was a job for a small child and she wanted to tell Colter so, but the words stuck in her throat.

"Keep at it, angelface. I'll fix some milk." Colter and José disappeared into the stockroom, and Marisa watched as Ellie worked. The animal made a whimpering sound, and Marisa realized that the little thing was in pain. She didn't know what it was—the thought of the pain or the thought of this small animal without a mother—but she found herself sinking down into the hay, reaching for a glove. In silence, she and Ellie cleaned and medicated every wound.

Colter came back and stopped as he saw Marisa helping Ellie. This was something he hadn't expected and the sight was a little unnerving. He could've sworn Marisa wouldn't touch the animal, but he was wrong.

"We're through, Daddy." Ellie's voice interrupted his musing.

"Good. The milk's ready." He knelt down and tried to get the fawn to suck from a bottle, but the little creature didn't respond. She just lay limp, stretched out on the hay as if she was ready to die.

"José, bring me the force feeder," Colter said.

He poured the milk into a bottle with a long tube that had a sort of squeeze pump. He opened the fawn's mouth and pushed the tube down her throat. As he squeezed the pump, gently, the milk flowed into her throat to her stomach. The fawn's throat convulsed, and Marisa had to look away.

"There, that should do it," she heard Colter say, and she turned back. The poor thing was still trembling, and the sight was more than Marisa could stand.

"Can't you stop her from shaking like that?" she asked Colter.

"I've given her an antibiotic and an anti-inflammatory. The pain will ease as soon as the medicine takes effect."

Marisa didn't want to wait that long. She got to her feet and found a horse blanket, then covered the small body, hoping the warmth would stop the quaking.

Colter watched her with a strange expression on his face, but he didn't say anything.

"Daddy, is she gonna live?" Ellie asked anxiously.

"I don't know. We'll keep an eye on her and feed her again this evening. That's about all we can do."

Marisa checked on the animal several times that afternoon. She couldn't seem to stay away. She wanted to do something to ease the fawn's pain, and that thought was as startling to her as it was to everyone around her. Whenever she headed for the barn, she could feel Colter's eyes on her.

When they went to feed her that evening, Marisa rushed over, hardly able to believe her eyes. "Look, Colter! She's not trembling anymore. That means she's out of pain, doesn't it?"

He stared into her eager eyes. Clearing his throat, he answered, "Yes. Now let's see if we can get her to suck."

The little fawn still didn't respond, so Colter squeezed more milk into her stomach. Marisa's heart sank. She'd felt sure the animal was improving.

She kept thinking about the fawn, but she soon got caught up in Ellie's exuberance about Christmas. They made oatmeal cookies for Santa, under Tulley's guidance, while Colter sat at the kitchen table drinking spicy apple cider.

"They have to be real good, Tulley," Ellie said, "so don't forget anything."

"Are you saying I'm forgetful?"

"No, yes, maybe." Ellie giggled.

Marisa laughed, a soft happy sound, and Colter reflected that this was what it would be like if they were married. He didn't push the thought away as he normally would, and realized he was finally seeing Marisa for the woman she'd become. He liked what he saw—a warm, giving, loving person.

Tulley closed the oven door. "The timer's set, so all you have to do is take 'em out when it dings."

"I can handle that," Marisa told him. "And I'll clean up the kitchen."

Tulley removed his apron. "Thanks, and ladies, this is about as much fun as I can stand for one night. I hear my bed calling."

"He always hears his bed calling," Ellie whispered to Marisa.

"I heard that," Tulley said as he walked toward his room.

"I love you." Ellie ran over and gave him a kiss.

"Aw, shorty, that makes everything okay. 'Night, everyone."

Marisa began to load the dishwasher and wipe counters, and Colter helped. They worked side by side in comfortable silence. Just as she turned the dishwasher on, the oven dinged. She removed the cookies and set them on the stove to cool.

Ellie pulled a chair to the cabinet and got down a plate with a Santa face on it.

"This is Santa's plate." She jumped down, then handed it to Marisa, who placed several cookies on it. Ellie carried the plate to the table and rushed back to the refrigerator to pour a glass of milk.

"Santa's gonna love these," she said, munching on a cookie. "Tulley didn't forget a thing."

Marisa took a bite of one and agreed—they *were* good. She should've written the recipe down, but she could always ask Tulley. She became still as she envisioned herself always here—with Ellie. And Colter.

"Bedtime, angelface," Colter said.

"Okay, Daddy, but first I have to do something." She raced to her room. For once, Sooner didn't follow. He was busy eating a piece of cookie Ellie had given him.

Colter looked at Marisa. "What's she up to?"

"I have no idea."

A few minutes later, she was back and set a piece of paper by the plate. "*Now* I'm going to bed." In a whirlwind she and Sooner were gone.

Marisa and Colter walked to the table and glanced down at the paper. In bold letters Ellie had printed:

Dear Santa,
Thank you for sending me my mommy for Christmas.
Love,
Ellie Kincaid

Tears rolled down Marisa's cheeks. At the sight, Colter's stomach seemed to tie itself in knots and he drew her into his arms. With one hand, he caressed the tears from her face. She looked up at him, and unable to stop himself, he kissed her. At first he kept his touch gentle, but then she whimpered deep in her throat, her hands sliding up his arms to his neck. At her response, he deepened the kiss. Rational thought was impossible as heated passion, too long denied, took over.

He had only meant to comfort her, but the touch of her soft skin, the feel of her in his arms, was his undoing. God, he wanted her. Eight years of hate, bitterness and love had fueled a flame so intense that both were oblivious to everything but the passion consuming them.

"Daddy, Mommy," Ellie called, shattering the moment. Marisa pulled away instantly and went to Ellie.

Colter stood for a moment, trying to get his emotions under control, but all he could feel was Marisa. He didn't have the strength to continue fighting a battle he was losing.

Slowly he made his way to Ellie's room, feeling as if he'd just been thrown from the meanest, baddest horse in Texas.

THEY PUT THEIR GIFTS under the tree. Then Marisa climbed the stairs to her room, while Colter talked to Becky on the phone. Marisa showered, then called Hazel to wish her a Merry Christmas. She'd sent her former landlady and friend a holiday flower arrangement, which Hazel had loved. Marisa promised to visit after Christmas.

She crawled into bed with thoughts of Colter. He'd kissed her with a passion she remembered from the past, and she wondered if he could kiss her like that without loving her.

Love and sex went hand in hand for her, and she finally had to admit she loved him as much as she ever had—the years, the heartache and separation hadn't changed a thing.

But how did he feel about *her?* He desired her; she knew that. This time, though, she wanted it all—love, home and a family. And she wanted it with Colter.

The wind wailed outside and the temperature had dropped to the low thirties. With the cold, she wondered if the fawn was trembling again. She sat up in bed, holding her hands to her face. Why was she so deeply concerned about this small animal? Was she somehow comparing her and Ellie's situation to the fawn's? She didn't know. All she knew was that she had to check on her once more.

She quickly slipped on her clothes and headed downstairs, grabbing her coat from the hall closet. As soon as she opened the back door, she heard a howling in the distance and the blackness of the moonless night seemed to engulf her. Thoughts of wild animals ran through her mind, but she walked stoically toward the barn.

Opening the door, she flipped on the light. The fawn was where they'd left her, stretched unmoving on the hay. Marisa knelt and tucked the blanket tightly around her. The little thing wasn't shaking, so that had to be good.

She stroked her face. "You *have* to live, little one," she whispered. "I know you don't have a mother, but I'll be your mother. I'll take care of you. I don't know anything about deer, but Colter does and I'm sure he'll help me."

Everyone should have a mother, every living creature. She thought about her own mother, and Marisa recognized that Vanessa was probably in pain at losing her. A sob left her throat, as she gazed toward the ceiling. "If you let the fawn live, I promise to talk to my parents and maybe I can find a measure of forgiveness." Suddenly she felt a sense of peace.

"What are you doing?"

Her head swiveled around. "Colter?"

He squatted beside her. "What are you doing?" he repeated.

"I had to check on her one more time." She rubbed the fawn's head.

"What is it with you and this baby deer?" he asked, his voice low.

"I can't explain it. I just don't want her to be in pain and alone."

"Is that how you felt?"

She let her eyes cling to his, knowing exactly what he meant. "Yes," she said hoarsely. "After losing my baby, the pain was so bad I didn't think I'd survive, and at times I didn't want to."

He swallowed hard. "I'm sorry for all you've been through."

There, in the quiet of the barn, the past came full circle and slid into the present. He knew that all he had to do was reach for her to obliterate the remaining sadness.

Instead, he helped her to her feet. "Let's go back to the house. It's cold out here."

She stared at the deer. "Will she live?"

"Maybe. Maybe not. We'll know by morning."

He took her hand, then flipped off the light and they stepped into the darkness, the wind whipping fiercely around them. They could hear howling in the distance. Marisa instinctively moved closer to Colter and he squeezed her hand.

"It's only a coyote foraging for food. They don't come near the ranch."

His touch and his words warmed her against the chilly night.

As they walked into the house, he asked, "Now can you get to sleep?"

"Yes," she answered, taking off her coat. "Thank you."

He watched the light in her eyes, then touched her cheek with his fingers.

The unexpected touch made Marisa catch her breath. Her eyes flew to his and she saw an emotion that stole her breath. *He wanted her.* His hand curved around her neck and she swayed toward him. "Colter," she whispered a moment before his mouth covered hers. Her lips parted eagerly as longing enveloped her. His tongue moved into her mouth, to taste, to probe, and a fire coursed through her. She quivered uncontrollably.

"Marisa," he groaned, his body trembling. He pulled her closer, kissing her hard and furiously. They strained together, lips touching lips, heart on heart, striving to say with their bodies what they hadn't been able to say with words. Marisa's hands traveled hungrily over his face, as if she were trying to imprint the feel of him on her fingertips. Colter kissed her again and again.

He felt himself exploding with all the emotions he'd kept inside, and he gave them full rein. He didn't want to think. He just wanted to *feel*—to feel all those wonderful sensations that were a part of her. Nothing else mattered, not their differences, not the past—just this moment, this feeling.

As he slid a hand beneath her blouse and caressed her heated skin, she couldn't control the whimpering deep in her throat. She wanted him, plain and simple, and she couldn't hide it. She returned his kisses with equal fervor, each taking and giving until nothing existed but the two of them. Finally, he rested his forehead against hers.

"Marisa…"

She placed her fingers over his lips. "Please don't apologize. Please…"

They stared at each other, both realizing that their anger was gone. Hers had faded into nothingness, and she could tell his had, too.

"I'm not." He drew a ragged breath and released her. "But we should slow down."

"Yes," she said, knowing he was right. This time they had to be clear about what they wanted. She gave him a brief smile. "It's Christmas Eve—Santa's going to be here soon."

He grinned. "You've been listening to Ellie too long."

She ran for the stairs singing, "You'd better watch out, you'd better not pout, you'd better not…"

Falling into bed, she felt young and very much in love. She touched her lips, still tender from his kisses. She loved him and wanted to be with him, but she couldn't make love with him unless she knew he loved her just as much. Maybe she was wishing for the impossible. Maybe the forever kind of love didn't exist in real life. Like Ellie, though, she believed.

And it was Christmas.

CHRISTMAS MORNING CAME very early and Ellie's excited shouts echoed through the house. She tore into her gifts like a hurricane, hardly giving Marisa and Colter time to fully wake up.

Pulling out the rhinestone studded jeans, she screeched, "Oh boy. Oh boy." Then she immediately slipped them on over her pajamas.

"Ellie," Colter sighed, but Ellie wasn't listening. She proceeded to dress completely in the outfit, whirling around for everyone to see.

"Don't I look cool, Tulley?"

"You're so cool I'm about to get frostbite," Tulley joked, working the video camera.

"My mommy gave them to me." She hugged Marisa, and Marisa held her tight, her eyes meeting Colter's. Their first Christmas…

Marisa could hardly breathe as she opened Ellie's gift. It was a plaster of Paris imprint of two hands, with Ellie's name and the date written beneath it. "That's my hand," Ellie said, as if she needed to explain. "I made it in kindergarten for Daddy, but he said I could give it to you. And I got you this, too." It was a school photo of Ellie in a silver frame. "You can put it on your nightstand and see me all the time."

"Thank you, baby. I love them."

A feeling of anticipation flowed through her as she watched Colter open his gift from her. She'd been torn with indecision about what to get him on such short notice. A sigh of relief escaped her when he seemed pleased with the green pullover sweater she'd finally chosen. And Tulley liked the leather gloves she'd given him.

Colter handed her a large box and she quickly unwrapped it. A pair of dark brown cowboy boots lay inside. "Oh, my," she whispered.

"I had them specially made at our factory. I got your shoe size from your heels."

She kicked off her slippers and pulled on the boots. Then she stood up and whirled around. "What do you think?"

"Cool, Mommy—just like a cowgirl," Ellie said. "Except you probably need to wear jeans instead of a bathrobe."

Marisa made a face.

Colter couldn't take his eyes off her, but forced himself to reach for another gift. And these—" he gave her the package "—are for when you're mucking around in the corrals with Ellie."

She removed a pair of black rubber boots from the box. "Thank you." She smiled and leaned over to kiss his cheek.

"You're welcome," he said, looking into her eyes.

"Daddy, Mommy," Ellie shouted, interrupting their silent communication. "Come on! I gotta ride my bike."

They spent the next hour teaching their daughter to ride her new bicycle. With Colter on one side and Marisa on the other, Ellie was soon off on her own, Sooner barking and racing after her. As she circled the driveway, the darkness of the night faded into another Texas winter morning. The wind whistled through the trees and the dew glistened on the grass like happy tears. It was going to be a chilly yet beautiful day.

"Becky's on the phone," Tulley called from the foyer.

Colter went inside, and Marisa continued to supervise Ellie's cycling. The child pedaled up the walk and Marisa caught the bicycle because Ellie hadn't learned to brake yet.

A few minutes later, Colter came running out. "They had

to take Jen to the emergency room and the doctor admitted her. They were able to stop her labor, thank God. She's doing fine, but the doctor wants to keep an eye on her." He took a breath. "That now means we'll be staying home for Christmas."

"I'll see what I can rustle up for lunch," Tulley said.

"Are we going to the hospital, Daddy?"

"This afternoon we'll all go." He glanced at Marisa. "Is that okay?"

"Yes," she answered, touched that he was including her.

Before breakfast, they went to check on the deer. When Colter opened the door, a surprise met them—the fawn was holding her head up, gazing around with wide-open eyes!

Ellie dashed over to her. "Look, Daddy! She's better." The fawn started to lick Ellie's hand. "And she's hungry."

This time she sucked her bottle readily as Marisa and Ellie hovered over her. "Isn't she beautiful?" Marisa gently stroked the little head, examining the white spotted body.

"Let's call her Beauty," Ellie suggested.

"Wait a minute." Colter held up a hand. "When she's healthy again, I'll call the game warden and—"

"No, Daddy! No." Ellie cried. "He'll take her away. Why can't we keep her? I'll take care of her."

"And I'll help," Marisa said, her dark eyes holding his.

Colter stared at Marisa, then at Ellie and then back at Marisa. "Okay." He gave in with a frown. "But just remember. When she gets old enough, we have to let her go. She's a wild animal and needs to be free. It would be inhuman to keep her penned up."

Marisa felt a moment of pure joy. His acquiescence meant he accepted her presence here in the future. The thought gave her hope—hope that one day he'd love and trust her again.

A warm glow lit her heart, and the holiday spirit seemed to embrace them in a world all their own.

Chapter Seventeen

They all pitched in to help Tulley with dinner. He had a chicken roasting and had made corn bread for the dressing. Green beans and yams waited on the counter. It was plain that he had everything under control.

Marisa and Ellie set the table in the dining room, and Colter prepared iced tea and apple cider. They were happily absorbed in their tasks, and Marisa soaked up the atmosphere and that sense of family, something she'd never felt before. Most of all she just watched Ellie, and she had to resist the impulse to hug Ellie every few seconds.

The phone rang, interrupting the silence. Colter answered it and talked for a few minutes; he hung up, saying, "That was Becky. She's on her way over with dessert. She said she's not going to miss seeing Ellie at Christmas."

"Oh boy. Oh boy." Ellie jumped up and down. "Now you can meet my Aunt Becky. She's real nice."

Marisa couldn't believe how nervous she was at the prospect of meeting this woman who probably hated her. She busied herself picking up discarded Christmas paper and straightening the den. Turning, she bumped into Colter.

He took the paper from her. "Relax. Becky won't do anything to spoil Ellie's day."

"I guess I needed to hear that."

"Becky's here, Becky's here, Becky's here," Ellie

shrieked, running through the house with Sooner on her heels.

"Guess Becky's here," Colter said. "I'd better help her get things out of the car." He took a step, then turned back. "Do you want to come?"

She shook her head. "No, thank you. I need a moment."

"Okay." He gave her a sympathetic smile and walked out.

Taking a deep breath, she looked down at her clothes—jeans and a cream-colored silk blouse with her new boots, which she found very comfortable. She was fine…if only the tenseness in her stomach would go away. Maybe a little lipstick. No, she didn't have time. She could already hear Ellie's chatter.

Ellie was pulling a brown-haired woman with Kincaid green eyes into the room. She was the same height as Marisa and about the same size—the reason Marisa could wear her clothes.

"This is my mommy." Ellie pointed to Marisa. "Her name is Marisa and she's gonna stay with Daddy and me forever."

Complete silence followed that statement.

Ellie glanced at Colter and back at Marisa. "Why's everyone looking so funny?"

"Your mother is here for the holidays, angelface," Colter said. "We haven't discussed anything beyond that."

Ellie stared at Marisa. "You're gonna leave?" Her bottom lip trembled, and Marisa hurried over to gather the child into her arms.

"I'm never leaving you again, baby. I promise."

What about me? Colter stood there, somehow needing an answer to that question. But he didn't get one. All he felt was the empty hole in his chest. Trying to conceal his sudden grief, he quickly carried the desserts into the kitchen.

"Nice to meet you." Marisa shook Becky's hand.

"Me, too. You're all Ellie's been talking about."

"Santa sent me my *real* mommy," Ellie said, her earlier distress forgotten.

"That's because you're special." Becky kissed her cheek.

"I'll get the presents out of the car." Colter headed for the door.

"I brought the poinsettias that were delivered to the office. I knew you'd want them today."

"Thanks, Beck."

Ellie ran after him, shouting, "I'll help, Daddy."

Marisa's throat felt tight and she was glad Becky walked into the kitchen just then and hugged Tulley. "How you doing?" she asked him.

"Fine. How's Jen?"

"Great. When I left, she and Bart were both sleeping."

"Just glad everyone's okay," Tulley said.

"Yeah, but when my sister's feeling better, I think I might kill her. She ruined my beautiful Christmas dinner. For once I was going to outshine her in the kitchen, but what does she do? Have premature labor pains and scare Bart and me to death. The doctor wants to monitor her to make sure it doesn't happen again."

"We're planning on going to the hospital this afternoon. Hope it's okay."

"Yeah. Jen will be heartbroken if she can't see Ellie on Christmas."

Marisa listened attentively; it was clear how much Tulley loved Colter and his sisters and how much they loved him. He was the only father they'd known, and she envied that closeness.

But she was still reeling from Ellie's announcement. She wouldn't leave Ellie—she was sure of that. It was Colter who worried her; he apparently felt some need to point out that she was leaving after the holidays. She had a week to change his mind—and she intended to do just that.

"Look what else Aunt Becky brought," Ellie said, placing a pie carefully on the table.

"I made homemade apple pie just like Mama and Cora used to, plus Colter's favorite four-layer cake."

"You did good, girl." Tulley patted her shoulder.

"Hmm." Colter laid packages under the tree. "Better wait until we taste it."

"Colter Kincaid!" Becky rested her hands on her hips.

The rest of the day Marisa listened to their easy banter, and if she expected animosity from Becky, she didn't get any. Becky was lively and energetic, with an irrepressible sense of humor, and Marisa suspected that Ellie had inherited some of her aunt's exuberance. By the middle of the afternoon, Marisa and Becky were talking like old friends. Becky reminded her a lot of Cari in her zest for life.

After dinner, they opened presents. Becky liked the mirror and said it was definitely something she would use. She handed Marisa a large package. "This is from Jen, Bart and me."

Marisa unwrapped it carefully and gasped when she saw what it was—a framed collage of photographs showing Ellie from infancy to the present. Tears trickled down Marisa's cheeks. Hugging Becky, she whispered, "Thank you. I love it."

Afterward they got ready to go to the hospital. Ellie wanted to wear her new clothes and she asked Marisa to do her hair in a French braid with a pink ribbon.

Becky took her own car, since she wasn't coming back to the ranch. Colter, Tulley, Marisa and Ellie rode in Colter's truck, but not before Ellie had given Sooner a long talk about why he couldn't go. They left him in the backyard.

Marisa wasn't nervous. She'd weathered one Kincaid, so she figured the rest couldn't be so bad. And she was right.

Colter helped Ellie carry in one of the big poinsettias. Jen's eyes lit up, and she welcomed Marisa warmly. Jennifer was an older version of Becky, but much more serious. Marisa thanked her for the photo collage, and Jen accepted her gifts, smiling serenely.

Bart's brother, Ted, and his wife, Susan, and son, Jarred, arrived soon after, and they all crowded into Jen's room. She was half sitting in the raised hospital bed, wearing a bright red robe with holly on the collar and cuffs.

Ellie introduced the boy. "This is Jarred. He's in my class at school."

"Hi, Jarred." Marisa smiled, pleased to meet Ellie's classmates.

He raised a hand in greeting and sidled closer to his father, obviously embarrassed by Ellie's attention.

"I'm sorry, big brother," Jen said. "I ruined Christmas."

"There's no way you could ruin Christmas. Just take care of yourself and the baby."

"Golly, your stomach's big," Ellie said, staring at her wide-eyed.

"Ellie—"

"Yes," Jen interrupted Colter. "My stomach's big. I feel like a bloated cow."

Ellie looked at Marisa. "Did you have a big stomach with me?"

"Enormous. I didn't think I was ever going to see my feet again." She couldn't believe it was so easy to talk about—especially in front of Colter and his family.

Colter glanced at her, and for a brief moment she remembered those months, being pregnant and feeling miserable. There were so many things about that time she wanted to share with him, good *and* bad.

"Daddy, can Jarred and me go look at the babies?" Ellie asked.

"Yes, but come right back," Colter replied, sitting next to Marisa.

Ellie and Jarred flew out the door, and the adults continued to talk about Christmas, babies, horses and business. They included Marisa, who was grateful they made her feel like part of the family.

"Thank you for being so nice." She felt she had to say that as she gathered up her purse and coat at the end of the visit.

"You're welcome," Jen said. "I admire your strength in dealing with everything you went through. I think I'd lose my mind if someone took my baby." She rubbed her stomach as she was talking.

"I was close to it when I found out the truth, but seeing Ellie saved me." She got to her feet. "She's been gone for a while, so I should check on her. And thanks again, everyone." She moved toward the door.

"I'll go with you," Colter said. "We should be heading home. You probably shouldn't have a lot of company, but we couldn't let this day pass without seeing you." He kissed Jen and Becky and followed Marisa out. Tulley was still saying his goodbyes.

In the hallway, Marisa hardly recognized her child. Her clothes were askew and her hair straggled out of its braid. She held the crumpled ribbon in one hand.

Marisa ran to her, pushing the blond hair from her heated face. "Baby, what *happened?* Are you all right?"

Ellie shrugged her shoulders. "Sure."

"What happened to your clothes and hair?"

"Are we going home?" Ellie asked instead of answering, evidently trying to change the subject.

"Ellie." There was a stern note in Colter's voice.

Jarred darted into Jen's room, but Marisa barely noticed. Her eyes were on Ellie.

"What happened?" Colter asked.

Ellie shuffled her feet.

"Ellie."

"Jarred pulled my hair and said I looked like a girl, and I hit him and he hit me back, then I pushed him and he pushed me." She shrugged again. "I guess we got into a fight."

"Jarred *hit* you?" Marisa was aghast, unable to believe someone would do this to her child.

"Don't overreact," Colter warned, obviously seeing the anger that filled her eyes.

Ted stepped into the hall holding Jarred's hand. Jarred stared at his shoes. He pulled the boy forward.

"I'm sorry," Jarred mumbled. For the first time Marisa

looked at him; his hair was disheveled, his shirt hanging out of his jeans, and a sleeve was ripped at the seam.

"It's okay," Ellie said, hanging her head.

Colter cleared his throat.

"I'm sorry, too," Ellie added quickly.

Colter and Ted talked for a minute, and then they left. Marisa was still in a state of shock. She didn't want anyone hitting her child and she didn't want Ellie in school with someone who'd do such a thing.

On the way home, they stopped at the cemetery to put the flowers on Colter's parents' graves and on Tulley's wife's.

When they got back to the ranch, Tulley fixed a light supper while they fed Beauty. The fawn was standing up now, so Colter put her in a horse stall.

These activities, and her pleasure over the fawn's recovery, eased Marisa's tension over Ellie somewhat.

LATER, MARISA PLAYED SOME Christmas songs Ellie wanted to hear, followed by "Ave Maria" and "O Holy Night," ending with parts of Tchaikovsky's "Nutcracker Suite." The day had come to an end, but she wanted to hang on to every second. Ellie nodded sleepily beside her.

Marisa kissed her. "Time for your bath."

"Okay." Ellie slid off the bench and went to her room, Sooner behind her.

"That was beautiful," Tulley said, pushing out of his chair. "Now I hear my bed calling."

"'Night, Tulley. And Merry Christmas."

"'Night," he called. "And same to you."

She turned to Colter, who was sitting on the sofa looking relaxed. "I'm having a hard time with Jarred hitting Ellie," she admitted.

"She hit him first," he said.

"He was baiting her. He said she looked like a girl."

One dark eyebrow rose. "She *is* a girl."

She shook her head. "That's beside the point. He only said it to taunt her."

"Marisa…"

"No." She refused to be put off. "I will not have someone hitting her. I think we should talk to her teacher and have her removed from that class. I don't want her anywhere near Jarred."

Colter leaned forward and rubbed his hands. "Have you asked Ellie how she feels about this?"

"No, of course not. She's just a child. She doesn't know what's best for her." An eerie calm came over her as the words resounded in her head. She'd heard them before, many times, but they'd been spoken about her. For a moment she was paralyzed as she fought for control over the emotions that gripped her.

Ellie came racing into the room in pink-and-white flannel pajamas, Sooner obediently by her side. "I'm ready for bed." She smiled at them.

"Angelface, your mother's upset because Jarred hit you. She wants to take you out of Jarred's class. How do you feel about that?"

Ellie's face crumpled. "No! Don't do that," she cried, staring at Marisa.

"Tell us why you feel that way," Colter said.

"Well." She twisted on her bare feet. "I like him and I think he likes me, too. That's why he was teasing me. If you move me to another class, I'll never see him again. *Please* don't do that."

Marisa could hear her own voice saying almost those same words when she was seventeen. *Please, I love him. If you make me go, I'll never see him again. Please.* But her mother hadn't listened to her. She was considered a child, her feelings and opinions inconsequential. Fear overwhelmed her as she realized she was treating Ellie the way her mother had always treated her.

Kneeling on the floor, she gathered Ellie into her arms. "Don't worry, baby." She smoothed her hair. "I won't do anything that'll upset you. I'm just overreacting. I'm new at this mother thing. You have to be patient with me." She kissed the tip of her nose. "But I still don't like anyone hitting you."

"It was just a tap," Ellie assured her.

"We'll discuss this 'tapping' later," Colter said. "Now off to bed."

"Gosh," Ellie grumbled, heading for her room, Sooner trailing behind her. "Does anyone love me enough to tuck me in?" Her voice echoed from the hall.

"We'll see," Colter called.

"Parents" they heard faintly.

Colter raised an eyebrow. "I guess you're included in that."

"It's not one of the ways I was looking forward to being included." She rose to her feet. "I'm sorry. I got carried away."

"If I thought for one minute that he'd hurt her or intended to hurt her, I would've been the first to box his ears. But they were just playing, and I seriously suspect Ellie was trying to get his attention." At her confused look, he added, "She has a crush on him."

"I should've known you had everything under control. I just—" She tried to explain and couldn't. Instead she said in a rushed voice, "We'd better say good-night before she thinks we've forgotten about her."

As soon as Ellie went to sleep, Marisa made a quick exit.

She grabbed her coat, exchanged her shoes for the new rubber boots and hurried out to the barn. The night sounds no longer bothered her. She had to get away, to sort out these new emotions that were tearing her apart. And she wanted to make sure Beauty was comfortable.

She opened the barn door and turned on the light, then entered the stall. Beauty was curled in one corner, blinking up at her in the sudden brightness. Marisa sank onto the hay and leaned back on her heels, stroking the fawn's soft body. Beauty licked Marisa's fingers.

"Hi, Beauty," she cooed. "Are you okay? Did you have a nice Christmas? Do you miss your mommy?"

A bubble of laughter escaped her. Here she was sitting in a barn, talking to a deer. And it felt…right. This New York City girl liked living on a ranch—because her daughter was here…and so was the man she loved. No, it was more than that. She *wanted* to be here and she was beginning to feel a connection with the animals. She couldn't explain what had happened. Maybe she'd grown up. But something still tormented her, a deep-seated pain she had to face.

"Marisa."

Her head jerked toward Colter's soft voice.

He walked in and knelt beside her. "Why didn't you tell me you were coming out here? I would've come with you."

"I just wanted to be by myself and think."

"Are you still worried about Jarred?"

"No." She sighed heavily, feeling all those buried emotions gathering force inside her. She couldn't stop the tears that filled her eyes. Quickly, she tried to brush them away, hating that she couldn't control this weakness.

He caught her hand. "It's all right to cry."

"I thought you didn't like it when I cried," she mumbled, remembering that from Vegas when it didn't take much to make her tearful.

Tenderly, he brushed the tears away with his thumb, his gentleness threatening to open a floodgate. "Sometimes you try to be too strong," he answered. "So, what are the tears about?"

"It's just…" She had a hard time finding the words, but she knew she could share anything with him. That was how it had always been. He was probably the only person who'd understand what she was feeling. "Tonight I saw my mother in me. She treated me like a child without feelings, she never asked what I wanted or how I felt, and I was doing the same thing to Ellie. I've always thought I was nothing like my mother, but—" She choked back a sob.

His hand curved around the nape of her neck and she

rubbed her cheek softly against his arm, feeling warmth and comfort.

"You are nothing like your mother," he said, his voice husky. "She was manipulative, driven and deceitful. You are a loving, caring woman, and you don't have a deceitful bone in your body."

She wanted to believe his words, but she wasn't sure she could. She pulled away from his hand. "Don't say that just to pacify me."

"I'm not. I mean it."

"No, you don't," she replied. "If you meant it, you wouldn't keep this distance between us. Today when Ellie said she wanted me to live here forever, you looked as if you'd been kicked in the stomach."

"Marisa. Let it drop."

"No, I won't," she snapped. "What is it? Why can't you let the past go? Why can't you trust me?"

"It's nothing, really," he murmured, obviously trying to put her off.

"No, it's something, and I want to know what it is."

There was a moment of hesitation. "In all the time you've been here and all the times we've talked, not once have you mentioned the note."

She frowned. "What note?"

"God." His jaw clenched. "How could you write something like that and not even remember it?"

"What are you talking about?"

He reached in his back pocket and took out his wallet. Flipping through it, he removed a piece of paper and handed it to her. She unfolded the worn sheet and quickly scanned the contents.

"No." She shook her head as each word pierced her. Her mother had done this, had left Colter this awful note. A cold shiver spread through her as all her bitter feelings toward Vanessa began to surface. But she knew, with everything in her, that her mother had done this because she loved her. Vanessa had wanted what she considered best for her daughter. She had done all the wrong things for the right reasons.

She stared at the note, wishing her mother had known Colter the way she did, but those doors to the past had been irrevocably closed.

Why had he kept this terrible note all these years? The answer came swiftly—because he thought she'd written it. And this was the reason he wouldn't admit he felt anything for her. He couldn't trust her feelings.

"I didn't write it," she told him in a shaky voice. "Surely you know I never felt that way about you and never will."

"You...didn't write it."

"No. I was crying so hard I couldn't write a word. I planned to get in touch with you later—remember, I told you? I guess Mother decided to leave the note to ensure that you wouldn't come after me."

For a moment his body went still, then he reached for the note, crushing it in his hand. "Another damn lie, another deception," he said in anger.

Marisa had to get away. So much pain, so much suffering, and it still wasn't over. This last blow brought all her hopes and dreams crashing down around her. She couldn't fight the inevitable anymore.

"I was hoping that in time we could put the past behind us, but I can see that's never going to happen. If you can believe I ever felt that way about you, then there's no future for us." She stood. It was too late. Nothing could help them now. She walked from the stall on heavy feet.

He let her go.

Chapter Eighteen

"Marisa."

She stopped. Had he called her name? No, she'd just imagined it. She told herself to keep walking. Tears stung her eyes and her stomach churned with a sick feeling, but her feet wouldn't move.

"Please don't ever leave me again."

This time the voice was faint, but she heard it. His words were full of pain and entreaty and seemed to come from somewhere deep within him. Or was she hearing things? Still, she couldn't walk away. Slowly she turned around. He stood, a solitary figure with his shoulders slightly hunched. Her heart contracted as she saw the tears glistening on his cheeks. She took a couple of steps toward him.

"What are you saying?" she asked, her voice trembling.

He gave a harsh laugh, a desolate sound that seem to echo between them. "I'm afraid," he admitted. "Big, fearless Colter Kincaid is afraid. I've tamed wild horses, but I'm afraid of the emotions I feel for you. Help me, Marisa. Because everything I believed about you is lies. I don't know what to think or feel anymore, but I'm certain of one thing. I'm tired of fighting you, I'm tired of fighting myself, but most of all, I'm tired of fighting all these emotions inside me."

"What emotions?" she asked, not daring to breathe.

"I've tried to hate you, to forget about you, but I've never succeeded. Even when you came back and we learned the truth about Ellie's birth, I still couldn't accept you in my life. I told you our love was like ashes and could never be rekindled. That was just another lie to protect me from the way I knew I'd feel when you tired of that rodeo rider who'd fathered your child. When you left me for the second time."

She whimpered in protest, but he didn't seem to hear as he continued. "So I tried to keep a distance between us because I knew I couldn't survive you leaving me again."

She took a step closer to him. "I've never really left you."

"What?" His eyes centered on her face.

"Eight years ago, my mother took me away, but you were always here—" she placed a hand over her breast "—in my heart, and you always will be. No one can take that from me— not even you."

"Marisa—"

He blinked back tears, and she could see that the battle within him was raging, but this time, she was winning.

"I need you," he whispered.

"I need you, too," she whispered back, wanting to throw herself into his arms, but she couldn't. He hadn't said the words she wanted to hear, and she didn't know if he ever would. "But needing isn't loving," she added. "And I need you to love and trust me. Without that we have nothing."

"I trust you with our child. Doesn't that tell you how I feel?"

"No, that only tells me how you feel about Ellie and me. I have to know how you feel about *you* and me."

He drew a ragged breath and placed a hand over his heart. "Even after all the times I've denied it, and all the times I've hurt you, this heart beats only with love for you." They stared at each other for endless seconds, both absorbing the truth. Then, with a muffled exclamation, he reached for her, gathering her into his arms. "Can't you feel how much I love you? My life has been so lonely and empty without you."

"I love you, too," she said with a tremor in her voice. It seemed as if she'd waited forever to hear those words, and she gave a sigh of pure happiness. "Say it again."

"I love you," he breathed against her face a moment before his lips covered hers, his arms molding her against the hardness of his body.

Her lips softened voluntarily, her hands curling into his hair. At her submission, he deepened the kiss, his tongue probing, tasting the sweetness of her. The kiss went on and on. They didn't seem to need to breathe. Their lips, tongues and hearts gave them the sustenance they needed.

He rested his forehead against hers. "Now do you believe me?"

Breathing heavily, she had trouble thinking above the hammering of her heart. But she knew with certainty that the wounds of the past had finally healed.

"Yes," she cried, her arms tight around his neck.

"Marisa," he groaned, gathering her closer. "I love you. I've always loved you. Even when I hated you, I loved you."

She touched his cheek gently and they swayed together like two drifting leaves in the wind. They stood for minutes just holding each other, both needing the comfort and reassurance that only touching could bring. Finally, Colter stared into her dark eyes, seeing all the love he would ever need.

"God, I love you," he murmured, kissing her deeply. "It feels so good to be able to say that."

"I know," she said, realizing how hard it had been for him. Tilting her head, she looked at him with dreamy, love-filled eyes. "I wish you'd mentioned the note earlier."

"I was waiting for you to bring it up, and when you didn't, I assumed you wanted to forget about it."

She tasted the tears on his face. "But *you* never forgot it. I'm so sorry for the pain that note caused you. In Mother's eyes, you were wrong for me, and she stopped at nothing to keep us apart. I've had all this anger and bitterness inside me.

I couldn't understand how she could do that to me, how she could hurt me like that. But tonight with Ellie, for a brief moment, I got a glimpse into her motives. Everything she did, she did because she loved me. For my sanity, I have to believe that."

"You're very forgiving" was all he said.

She cradled his face in her hands, staring into his eyes. "When I was seventeen and I looked at you, I got this wonderful feeling inside. I've never felt anything like it before or since. I felt it the day I met you again, although I didn't want to admit it, and I feel it every time I look at you now. I can't describe it, but I know it's love and I know I'll never feel it for any other man. I want to spend the rest of my life with you, more than anything in the world."

"Oh, Marisa." He buried his face in the warmth of her neck.

She understood that he'd opened his heart to her and allowed her to see his vulnerability, his uncertainty and fear. All his defenses were down, showing her just how much he trusted her. How much he loved her. That love flowed through her body.

"I'm so happy." Her fingers caressed his neck.

Slowly, her lips replaced her fingers, her tongue gently stroking the pulsing nerve at the base of his throat. Urgently turning his head, his mouth captured hers with a mindless, burning need that left her limbs trembling, her senses spinning, and her body aching for the ecstasy that only he could give.

Fighting for restraint, she drew back slightly, wanting to be sure. "Does this mean we're going to be a family now?"

He grabbed her hand and headed for the house.

"Colter, where are we going?"

"Shh." He put a finger to his lips.

She followed him to the house through the back door and to his study. "Colter?"

"Shh," he said again. "We don't want to wake our daughter."

He closed the door, and Marisa stood transfixed, staring at an object in the corner. The Christmas Cradle was there, and for a moment she couldn't believe her eyes. She blinked, but it was still there. She walked over and touched it lovingly. "Where did this come from?" she whispered.

Colter was busy getting something out of a drawer and he swung to face her. "What? Oh, the cradle?"

"Yes. Where did it come from?"

He set something on the desk and came to her. "I bought it that day I met you in Dalton's. I thought it was beautiful and would make a great gift for Jen. They delivered it to the office. I brought it home the other day and stored it in here."

"Do you know it's called a Christmas Cradle?"

He shook his head. "No. It just caught my eye. The saleslady wanted to explain, but I didn't have time."

She pointed to the figures carved in the wood. "These depict The Twelve Days of Christmas and it's all carved by a craftsman in Austin. His wife is from England and she sews the lovely bedding. See, the song starts here at the head of the cradle with a partridge in a pear tree, two turtle doves, three French hens and so on. You can see the song depicted along the sides of the cradle and at the base. On the rockers are eleven pipers piping and twelve drummers drumming." She smiled mistily. Dalton's orders one every year. The cradle takes a long time to carve and the craftsman only makes a few. See? It's made from one block of wood and is unique in its design. I love just looking at it and I looked at it that very same day and—and…it was something I always had to do. Every year. I could almost see my baby in it. I could…"

He slipped his arms around her waist from behind.

"I was wondering that same day who would buy it." She rested her head against his chest. "And you did. I would never have guessed. Jen will love it."

"I don't think so."

She turned in his arms. "What do you mean?"

"I'd never give that cradle to anyone but you. I can hear the love in your voice when you talk about it."

"No. You bought it for Jen."

"Not really," he said. "I think I must've bought it for myself—call it fate or whatever. I don't usually believe in those things, but subconsciously I must've sensed your interest in it. Becky told me Jen didn't need it—she's using Bart's bassinet from when he was a baby. I bought it anyway."

"Oh, Colter." She wrapped her arms around his neck. "Thank you."

"You're welcome." He kissed her briefly and reached for something on the desk.

Puzzled, she watched as he opened a small velvet box. Her heart skyrocketed as she stared at a diamond ring.

"I was going to give this to you the day you left." A wistfulness entered his voice. "Afterward, I planned to return it, but I never did. Later, I decided to keep it for Ellie. But now—" he looked deep into her eyes "—I think the woman I purchased it for should wear it."

"Oh, Colter, it's beautiful!"

He slid the ring onto her trembling finger, saying, "Marisa Preston, will you marry me?"

"Yes, yes, yes." She threw her arms around his neck.

He kissed the side of her face and picked up a document on the desk, which he handed to her.

It was Ellie's birth certificate.

Tears gathered in her eyes as she saw Ellie's birth name. "You named her Marisa Ellen."

"Yes. I wanted her to have a small part of you. Later, I regretted that impulse and I never told Ellie. Tulley's the only one who knows."

"I'm not sure what to say."

"Say you love me," he said in a hoarse voice.

Her eyes sparkled. "I love you, forever and always."

His arms tightened around her and he let his lips travel from her mouth, to her cheek, to her hair. "Oh God, Marisa, I love you so much it's killing me. These last few days, every time you responded to me you seemed to hate yourself and me afterward." She smoothed his dark hair and he breathed a kiss behind her ear. "When I saw you in Dalton's, I was so angry. Then you came here to the ranch and the moment I saw you beside Ellie, I knew you weren't out of my system."

"You were thrown from that horse and got hurt." Her finger touched the quivering muscle in his jaw. "I don't think I ever told you how sorry I was about that."

"It wasn't your fault," he told her. "The first thing a rodeo rider learns is concentration, total concentration. Lose that for even a second and, well…you saw what happened."

His voice grew weaker and weaker as her lips touched his jaw. He turned his head, his mouth covering hers once again with a driving need. She reveled in the mastery of his kiss, her senses spinning, her body aching.

"Marisa," he groaned into her throat. "I want you so badly that I'm burning up with it."

"Me, too." She left a trail of moist kisses from his jaw to his ear. His body quivered, and she slowly began to unbutton his shirt, then splayed her hands across his chest. She took his hand, then led him toward the hall.

They ran up the stairs like two excited teenagers. As soon as the door closed, they were locked in each other's arms. She clung to him, her blood raging like a river, sweeping her along with a passion her body remembered well.

Within minutes, their clothes were a heap on the floor. Colter paused to slip off his boots and his jeans, his eyes lingering on the silken smoothness of her body. Her skin tingled at his dark gaze.

"You're more beautiful than ever," he murmured, swinging her up into his arms and placing her on the bed. His fingers skimmed her heated flesh. "I've dreamed of this moment so many times, but the fantasy is nothing compared with the reality."

He pressed his lips to every inch of her skin. Tiny flames ignited in the pit of her stomach, but before the flames consumed her, she wanted to tell him.

"Colter," she managed to say between gasps of air.

"Mmm?"

He kissed one breast and then the other, and she forgot what was so important—but only for a second. "It's…it's been a long time."

"I know." His tongue explored one rosy nipple, and all rational thought was fast leaving her.

"No. I mean it's really been a long time for me." She spoke in a rush. "There…there hasn't been anyone since you."

He raised his head, his eyes glazed. "My God, why not?"

"After losing my baby, I lost interest in everything, including men. When I did start dating, I was careful not to let my emotions get involved. I didn't want to be hurt again." She smiled tentatively. "I'm telling you this because in Vegas I neglected to tell you I was a virgin. I want everything to be right this time."

His eyes clouded for a second. "That means you're not on the pill?"

"No…"

"I don't have any condoms, and we should be adults about this. Responsible."

"We were the last time, and look what happened."

"I know, but…"

She caressed his face. "I see this as a commitment to our life, our future."

"Then you wouldn't mind another child?"

"I've been given a beautiful cradle, so what do you think?"

His sweet smile and loving kiss evoked a response deep within her. They made love to each other as they had years ago. Everything came just as naturally as it had before, but it was all so much better. Their responses were stronger, more ardent, because they knew all those secret little joys that brought each other pleasure. They gave of themselves without holding back. When the ecstasy came, it came with a fierce abandonment that left them both sated, content, wrapped in the arms of love.

Later, his head lay possessively on her shoulder and her hand lazily stroked the muscles in his back.

"Colter?"

"Mmm?" His lips nuzzled the curve of her neck.

"Merry Christmas."

He raised his head. "Ah, you're the best Christmas gift I've ever been given."

She ran her fingers over the stubble that was beginning to show. "I've changed, haven't I?"

He rolled away, pushing up against the headboard, and pulled her into his arms. "The younger Marisa was insecure, afraid of a lot of things and dominated by her mother. I loved her anyway. The older Marisa's independent, making it on her own and stronger than I ever thought she could be. When you learned about Ellie, I thought you'd fall apart, but you didn't. And I loved you even more."

They shared a long deep kiss. "You gave up so much to raise our daughter," she said. "You're a very special father, Mr. Kincaid. I hope I can be as good a mother."

"You will be. Ellie adores you already."

She remembered a time when she'd adored her own mother.

"What is it?" Colter asked, seeing her sad expression.

"I was thinking about my parents—especially my mother."

His arms tightened around her. "Our future's together, but what kind of future can we build on bitterness and resentment? I want more for Ellie."

"Me, too." She idly caressed the firm muscles in his arms. "I never thought I'd see the past from my mother's point of view. But I've had these insightful moments ever since that night you wondered what you'd do if Ellie had my talent and got pregnant at seventeen. I couldn't really answer. And tonight the incident with Jarred opened my eyes even more. She did the things she did because she loved me. She just didn't *know* me. I don't want to make that mistake with Ellie."

She snuggled close to his body and a comfortable silence enveloped them both.

The future was so bright she could almost touch it. But as Colter had said, what kind of future could they build if she continued to harbor bitterness and resentment toward her parents? She knew what she had to do, and it wouldn't be easy.

He kissed the top of her head. "You can do it."

She looked up at him. "How did you know what I was thinking?"

"Because I'm thinking the same thing. You've been through hell, but you're not going to be completely happy until you talk to your parents." His lips took hers again, and they forgot everything but each other.

Sometime toward morning, Colter placed a gentle kiss on her lips and slid from the bed.

"Colter," she murmured sleepily.

He tucked the covers around her. "Go back to sleep. I'm going to my own room so Ellie won't find me here."

"I love you."

"Love you, too." He found his clothes and quickly left.

Marisa turned over, feeling lonely without his warmth. She glanced at the clock—5:00 a.m. Soon Ellie would be bouncing on her bed. Soon they'd tell her they were getting married. Soon they'd be a real family.

First, though, she had to see her parents. Without forgiveness, there could be no happiness, and she wanted true happiness for Ellie, Colter and herself.

But could she actually forgive them for taking her child?

Chapter Nineteen

"Mommy, wake up! Mommy."

The precious voice tugged at her brain and Marisa slowly opened her eyes. "Morning, baby."

"Morning, Mommy," Ellie said, and crawled in beside her; predictably, Sooner, too, jumped onto the bed, and Marisa stroked his sleek fur. "Did you sleep good?"

Better than I've slept in years. Colter's touch, his kiss, was still with her.

She pulled Ellie into her arms. "Yes, and how about you?"

Ellie shrugged. "I don't know. I fall asleep and I don't remember anything. I just wake up."

Marisa kissed her good-morning. "Is your father awake?"

"Yeah. He and Tulley are drinking coffee."

"Then let's join them."

"Okay." Ellie scrambled off the bed.

Marisa reached for her robe. She didn't want to take time to dress, she just wanted to see Colter.

They hurried downstairs and she paused in the kitchen doorway, her eyes on Colter. He was smiling as he noticed her, and she was, too. They couldn't seem to stop.

Ellie slid onto Colter's lap.

"What do you want for breakfast?" he asked Ellie, his eyes never leaving Marisa.

"I don't…"

As Marisa pushed her hair behind her ears, her diamond ring caught the light—and Ellie's attention.

"What's that, Mommy?" Ellie pointed.

"Yeah, what's that?" Tulley asked, grinning.

Marisa and Colter exchanged a secret smile. "Well, you see, angelface, last night I asked your mother to marry me and she said yes."

Ellie's mouth fell open and then she jumped off Colter's lap, shouting, "Oh boy, oh boy, oh boy, this is big—bigger than Christmas. I gotta call Aunt Becky, Aunt Jen and Lori. Golly, this is the best Christmas *ever.*" Sooner barked in a frenzied manner as Ellie bounced around the room.

Colter finally grabbed her by the arm. "Okay, baby girl, calm down."

"I can't, Daddy. I'm too excited. My mommy's gonna live here forever. I'll never be without a mommy again."

She ran to Marisa and threw both arms around her waist. Colter came to stand beside them, sliding an arm around her shoulder.

"I believe in Santa Claus—don't you, Mommy? Daddy?"

"Ellie," Colter sighed.

Marisa smoothed Ellie's hair, gazing into Colter's eyes. "Oh, yes, I believe."

Looking at her, he believed in the unbelievable, the impossible. "Daddy believes, too," he said.

Tulley stood and scooped up his hat. "If that don't beat all. I'm beginning to believe myself."

Ellie giggled as Tulley ambled out the door.

They ate breakfast with Ellie asking a million questions. She couldn't sit still for one second—up and down, up and down, until Colter said it was time to feed Beauty. Marisa and Ellie changed into jeans and boots and headed for the barn. Colter tagged along, unable to stay away from them.

Marisa prepared the milk and poured it into the bottle. Beauty was walking around in her stall, hardly resembling the fawn of two days ago. Ellie fed her the bottle, and Marisa knelt in the hay applying ointment to the sores still evident on the small body. Happy and content, Beauty curled up on the hay and went to sleep.

Marisa then helped Ellie tend to her horses. They filled buckets with horse and mule feed and carried them to the long troughs in the pasture. Dandy and Sassy immediately galloped toward them. Marisa pulled a chunk of carrot from her pocket, which Dandy ate from her hand.

Colter observed all this with a sense of wonder. She seemed at home here on the ranch and with the animals. She was nothing like the frightened young girl of eight years ago, but she had the same big heart, the same innocence and beauty he'd never forgotten. And never would. This time she was in his life to stay.

But he saw the sadness that lingered in her eyes. He'd thought he would never forgive Richard and Vanessa Preston, but love had miraculous healing powers. Now Marisa had to find the strength to do the same, and he would be right beside her.

"Mommy." He heard Ellie talking. "I'm gonna put on my new outfit and ride Dandy. Please fix my hair in a French braid with a red ribbon. I'll look so cool."

Marisa sat on a bale of hay and pulled Ellie to her side. "Mommy has to go into Dallas for a little while."

"Why?"

"I'd like to go see my father."

"Oh." Ellie twisted on her boots. "When will you be back?"

Marisa caught her hands. "About lunchtime, and then I'll fix your hair and watch you ride Dandy."

"Okay," Ellie said, but she didn't look up, and Marisa knew something was bothering her.

"Mommy?"

"What, baby?"

"Is your daddy gonna be mean to you?"

"Oh, baby, no." She gathered her child in her arms. "He loves me."

As she said the words, she knew they were true. For days she'd been telling herself that her parents had to love her to do what they'd done, but she hadn't fully believed it until now. She'd grasped it intellectually but not emotionally. Until now. She knew her parents would never intentionally hurt her. They'd sheltered and protected her from the world; and at seventeen she'd had no clear idea of what was out there. Their decisions had been wrong for Marisa. They'd had no way of knowing that, though, because communication was not a strong suit in their family.

Thank you, baby. It took her child to make her fully understand—and accept—the past.

Within the hour she was dressed and ready. Colter walked her to the car holding her hand. Ellie was riding her bicycle, completely competent at stopping and turning after her Christmas Day lesson and this morning's practice.

"If you wanted me to, I'd go with you," Colter said, "but I know you have to do this by yourself."

She touched his face, loving him all the more for realizing that. "Yes, I do." She went into his arms and he held her for a second, then she got in the car and drove toward Dallas.

Colter watched until the car was out of sight. He felt as though the sun had just stopped shining in his world. It wouldn't shine again until she was back.

Hurry home, Marisa.

MARISA TRIED NOT TO THINK about the meeting ahead. She didn't even know if her father was home. Her mother had gone on a cruise, and she didn't have a clue to where Reed was. He had said he'd call over the holidays, but so far he hadn't.

She picked up her cell phone and called Cari. They talked until she turned in to Highland Park. Cari was thrilled to hear that she and Colter were getting married, and Marisa could hardly contain her own excitement. But as she pulled up to the gates, all she felt was apprehension.

She punched in the code and thought that maybe she should've called, after all. With the upheaval in the family, her father might have gone away for the holidays. If so, she'd go back to Colter and Ellie and wait until after New Year's. She knew she had to do this.

As she drew closer to the house, she noticed Reed's sports car parked in front. Had he been in Dallas all along? Why hadn't he called her? Maybe he'd reconciled with their father and didn't know how to tell her. She got out and ran to the front door and rang the bell.

Winston opened it immediately. "Miss Marisa, how nice to see you."

"Thank you, Winston. Is my father home?"

Winston stepped aside. "Yes, ma'am. They're in the library."

"They?" She walked into the foyer.

"Mr. Reed and Mrs. Preston are here, as well."

"Oh. My mother's back from her cruise?" She could see both her parents at the same time; she hadn't expected this.

"She cancelled her holiday plans," Winston replied. "She spent Christmas with Mr. Preston."

"Really?" It was hard to keep the shock out of her voice. For years she and Reed were the only thing that had kept her parents civil. Had they actually managed to spend time together without tearing each other apart?

Marisa walked toward the library, her mind whirling. Her mother was still here; apparently she'd never left. And Reed was here, too. What was going on? As she reached the library, she heard raised voices. She didn't want to eavesdrop, but she didn't want to interrupt, either.

"Those are my conditions, take them or leave them." That was Reed and he sounded angry.

"I don't like ultimatums, son," her father warned.

"And I don't like how you've controlled and manipulated

my life. You've been grooming me for years to take over Dalton's, but I'm nothing more than a figurehead. I have no real responsibility or power. Marisa felt the same way."

"Have you seen your sister?"

"No. I've given her the time she needs with Colter and their child."

"I thought she'd call over the holidays," Richard said plaintively.

"Why would she do that?" Reed asked with a touch of sarcasm. "You and Mother have treated her like a porcelain doll, unable to live her own life because of her great talent. Well, you've finally shattered her life into so many pieces, I'm not sure she'll ever be the same."

"I'm fine, Reed," she said, stepping into the room.

All three looked at her. "Oh, my darling, you're home," Vanessa said. She was standing by the fireplace drinking a cup of tea. Putting the cup down, she hurried toward Marisa, but halted abruptly a few feet from her.

Her father seemed unable to speak.

Reed came and hugged her, smiling broadly. "How are you doing? You look great."

"I am great." She smiled back. "I have my daughter."

"I'm glad you're home," her father finally said.

"I'm not home." She wanted to make that point clear. "I just came to tell you I'm getting married."

"Oh." Vanessa blinked.

"So you're marrying him?" was Richard's response.

"Yes. I've never stopped loving him." She looked directly at her mother. "I think you know that."

"After I told you the baby was stillborn and you sank into such a deep depression, I felt we'd done the wrong thing. But when you refused to play the piano, I knew for sure that we had. I just didn't know how to make it right without hurting you even more."

"I thought I'd never recover," she said, wanting to be completely honest. "But Colter and Ellie have made me see things in a new way—well—I'm playing the piano again."

"Oh, darling, that's wonderful." Vanessa clapped her hands together.

"Colter had never heard me play and he said he hadn't realized I was so talented. He wondered what he'd do if Ellie had that kind of talent and got pregnant at seventeen. I really couldn't answer until yesterday. Ellie was playing with a friend from school and they got into a disagreement and he hit her. I was furious. I wanted Ellie removed from that class. I wanted to get her away from him—that was all I could think of." She took a breath. "Colter asked me if I'd asked Ellie what *she* wanted, and I told him she was a child and didn't know what was best. And I began to understand that was exactly how you felt about me. I was young, so young."

"Yes, darling, you were."

"Today when I told Ellie I was coming here, she was afraid you might hurt me."

A strangled sob left Vanessa's throat, but Marisa continued. "I knew then that you didn't intentionally hurt me. You've loved and protected me all my life, yet you've never really known me. I hated the long hours of practice and I wanted to be like other girls—having fun. In rebellion I made some bad choices, but I will never regret loving Colter."

There was silence for a moment.

"I want to thank you for giving my child to Colter," she said quietly. "He's done a great job with Ellie."

Vanessa twisted the pearls around her neck. "He kept demanding to see you. I had to tell him another lie—that you didn't want anything to do with him or the baby. I could see how much that hurt him."

"Yes," Marisa said, staring down at her hands. "He's been hurting for a lot of years."

"Just like you," Reed put in.

"Yes, just like me." She looked at her father. "Why didn't you tell me you were there when Ellie was born?"

His eyes didn't waver from hers. "I didn't want you to know," he said with more honesty than she'd expected. "When Vanessa called, I saw it as a way to get what I wanted—you, back in Texas. I told her I'd help if she didn't pressure you to stay in New York. She kept her word, and you came home with me." He drew a long breath. "That doesn't make me look very good, but you're being honest and I have to do the same. I've always been angry at Vanessa for taking you away, and I saw this as my chance to have both my children with me. But giving up your baby was not an easy thing to do."

After another long silence, he resumed. "I grew up poor, as you know. My parents died when I was small and I lived with an aunt and her family. I started working when I was twelve, mowing yards and helping people in the neighborhood, but there was never enough money to go around. I studied hard and got a university scholarship. I was determined to have a better life. I worked in the men's department at Dalton's while I went to college. When I graduated, I applied for a management job at Dalton's and was hired as an assistant to the vice-president of sales." He walked to the fireplace and stared into the fire.

"I knew what I wanted, but I wasn't sure how to get it—until I met Vanessa. Her father doted on her and I set out to marry her. She was my stepping-stone to the big time. She was home for the holidays, and by New Year's we were heavily involved. But Vanessa had no plans to marry me. She went back to New York and her career." He picked up a poker and stoked the fire. "Fate intervened, though. When her parents discovered Vanessa was pregnant, I was called in to Mr. Dalton's office. He said, 'Buy a tux, boy, you're marrying my daughter.' And that was it. Vanessa and I did the right thing, but we fought all the time. She blamed me for everything that had happened. However, Mr. Dalton took me under his wing and taught me everything he knew—and I learned fast. I had what I wanted. My kids wouldn't have to work a day in their lives."

He turned to look at Reed and Marisa. "I did everything for you, and both of you complain that you don't have any responsibility. With responsibility come long hours and hard work. I didn't want that for you. I wanted you to enjoy life— and I was wrong. You have to learn, to grow. You have to experience pain in order to be strong. I tried to spare you all that, but I made a mistake. You have to experience the losses as well as the rewards. That's what creates character, and Marisa, I've never been prouder of you than I am today. I'm sorry for the pain I've caused you. I wish you nothing but happiness in your marriage." His voice wavered on the last word.

She'd never seen her father so humble and sincere, and she knew he meant what he'd said. "Thank you, Father."

Richard turned to Vanessa. "I'm sorry for the years I wouldn't listen to how you felt, but I'm not very good at sharing and I'm afraid I don't hear anyone's viewpoint but my own."

Vanessa brushed away a tear.

"And, Reed, I agree to all your conditions. By the time you're forty you will be CEO of Dalton's, and in the meantime, I will gradually ease into retirement."

"Thank you, Father," Reed said. "And maybe *you* should try to enjoy the life you've built."

"I'm going to try." Richard glanced at Vanessa. "Your mother and I are going to New York for New Year's and she's going to show me her city."

Marisa and Reed were speechless. Their parents hadn't gone anywhere together that Marisa could recall. She felt as if she'd stepped into some fantasy realm where fact and fiction were closely entwined. But this was completely real. She could look at her parents and see how they'd changed. Ultimately the tragedy had changed all their lives—for the better.

"Marisa," her father said. "There will always be a place for you at Dalton's."

"I'm not sure what direction my life will take, but I do know I'll be a wife and mother and I will continue with my music."

"Oh, darling," Vanessa whispered through her tears.

"Then you're not going back to Madame Hélèna's?" Richard asked in a controlled voice.

"Hélèna helped me when no one else would, and I will fulfill my commitment to her—even though I suspect she only hired me to get back at you."

"She's a spiteful old witch."

"She's a brilliant designer and her clothes should be in Dalton's."

Richard smiled. "Then make it happen."

She smiled back, admiring his cleverness. "It's not that easy, Father. My life is now with Colter and our child. I'll leave the business deals to Reed. I had to tell you I've forgiven you, but it'll take me a while to forget—if ever."

"Thank you, darling." Vanessa stepped forward and hugged her, and Marisa hugged her back.

She couldn't go into the future with one foot in the past. She found she could make the transition easily now because so much was waiting for her.

"I'd better go. I don't want to stay away from Ellie too long." Marisa saw fresh tears in her mother's eyes, and if she felt any residue of resentment, it completely dissipated at the sight.

"Do you…do you think you might one day allow us to see Ellie?"

Marisa swallowed. "That'll be up to Ellie and, of course, Colter."

"Tell us about her," Reed invited.

She nodded readily. "Ellie's the most wonderful little girl. She's bright, funny and she never walks, she's always running. She has a dog named Sooner who she swears talks to her, and she's not afraid of anything. She has two horses named Dandy and Sassy, and she rides almost as well as her father."

"I can't wait to meet her," Reed said.

"Maybe soon," she replied. "Now I have to go."

"Goodbye, Marisa." Richard embraced her. "Just be happy."

"I am," she said, fighting tears.

She quickly left and ran to her car, then headed for home—her home, the place she'd been searching for. She'd done the right thing in seeing her parents. Now she could love Colter completely.

COLTER CHECKED HIS WATCH again. It was just after twelve. Marisa should've been home by now. A farrier was shoeing a couple of his horses; Ellie was watching closely, which kept her occupied. She knew her mother loved her and would be back. He knew the same thing, but he didn't want Marisa hurt or upset. He checked the time again.

"If you look at that watch once more, you're going to burn a hole through it." Tulley leaned on the fence beside him.

"I wish I knew what was happening."

"She'll tell you all about it when she gets back."

Colter jammed his hands into his coat pockets. "Yeah. I'm just nervous for her and—"

They both saw the car coming down the road, and Colter raced for the gate. Marisa parked by the garage, then got out and ran toward Colter. He met her halfway, caught her and swung her around and around. He set her on her feet, kissing her deeply. Finally he held her face with both hands.

"How'd it go?"

"Better than I ever dreamed. In some ways it's as if they've become different people. They're feeling a lot of pain over their actions, but I've forgiven them. It felt so good to be able to do that. By letting go of the heartache, I'm free to live a whole new life with you and Ellie."

"I love you," he whispered, running his fingers through her long blond hair.

She held his gaze. "I will love you forever."

"Mommy, Mommy, Mommy," Ellie shouted, racing toward them.

"Later," she whispered.

Ellie wrapped her arms around Marisa's waist. "I missed you."

"I missed you, too." She kissed the top of Ellie's head.

"Guess what, Mommy?"

"What?"

"Mr. Harvey is shoeing some horses and his son is gonna build Beauty a pen. Daddy asked him to."

"Really?" Marisa looked at Colter.

"We can't continue to keep her in the barn. She needs to be outside. I'll have Rod make a shelter for her to get under when the weather's bad. But eventually we have to let her go."

"You're so wonderful." She gave him another slow kiss.

"Are y'all going to be doing that a lot?" Ellie asked, frowning at them.

"Yep, a whole lot," Colter said.

"Then Mommy's going to give you kisses in the morning and at night, too?"

"Yep." He grinned. "I've got two beautiful ladies. I'm one lucky man."

"Yes, you are." Ellie nodded.

Colter picked her up and groaned. "You're getting heavy."

"No, I'm not. You're just getting old."

"Old! I'll show you old." He tickled her rib cage and she giggled, squirming and squealing. Sooner barked agitatedly trying to reach her, and Marisa laughed.

"Help me, Mommy," she squealed more loudly.

"Oh, no, you got yourself into that one."

Ellie slid to the ground amid a fit of childish laughter. Sooner eagerly licked her face.

Colter slipped an arm around Marisa's waist, and she

rested her head on his shoulder. They had weathered the storm, and now laughter and sunshine would fill their days. When other storms came, they would face them as a family.

Epilogue

One year later
Christmas Eve

Colter knew Marisa was miserable, but he didn't know what more to do. He'd rubbed her back, her legs, her neck until his arms ached. At nine months pregnant, nothing helped much. She'd had contractions earlier, and they kept waiting for them to start again, but they hadn't.

He listened to her steady breathing. Finally she seemed to be drifting into sleep. That was what he'd been hoping for—that she could get a good night's rest. Both families were coming for Christmas dinner; so were Cari and Hazel. He didn't think it was such a good idea, since the baby was due on the twenty-ninth, but it had been a year of forgiveness, change and acceptance, and Marisa wanted it—so he gave in. He found he couldn't refuse her anything.

Holding Marisa, his thoughts drifted back over the past year. His wife was awesome, as Ellie called her. She'd worked at Madame Hélèna's until they discovered she was pregnant, then Hélèna had said she should go home and enjoy her family. Marisa was ready to do that because she was involved with Ellie's school. The teachers were grateful for the help she provided with parties and outings, and for the music programs she arranged.

After she left Madame Hélèna's, Reed had talked her into taking a seat on the board of Dalton's. Colter and Marisa discussed it for a long time, and in the end she accepted out of respect for Reed and the new ideas he was bringing to the company. Colter knew she'd made the right decision.

He marveled at her energy and her talent. Between her and Reed, they'd made a deal with Madame Hélèna and, come spring, her line of clothes would be carried at Dalton's for the first time. It was a major coup for the company, and Marisa had been the driving force behind it.

Not only that—Marisa and Reed had put their heads together with Becky and Bart, and Dalton's would now carry the Kincaid Boot. The boots would be in the stores in early March. Marisa and Reed were energized by the new ventures, and Dalton's was flourishing, reaching a younger clientele while continuing to satisfy their older customers.

Richard was still head of the board and CEO, but he kept a low profile. Vanessa had moved from New York to Texas and had taken an active seat on the board, but both Richard and Vanessa acquiesced to the ideas of their children. Vanessa now lived with Richard again, and although Marisa and Reed weren't sure about the relationship, their parents seemed to get along in a way they hadn't in all the years they'd been married.

Since Marisa was pregnant, Colter worried about her doing too much, but he had only to look at her to know she was fine. The pregnancy had gone smoothly, with no problems. She had more energy than ever. In the mornings, before taking Ellie to school, she and Ellie fed Beauty, whom they'd set free, but the deer never wandered too far from the barn.

In the evenings Marisa played the piano, and he could see how much she enjoyed it. She'd joined the Dallas Symphony Orchestra as a guest soloist; a week before, she'd performed in the Christmas concert and invited family and friends—her parents, Reed, Cari, Hazel and Hélèna were among them.

When she was introduced and came on stage, she faced the audience and said, "I dedicate this performance to my mother,

Vanessa Preston, whose dreams I never understood as a child. As a mother I see them clearly. So tonight I play for my mother and her dreams."

Marisa played brilliantly, and although he knew little about Tchaikovsky or Bach, he knew that he was hearing a very gifted young woman. He experienced a moment of guilt—that he had come between her and the career she so richly deserved. But he realized that career wasn't what she wanted. And these days Marisa knew *exactly* what she wanted.

When Marisa had made the announcement that night, Vanessa had begun to cry. Ellie had helped her find a handkerchief in her purse, saying, "Don't cry, Grandmother. Just listen."

Vanessa grabbed Ellie's hand and listened to the whole performance that way—holding on to Ellie. And that was wonderful to see. Ellie felt no resentment toward her grandparents, none at all.

When she'd met Richard and Vanessa for the first time, she'd asked in her usual, direct way, "Why didn't you want me?"

Vanessa had started to cry, and Ellie had done the same thing as she did later at the concert. She'd said, "Don't cry, Grandmother. Please don't cry."

Richard had sat down with Ellie and he'd told her how much they loved Marisa. He'd explained that out of their love, they'd made bad choices and decisions they regretted.

From that day forward, he and Vanessa had forged a relationship with their granddaughter. They took things slowly because that was the way Colter and Marisa wanted it. But as the weeks passed, he could see another miracle happening—the Prestons loved Ellie and the feeling was returned. Ellie now had grandparents.

He listened to Marisa's breathing and it wasn't steady anymore; it had become more labored. "You're not asleep, are you."

"No." She turned toward him, which was an effort because she'd gained a lot of weight. The doctor said the baby was going to be eight pounds or more. And they knew it was a boy. Not once had he heard her complain, though—both of them had thoroughly enjoyed the pregnancy. They were experiencing it together, and that made all the difference.

"Do you think Ellie's asleep?" she asked. "We have to put her gifts under the tree."

Colter crawled out of bed and reached for his robe. "You rest. I'll do it."

"No way, Colter Kincaid." She struggled to sit up. "I'm not missing any part of Ellie's Christmas."

He helped her up and held her for a moment. He didn't argue with her, since this was too important to Marisa.

Kissing the side of her face, he took her hand and they walked to the door.

"Wait," she said. "I have to go to the bathroom…again."

"I'll check and make sure Ellie's asleep."

Marisa came out of the bathroom and stopped abruptly as a sharp pain gripped her. She'd been having light pains lying in bed, but didn't want to alarm Colter or say anything until it was necessary. She grabbed the vanity as she realized water was running down her legs and pooling at her feet. *Don't panic. Don't panic. Be calm. Be calm.*

"Colter," she screamed, unable to still the anxiety in her. *Be calm. Be calm.* She squatted as another pain shook her.

Colter was inside the bathroom in a split second. "What is it? What's wrong?" he asked, kneeling beside her, his heart racing.

"My water's broken."

"What! OhmyGod!"

"The baby's coming," she breathed between pains.

He scooped her into his arms. "I'll get your bag and we'll go to the hospital."

Marisa shook her head. "No. We don't have time. The baby's coming *now!*"

Colter's eyes grew enormous. "No. It's too quick. We have to go to the hospital."

A pain ripped through her and it was a moment before she could speak. "Colter, listen to me," she said, each word slowly and carefully enunciated. "Put me on the bed and call 911, then call our doctor. The baby's coming. We don't have much time." The swift cyclic pains were the type she'd had right before Ellie was born. She wasn't having this baby in a vehicle.

"Okay. Okay."

His arms trembled as he laid her down, and she knew he was trying to be calm but failing miserably. Colter quickly dialed 911. She took several deep breaths, then a sharp contraction hit her. She bit her lip to keep from screaming again.

Tulley appeared in the doorway in his pajamas. "What's wrong? I heard screaming."

Colter slammed the phone down. "Marisa's having the baby."

"What!"

"Get dressed and drive to the entrance so the ambulance won't miss our turn," Colter said, the stress showing on his face.

"You got it." Tulley turned as Ellie came charging into the room.

"Why is everybody…" Ellie's voice trailed off as she saw Marisa in bed with her knees drawn up. "Mommy, Mommy," she cried, running to her, but Colter caught her before she could crawl onto the bed.

"Mommy's having the baby," he told her. "So be gentle."

Sooner barked from the doorway.

"Shh," Ellie told him.

Colter released her, and Ellie leaned toward Marisa, who wrapped an arm around her daughter.

"Are you hurting, Mommy?" Ellie asked softly.

"It's a good kind of hurt, Ellie," Marisa said, trying not to cry out. "Soon your baby brother will be here."

"Oh boy, I gotta call Grandmother and Aunt Becky." She whirled around and Colter caught her again.

"First go with Tulley so the ambulance won't miss our turn."

Tulley came back, fully dressed, with a pan of hot water, fresh towels and sheets, and placed them on the dresser. "You might need those. Come on, shorty. We don't want to miss that ambulance."

As they left, Colter picked up the phone and called their doctor. Marisa let out a long scream. She had to. She couldn't hold it in as a strong contraction clenched her whole body.

"Remember the breathing," Colter said to Marisa, listening with one ear to the doctor and switching on the speaker phone. "Quick panting breaths."

Marisa just screamed.

"Marisa," Dr. Gates said. "Breathe, breathe, breathe. Don't push just yet."

"Okay," she answered, taking quick breaths and trying not to scream.

"Colter," the doctor continued, "take a look and tell me what you see."

He pulled up her gown, saw the blood and fluid and almost lost it. Then he noticed the crown of his son's head and he was revived with wonder and strength. "I...I see the head," he said, his voice cracking. "OhmyGod! The baby's coming!"

"Calm down," the doctor instructed. "And don't push, Marisa. Breathe, breathe, breathe. Looks like the baby's in a hurry to get here. Colter, get lots of clean sheets and towels and something to tie the umbilical cord. The paramedics will cut it when they get there."

"Like what?" Colter asked in a frantic tone.

"Some type of string, and get a bulb syringe. I'm sure you had one when Ellie was a baby."

"Yes." He dashed into Ellie's room. Where the hell was it?

He ran to the utility room and found it in the medicine cabinet. He ran back. "I have the syringe and string from a kite. Is that okay?"

"Yes. That's fine. Cut a piece, then put several sheets beneath Marisa. Have towels ready and a washcloth to wipe the baby's face."

Colter worked quickly and efficiently. He cut the string and gently shoved sheets beneath Marisa, piling towels and everything else he needed on the bed.

"It's all there," he told the doctor.

"Now wash your hands and the syringe, and get ready to deliver your son."

A strong contraction almost overwhelmed Marisa, and she screamed and breathed at the same time. Sweat ran down her face and she clutched her knees with both hands. But as long as Colter was there, she'd be fine.

"Tell me what you see," the doctor said.

Colter crawled onto the bed and knelt between Marisa's legs. "The head's coming out," he shouted.

"Hold it with a clean towel. Do you see the face?"

"Yes, yes, yes. Oh my God, yes."

"Wipe his face, and clear his mouth and nose with the syringe."

Colter carefully held the baby's head and did as the doctor instructed, surprised his hands weren't shaking.

"Everything okay?"

"So far," Colter said raggedly.

"Okay, Marisa, time to push. Push hard. Push your son into the world."

"We're having a baby, sweet lady." Colter smiled at her. "How are you?"

"Gre—at. I love—you." Words locked in her throat as the pain became more severe. She would not pass out. She would not let go—that was a vow to herself. She had to be awake for her son's birth, and she had to see him, hold him.

"Honey, one more push," Colter said. "You have to push him out. Come on. One, two, three—push."

Marisa felt her strength waning. *Push. Push. Push.* She couldn't. She had to. Taking a deep breath, she pushed with everything in her. A scream left her throat and she fell back on the bed as their son slid into Colter's waiting hands.

Colter glanced at the clock and reached steadily for the string.

"Colter, is he okay?" Marisa asked in a faint voice. "Is he breathing? Colter, tell me!"

"Yeah, and it's definitely a boy."

"Tie off the umbilical cord," the doctor said. "The baby will be bloody and grayish, but don't worry about that."

Colter let out a long sigh of relief. He'd noticed the color, but everything was fine.

"It's done," Colter told him.

"Put him on Marisa's chest."

He placed their son on her chest and gazed at her face.

"Oh, he's so beautiful and so perfect," she whispered, her hands trembling against the small body.

"Take a towel and rub him vigorously all over." The doctor was still giving orders.

Colter began to rub him, and Marisa helped. Suddenly the baby started to cry loudly.

"That's what I wanted to hear," Dr. Gates said.

"Oh, oh, oh," Marisa cooed to him. "It's okay. Mommy's here." She kissed his face and touched his head, his stomach, counted his fingers and toes—and then she began to cry. She had her baby and no one would ever take him from her. In her weakened state that was all she could think about.

"Wrap the baby up. Keep him and Marisa warm."

Colter pulled a blanket around Marisa and the baby. He rested his face against hers. "How are you?"

"Wonderful and tired, but no one's taking this child. No one."

"Honey…"

Marisa grimaced.

"What is it?" Colter was immediately on the alert.

"I'm cramping."

"That's okay," the doctor said, still on the phone. "The placenta's coming out. Colter, reach down and gently tug on the umbilical cord."

He did. "Everything's out."

"Good. Congratulations! You have a son and you both did great."

Colter kissed the side of Marisa's damp face. "*You* were great."

"Look at him, Colter, just look at him." Her voice held awe.

"I am. He looks a lot like Ellie."

"Does he?" Her voice wobbled, and he knew she was remembering Ellie's birth.

"I love you," he said, and she rested against him and smiled into his eyes.

"Hey, you two. I'm still here," Dr. Gates teased.

The baby began to squirm, moving his head as if he was searching for something.

"He seems hungry," Colter commented.

"He probably is. You can nurse him, Marisa." The doctor's voice was very clear.

Marisa opened her gown and the baby latched on, sucking hungrily.

"Colter, can you see him?" Marisa asked. "He knows exactly what to do."

"I see, honey. He's a Kincaid."

Marisa stared into her husband's eyes and knew that nothing in her life would ever match this moment—the moment of giving birth with her husband's help and then holding and seeing her child.

There was a clatter at the door just then. The paramedics came through and immediately took over. Colter gave her a kiss and moved from the bed, letting them take care of Marisa and the baby. Tulley hurried down the hall.

"Everything okay?" he asked sounding concerned.

Colter nodded. "He was born at 12:05 a.m. He's a Christmas baby." His body shook with all the emotions he was feeling, and Tulley put an arm around his shoulders.

"You all right, boy?"

He nodded again. "I've delivered foals before, but this is the first time I've helped deliver a baby—my own baby. It's a little overwhelming." He brushed away a tear. "Where's Ellie?"

"Talking to Mrs. Preston on your cell phone."

Colter looked down and saw Marisa's blood all over him. "I have to clean up for the trip to the hospital. I have clothes in the utility room, so I'm going to take a shower. I won't be long."

In less than ten minutes he was back. As he got clothes for the baby and handed them to the paramedics, Ellie ran up to him.

"Daddy, Grandmother wants me to call her as soon as the baby comes."

Before Colter could answer, the paramedics emerged from the room. "Your wife refuses to go to the hospital, so I've checked her and the baby, and everything seems to be fine. I spoke with the doctor and he's agreed to let her stay home for Christmas, but he wants her and the baby in his office first thing the day after Christmas." The paramedic looked down at the papers in her hand. "On your digital scale, the baby weighs seven pounds, fifteen ounces, and is twenty-one inches long. Did you by any chance get the time of birth?"

"12:05 a.m.," he said.

"Good. Your wife gave us his name. She's taken a shower, and we cleaned the baby per the doctor's instruction. We also changed the bed. We don't usually do that, but it's Christmas."

"Thank you. And Merry Christmas."

The paramedics left, and Colter entered the room with his daughter. Marisa was sitting up holding the baby who'd been wrapped in a blue blanket with pictures of ropes and spurs on it. She smiled, and Colter kissed her and then his son, now sound asleep.

Ellie stood staring with big eyes. Marisa looked at her. "Come meet your new brother."

"Are you okay, Mommy?"

"I'm fine, baby."

"I'm not the baby anymore," Ellie said moving closer to the newborn.

Marisa smiled at her. "You will always be my baby."

Ellie nodded happily and sat by Marisa, staring at her new brother. "Now you have two babies, Mommy. Can I touch him?"

"Yes, but very gently."

Ellie caressed his cheek with one finger. "He's so tiny and cute."

"Yes, he is." Marisa kissed the top of his head. "Now I'd like everyone to meet this young man. His name is Jackson Aaron Colter Kincaid. We'll probably call him Jack."

There was no question about what his first name would be. Colter wanted to name him after Tulley, and Marisa was fine with that. Aaron was her father's middle name, and the fact that she was able to call her son after her father meant the old wounds had healed. The scar tissue was still there, but it couldn't hurt her anymore. She'd forgiven her parents completely—and she prayed that she and Colter would never make decisions that would hurt their children.

"Lordy, lordy," Tulley said, his eyes filled with tears.

They hadn't told him what they were naming the baby. Colter had wanted to wait until the baby was born.

"You're crying." Ellie pointed at him.

"Yep, I guess I am." He cleared his throat, hugged Colter

and kissed Marisa's forehead. "Thank you." He deftly took
the baby from her. "Hi there, little buckaroo. I'm gonna enjoy
getting to know you."

"Time for everyone to get to bed," Colter intervened. "Or
Santa's going to miss this house."

Ellie shook her head. "Santa's already been here. He
brought us Jack."

"It's still time for bed," Colter said, smiling.

Ellie gave lots of kisses. Tulley handed the baby back to
Marisa and gathered up the dirty laundry. "I'll put this in the
washing machine."

"Oh, no. I forgot. I gotta call Grandmother," Ellie said, and
ran to her room, Sooner on her heels.

And then it was the two of them with their son. Colter went
into the baby's room and brought the Christmas cradle, which
he placed beside the bed. "Time for Jack to get some sleep,
too."

"No. I want to hold him for a little longer."

Colter gently brushed back her damp hair. "Honey, no
one's taking this baby."

"I know—it's just—"

"You're afraid you'll wake up and he won't be here," he
finished for her.

"It's crazy, I'm aware of that, but I can't shake the feeling."

"With what you've been through in the past, I think it's a
normal reaction." He kissed her softly. "Trust me. This baby
isn't going anywhere." He lifted Jack out of her arms and laid
him gently in the cradle.

Marisa shifted onto her side, watching him. "So many
times over the years, I've looked at this cradle in Dalton's and
imagined our baby in it. It's kind of surreal to actually have
it happening."

Love brightened his eyes. "Have I told you how wonderful you are?"

She nodded, her eyes closing as exhaustion overtook her.

He looked at his son for a moment, knowing he'd witnessed another miracle, then slowly went to put out Ellie's gifts. First, he checked to make sure she was asleep—and she was. He got the gifts from the attic in the garage and arranged them under the tree. As he was about to turn out the light, he noticed a piece of paper lying on the table next to Santa's cookies and milk. He picked it up and read:

Dear Santa,
My friend Lori says there is no Santa Claus, but I believe. Even when I get as old as Daddy, I'll still believe 'cause you brought my mommy home and you gave us a brand-new baby. Everybody's happy. Thank you, Santa Claus. I believe.
Love,
Ellie Kincaid

A smile tugged at his mouth. Yes. They were happy—finally. He drank the milk and took the cookies, along with the letter, to show Marisa. He stopped when he entered the bedroom. Marisa was asleep on her side, one hand on the cradle.

When he lay down by his wife, she let go of the cradle and curled into him.

I believe, too.

A COWBOY AND A KISS

by Dianne Castell

Sunny Kelly wants to save the old saloon
that her aunt left her in a small Texas town.

But Sunny isn't really Sunny.
She's Sophie Addison, a Reno attorney,
and she's got amnesia.

That's not about to stop cowboy
Gray McBride, who's running hard for
mayor on a promise to clean up the town—
until he runs into some mighty strong
feelings for the gorgeous blonde.

On sale starting December 2004—
wherever Harlequin books are sold.

If you enjoyed what you just read,
then we've got an offer you can't resist!

Take 2 bestselling
love stories FREE!

Plus get a FREE surprise gift!

Clip this page and mail it to Harlequin Reader Service®

IN U.S.A.
3010 Walden Ave.
P.O. Box 1867
Buffalo, N.Y. 14240-1867

IN CANADA
P.O. Box 609
Fort Erie, Ontario
L2A 5X3

YES! Please send me 2 free Harlequin American Romance® novels and my free surprise gift. After receiving them, if I don't wish to receive anymore, I can return the shipping statement marked cancel. If I don't cancel, I will receive 4 brand-new novels every month, before they're available in stores! In the U.S.A., bill me at the bargain price of $4.24 plus 25¢ shipping & handling per book and applicable sales tax, if any*. In Canada, bill me at the bargain price of $4.99 plus 25¢ shipping & handling per book and applicable taxes**. That's the complete price and a savings of at least 10% off the cover prices—what a great deal! I understand that accepting the 2 free books and gift places me under no obligation ever to buy any books. I can always return a shipment and cancel at any time. Even if I never buy another book from Harlequin, the 2 free books and gift are mine to keep forever.

154 HDN DZ7S
354 HDN DZ7T

Name	(PLEASE PRINT)	
Address	Apt.#	
City	State/Prov.	Zip/Postal Code

Not valid to current Harlequin American Romance® subscribers.

Want to try two free books from another series?
Call 1-800-873-8635 or visit www.morefreebooks.com.

* Terms and prices subject to change without notice. Sales tax applicable in N.Y.
** Canadian residents will be charged applicable provincial taxes and GST.
   All orders subject to approval. Offer limited to one per household.
   ® are registered trademarks owned and used by the trademark owner and or its licensee.

AMER04R   ©2004 Harlequin Enterprises Limited

HARLEQUIN *Super*ROMANCE®

A six-book series from Harlequin Superromance.

WOMEN *in Blue*

Six female cops battling crime and corruption on the streets of Houston. Together they can fight the blue wall of silence. But divided, will they fall?

Coming in December 2004,
The Witness by Linda Style
(Harlequin Superromance #1243)

She had vowed never to return to Houston's crime-riddled east end. But Detective Crista Santiago's promotion to the Chicano Squad put her right back in the violence of the barrio. Overcoming demons from her past, and with somebody in the department who wants her gone, she must race the clock to find out who shot Alex Del Rio's daughter.

Coming in January 2005,
Her Little Secret by Anna Adams
(Harlequin Superromance #1248)

Abby Carlton was willing to give up her career for Thomas Riley, but then she realized she'd always come second to his duty to his country. She went home and rejoined the police force, aware that her pursuit of love had left a black mark on her file. Now Thomas is back, needing help only she can give.

Also in the series:
The Partner by Kay David (#1230, October 2004)
The Children's Cop by Sherry Lewis (#1237, November 2004)

And watch for:
She Walks the Line by Roz Denny Fox (#1254, February 2005)
A Mother's Vow by K.N. Casper (#1260, March 2005)

HARLEQUIN®
Live the emotion™

Visit Dundee, Idaho, with bestselling author

brenda novak

A Home of Her Own

Her mother always said if you couldn't be rich, you'd better be Lucky!

When Lucky was ten, her mother, Red—the town hooker—married Morris Caldwell, a wealthy and much older man.

Mike Hill, his grandson, feels that Red and her kids alienated Morris from his family. Even the old man's Victorian mansion, on the property next to Mike's ranch, went to Lucky rather than his grandchildren.

Now Lucky's back, which means Mike has a new neighbor. One he doesn't want to like…

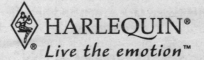

HARLEQUIN®
Live the emotion™

www.eHarlequin.com

HSRH001204